FLESH

AND
BLOOD

FLESH

AND
BLOOD

DANIEL DERSCH

Translated by Gerald Chapple

47N⬤RTH

The characters and events portrayed in this book are fictitious. Any similarity to real persons, living or dead, is coincidental and not intended by the author.

Published by 47North, Seattle

www.apub.com

ISBN-13: 9781477817469
ISBN-10: 1477817468

Cover design by Stewart A. Williams

Library of Congress Control Number: 2013948600

Printed in the United States of America

To B.

PROLOGUE

THE YOUNG MAN ARRIVED at the pasture shortly after sunrise. The clearing overlooked the city, less than an hour away on foot.

Of course, that's how long it took only if the sheep followed willingly. Because at the very end of the summer, when nights turned colder and the icy wind swept over the country, the sheep balked and became unmanageable. Neither kindly persuasion nor shouts helped. A not-infrequent whack with a stick was the only way to get them back onto the path. This time of year it could take almost twice as long for the whole flock to get to pasture.

But on this day the shepherd was lucky; no stragglers held him back. They all marched properly, following his lead. His two dogs were on either side of the flock, a little distance away. They'd crept silently through the underbrush, keeping an eye out for any danger. When the woods began to thin out, they returned to the flock and mingled with the sheep.

The dogs' white, shaggy coats were often hard for him to distinguish from those of his charges. They were good dogs, and thanks to them he hadn't lost a single sheep to the wolves that summer. They always jumped up at the slightest rustling in the woods, barked, and drove every would-be thief back into the darkness of the undergrowth.

Upon reaching the pasture that day, the shepherd sat down on a fallen tree trunk and warmed himself in the rising sun. Fishermen's sails billowed out in the city harbor in the morning breeze, and far out to sea, huge steamships sailed eastward.

The sea was calm and almost the same color blue as the sky. The two hues mingled in an impenetrable blur on the horizon. For a few moments the young man couldn't tell exactly where the sea stopped and the sky began.

He sat there for a while, looking upon the water and letting the sun shine on his face. After warming up a little, he took off his rucksack and made breakfast: just two boiled eggs and a crust of bread, but after the steep climb even this meager fare tasted downright sumptuous.

After his meal, he indulged in a swallow of ouzo from the bottle he carried in the breast pocket of his jacket. Its spiciness ignited a warm glow in his chest. His breakfast over, he had nothing more to do than sit and look to his sheep now and then. He got up from the log, leaned his bag against it, and then sank to the ground. His rucksack was worn and thin, but he could lean against a tree trunk on it all day without getting a stiff neck. "Even the smallest cushion is better than bare ground," his grandmother always used to say, and in the end she was right.

Once he'd stretched his legs out in the grass, he took a little book from his pocket, turned to the place he'd dog-eared, and began to read.

The book was written by one of his countrymen years ago after spending almost his whole life traveling the world. It was a collection of travelogues the author—a former trading ship's captain—had put together over the years. The good fellow got to know the four corners of the earth and put his impressions and experiences into the book. The young man liked the collection very much, though he'd never been more than a two-day trip away from his home in spite of his twenty-three years. He liked it so much that he was reading it for the fourth time, never bored for an instant. He knew the stories by heart, but he nonetheless followed the author's adventures feverishly, again and again, whether spending torturous days in the horse latitudes with the captain or encountering cannibals on a lonely island in the South Seas.

Despite the allure of the exciting stories and terrifying curiosities, the young man most enjoyed descriptions of all the foreign countries and cities.

He secretly asked himself whether Fate might grant him, too, a journey to foreign lands to find friends in far-flung cities the way the captain had. Maybe Hong Kong, Buenos Aires, or even New York? Time and again he paused during his reading and tried to imagine living somewhere else, in one of the many cities he knew only from the book.

As he'd done so often, the young man spent the morning lost in daydreams. Soon, he drifted further, nodding off in the sunshine.

But today his sleep was restless, his dreams confused. No matter where he turned, he was hounded. Instead of the captain and friendly foreigners, all the men he dreamed of were menacing, dark, evil figures with blood-red eyes. They looked at him eagerly, baring their teeth like mad dogs. He feared they would tear him to pieces in a brutal attack at any moment.

He startled awake with a slight headache and the strange feeling that he was being observed.

He looked around in alarm but couldn't see anything. The sheep were grazing peacefully, and the dogs . . .

Where are the dogs?

. . . were nowhere to be seen. He began to get anxious until he finally caught sight of the dogs lying off to one side of the pasture, in the middle of a little flock of sheep and looking toward the woods.

The young man settled down, assured that everything was fine. Nonetheless he couldn't help feeling he was being watched.

As soon as he turned away from the woods he sensed an icy stare burrowing into his back, cold as a knife edge. But when he peered into the trees, he didn't see anything. The forest looked deserted, as always. No sound but the rustle of treetops and the bleating of sheep.

He turned his back on the woods, sat down on the log, and opened his book again to take his mind off the uncanny sense of menace.

To no avail.

His eyes danced over the lines; he didn't understand a word despite his familiarity with the story. He tried several times, forcing himself to read each word carefully. But he couldn't concentrate. The feeling of being watched had grown so strong that he dreaded turning around.

Yet he got hold of himself and stood to brave another look at the woods. His heart beat wildly in his breast. All the while his brain rehashed his grandmother's old tales from his childhood. She had told him of the horrid things and the great terrors that befall disobedient children, stories of demons and other shadowy figures that go after naughty boys and girls.

He recalled them so vividly that he momentarily relived his grandmother's croaking voice in his thoughts:

"Be careful, my boy. There are *evil* creatures out there in the woods that are just waiting for a child to wander their way. A good child who obeys his parents' rules has nothing to fear. But bad children who roam around like stray dogs—demons will sooner or later . . . *gobble them up!*"

Yes, he recalled, that's what she had warned: *Bad children get gobbled up.*

He stood there motionless, looking across the clearing. The feeling of being watched had grown so strong that it preyed on his mind.

He reached into his pants pocket and pulled out the knife he'd cut his breakfast bread with. His palms were moist. The knife handle felt slippery, like a wet bar of soap. Drawing his knife reassured him somewhat.

"Is anybody there?" he shouted in the direction of the forest. But his voice sounded anxious, like a child's.

"Come out, come out whoever you are!" he shouted. Some of the sheep turned and looked at him; the two dogs perked up their ears and gave him an inquisitive look. Otherwise, nothing, just the rustling of the treetops that the wind kept inviting to come and dance.

He was about to turn away again when a voice resounded from the woods.

"Georgius!"

The young man jumped at the sound of his name as if it had been a pistol shot. His heart seized up, as did his whole body. He ducked his head and listened for a moment. No further sound.

"Who's there?" he yelled. Again he peered into the darkness of the forest, where waving treetops kept creating new patterns of light and shade.

"Georgius, come to me," the voice hissed this time. It was little more than a whisper, carried to his ears on the invisible wings of the wind.

"Who the hell's there?"

A laugh rang out from the tangle of shadows.

Georgius looked to the dogs. They'd stood up and were also staring at the edge of the clearing, ears back, the hair on their napes bristling. Nelka, a bitch, flashed her teeth. Her tail was tucked between trembling legs. Nemos, her brother, was off to one side, quaking all over. They both started to growl as if on command—a deep-throated sound that echoed across the clearing.

The young man had never seen his dogs behave like that. He remembered other shepherds telling him about this behavior, shepherds who remembered the times when the forest crawled with bears. But he knew that there hadn't been any bears in the area for decades. And definitely not any bears here or anywhere in the world that would call him by name.

"Come to me, Georgius," the voice called out again, commanding.

"Show yourself, whoever you are!" Georgius shouted.

There was a rustling in the thicket, and the young man was certain it wasn't the wind. Concentrating on that one spot, he thought he could make out a dark figure huddled in the bushes. But he knew that the dance of shadows in the underbrush could play tricks with his eyes.

Undeterred, he looked to see if the dogs had picked up a scent. But what he saw hit him like a blow to the stomach. Nelka was squatting and uncontrollably peeing on the ground. Nemos was howling like a pup, head back and eyes wide open. When another rustling sound came from the woods, both dogs turned and hightailed it.

"Nemos, Nelka—stay!" the young man screamed. But even before his words died away, the dogs were out of the clearing, leaving him alone with his flock. Even the sheep looked anxiously in the direction of the rustling sound.

"Come here, Georgius. Come to me, and we'll have a lot of fun with each other."

The voice had changed. It wasn't a hiss. Nor a whisper. It was a woman's voice. The words were breathy. Sensuous and maybe a little . . . *lascivious*.

He loosened his grip on the knife. His pants began to grow taut. A warm feeling flowed through his body, gradually washing away his fear. His desire mounted and eroded his reason. The young man wavered, indecisive, as he took the first step toward the clearing's edge.

"That's *very* good," the woman's voice cooed. "Come over here, and I'll show you a pretty little thing."

The voice was very near rejoicing. The young man took another hesitant step. And another. Finally, he walked through the sheep, who parted as if they were an honor guard. He neared the edge of the clearing with the uncertain gait of a sleepwalker.

"Come here," the voice moaned, "and something nice will happen to you, my sweetheart."

The words clouded his thinking like a thick fog. His grandmother's warning came to him again: *Bad children get gobbled up.*

But that caution from the past couldn't clear away the billows of lust-filled fog in the young man's mind. Invisible threads drew him faster and faster toward the forest. At last he stumbled to the clearing's edge.

"That's very good—and now come here!"

Fragments of his dream flared up in his thoughts as he pushed the bushes aside. And the more he saw of what lurked in the darkness, the more his dream—*dark figures with blood-red eyes staring at him coldly, baring their teeth like dogs*—turned into a horrifying reality.

The sight choked him. He tried to scream, but a mere rattle escaped his lips. The woman-like figure seemed not merely aware of his fear but greatly delighted by it. The thing stared at him with red eyes that sparkled like rubies in candlelight. Spines and thorns had torn parts of its pale skin. Under the skin tangled a dark web of veins where blood hadn't flowed for a long while. The creature was naked, and her breasts hung limply down her body like dried fruits. Insects and maggots crawled all over her, feasting on her dead flesh.

The young man's heart skipped a beat and then raced wildly. He tried to turn away from those flashing eyes, rush over the pasture, and get out of sight, as far and as fast as his feet could take him. But as much as he tried, he couldn't retreat from the horrifying visage. He couldn't move a muscle. His limbs were paralyzed with fear.

Before he could pull back, the creature had grabbed his shirt and dragged him into the dark. The last thing he saw was her flashing teeth . . . *long, pointed, curved* . . . before they sank into his neck.

His final thought was that he knew the woman in the thicket. He had recognized her at once in spite of all the changes she had undergone. With this knowledge, with his energy drained from his body, he resigned himself to his fate.

The creature that had so firmly bitten him in the neck had once been a fisherman's wife in the town. She'd disappeared suddenly the previous spring without a trace. One night she was asleep in her bed with her husband—the next morning, gone forever.

The shepherd had joined in the search for her, as had most of the other young men in the town. They'd scoured the woods and the gorges and the mountains.

No luck.

At some point a rumor made the rounds that she'd fallen into the sea and drowned. Everyone waited in vain for her bloated body to wash ashore.

But now she was back.

She was back!

Very soon the young man's mind sank into a blood-red mist, and his heart stopped beating.

CHAPTER 1

CLAIRE HAGEN FOUGHT BACK TEARS. Dr. John Harris leaned over his desk and handed her a tissue.

"Please, don't cry," he soothed. "There is no reason to be so upset."

Claire wiped the tears from the corners of her eyes and crossed her hands on her lap. Her fingers clutched the soaked tissue, and all the blood left her knuckles until they were white as polished ivory.

"What's going to happen to Amanda, Dr. Harris?" Her voice trembled. She found it hard not to burst into tears again.

Harris leaned back in his leather chair and looked at the ceiling as if everything that he needed to calm Claire down were written there.

Claire could tell by his tone of voice that he was simply reciting a litany, a sequence of hollow phrases he'd use to justify his work.

"Your sister has been medicating herself heavily, it seems, but still is in a pronounced state of agitation. It looks to me like a nervous breakdown caused by stress. A stay in the ward is appropriate for now; I believe it is in Amanda's best interest."

"So you think Amanda might hurt herself?" Claire asked. Her sister's image in the ward had burned itself onto her retinas. Whenever she closed her eyes, there was Amanda staring at her with that crazed look as she yanked at the ties holding her to the bed. Her tortured voice haunted Claire.

Please, Claire, get me out of here. I'm not safe here! HE will find me! My God, he'll find me!

"I don't think she is acutely suicidal," Dr. Harris explained. "To be sure, my experience with such patients has taught me to be cautious. You yourself have seen how quickly your sister's mood swings between fantasies of fear and normality. For this reason I think it safest to restrain her for the time being. But I assure you that this is only a temporary measure. It will continue only until we begin proper medication."

Dr. Harris's words were small comfort for Claire. Since she got the news of Amanda's hospitalization, she'd found herself unable to think clearly; her head was too busy whirling with self-accusations.

Though she hadn't heard anything from Amanda for more than a month, it was an older sister's instinct that persuaded Claire that she was responsible for Amanda's condition.

It was like when three-year-old Amanda broke her arm falling off the playground seesaw, all over again. Claire could almost still hear her father's angry voice blaming her for the accident.

It's your fault that this happened. Nobody else's! You're Mandy's older sister, and it was your responsibility to look out for her!

Those harsh words had wounded the ten-year-old Claire's psyche deeply. Almost twenty years later, Claire realized that she still hadn't gotten over it. The memory of the accident still seized her heart like an iron fist.

She took deep breaths and faced reality again, though it seemed increasingly like a confused dream.

"Will Mandy ever be normal again?" Claire realized too late how cold this question might sound to Dr. Harris's ears.

The doctor took off his glasses and placed them on his desk. He rubbed the fiery red marks the glasses had left on his nose.

"I will be honest with you," he said, looking her straight in the eye. "If it is a stress-related nervous collapse, then the odds in favor of recovery are statistically at least as good as in the case of pneumonia. It might take some time, but we will certainly have your sister back on her feet again. The overwrought state of your sister's nerves and her mental confusion could be simply the result of an acute reactive disorder—a nervous breakdown. These types of symptoms can be treated with medication and relaxation therapy without any problem.

"But if your sister continues to present the same kinds of psychotic symptoms that precipitated her admission, we would have reason to suspect schizophrenia. That would, of course, call for a completely different therapy."

Harris paused for a moment, and then folded his arms across his chest. Claire recognized this body language as a defensive position; she'd seen that stance in many critical interviews she'd done as a reporter for the *New York News Review*. She intuited that Dr. Harris was on the brink of telling her the whole truth about her sister's condition.

"What I am most worried about is the advanced manifestation of her fears. Psychosis aside, your sister's illness did not spring up overnight. Actually, I suspect she has been fighting her fears and delusions for quite some time."

"What's she so afraid of, Dr. Harris?" Claire asked.

"Vampires, Miss Hagen. Your sister is afraid of vampires. Or to put it more accurately, she dreads one vampire in particular. She is firmly convinced that this vampire visits her night after night to drink her blood."

CHAPTER 2

SAYING GOOD-BYE TO AMANDA did not take long.

After talking with Dr. Harris, Claire wanted to see her sister again. A nurse took her to a room tiled to the ceiling, with stout iron bars on the single window. The nurse explained that Amanda had been given a strong sedative and could probably not say much. She opened the door to Amanda's room and left Claire alone with her.

Claire went to the bed and looked carefully at her sister, the most important person in her life since their parents died. Mandy's head was turned to one side, and her eyes were closed.

Madness and fear were completely absent from her features for the moment. A breath of hope wafted through Claire.

"Oh, Mandy," she said, running her fingers through her sister's dark blond hair. "What is going on with you?"

Amanda opened her lids hesitantly and looked up at her sister with glassy eyes and dilated pupils. Mandy's gaze was vacant and expressionless, and for a minute it seemed to Claire that she was peering down a dark, dried-up well.

Claire suppressed the thought, knowing Amanda's vacant look was probably a side effect of the sedative.

"Claire," Amanda said.

"Yes, hon, it's me. I'm here. How are you?"

A fleeting smile appeared on Amanda's chapped lips. Then she scowled.

"Claire."

"Shh, sis. It'll be OK. Just get some rest to make sure you get better quickly."

"Claire, please help me," Amanda said. Her voice sounded as if she'd drunk too much. She slurred her words, which came laboriously through her lips. At the same time all the calmness left her face. She furrowed her brow, and her lips began to tremble.

"Claire, you've got to get me out of here. Please, Claire, I can't stand it anymore. He'll find me. I'm not safe here."

Mandy's words hit Claire like an unexpected punch, and the little spark of hope she'd been harboring was extinguished in a sea of anxiety. Bitter tears welled up in her eyes, and her sister's face dissolved in a jumble of streaks. Nevertheless, she refused to cry.

"Everything's going to be OK, Mandy, I promise. Just relax, and everything will be all right."

Amanda's face grew less tense. She closed her eyes, and Claire could see from her slow, regular breathing that she'd fallen asleep. Claire bent down and gave her sister a kiss on the forehead.

Then she left the room.

She hurried through the clinic's many dark corridors, feeling as if she were in a dream. Her thoughts were inextricably held in a welter of self-doubt and reproaches:

Would Amanda ever be healthy again? Was what happened to Mandy her fault? How had things gotten so far? Had she been thinking only of herself lately and lost sight of her sister?

These and similar questions flew through her head like startled bats in the timbers of a house. She didn't allow the tears to flow until she'd gotten into her car and slammed the door. She gave in to her emotions while a light drizzle started up outside.

The tension drained out of her as if through a safety valve, like floodgates had been opened. The intensity of her crying washed away all her worries.

After her crying spell was over and only a gentle sobbing rattled Claire's self-control, she looked at herself in the rearview mirror. Her eyes were red, her makeup smeared. She dug a tissue out of her purse and wiped the dark smudges from her eyelids and cheeks. Then she took a deep breath and forced a smile.

"Everything's going to be OK again," she reassured herself.

She rummaged around in her purse again until she found her cell phone and called up Arthur Flynn, the editor-in-chief of the *News Review.*

The phone rang, and finally the ever-harried-sounding voice of her boss answered.

"Claire, where the hell are you? If you flake on me in the middle of an election, you might as well pack your bags, darling. There's a bunch of reporters drooling for your job."

"Art, I'm sorry. My sister had a . . ."

A what, Claire? What did she have? A touch of insanity? Is that what your sister had?

". . . an accident, and I had to go see her in the hospital."

There was absolute quiet for a moment at the other end.

"Oh my God, Claire. Why didn't you say so right away? I hope it's nothing serious. Holy shit, if I'd known that, I wouldn't have given you such a hard time. I'm so sorry. Sometimes I'm a real asshole."

"It's OK, Art—don't worry. My sister's already a little better. Still, I wanted to ask if I could have the day off to be here for her."

"That's the least I can do, Claire. Morris will take over your deadlines, and I'll personally see to everything else."

"Thanks, Art. You're the best."

"I couldn't agree with you more, sweetheart. Arthur Flynn, always at your service."

Claire could hear the smile in his gruff voice.

"Idiot," she said.

"Guilty as charged," he admitted. "Let me know if you need anything—whatever, I'm here. Have a good day, kiddo. See you tomorrow."

"Thanks for everything, Art. Talk to you tomorrow."

Claire hung up. The chat had been enough to calm her down, at least for a bit. And even if Art's words maybe just amounted to a few empty phrases, she thought, this little shot of encouragement was pure balm on her troubled soul.

As Claire stuffed her cell back into her purse, she saw Amanda's personal effects, which Dr. Harris and his staff had given to Claire.

It wasn't much: a cell, lipstick, and the key to Amanda's apartment in Greenwich Village.

As she held the apartment key, the personality traits that had been earning her a living for more than five years kicked in: her journalist's curiosity and her street smarts.

If anything could help her explain Amanda's condition, it was the apartment. It had been a month since Claire had been there, and she wasn't sure what she hoped to find. Still, she decided that it couldn't hurt to take a little look around within her sister's four walls.

She started the car, left the parking lot, and merged into the traffic going downtown.

While heading south she remembered Dr. Harris's bizarre words . . .

Vampires, Miss Hagen. Your sister is afraid of vampires.

. . . and an icy shiver ran down her spine.

CHAPTER 3

AMANDA'S APARTMENT was on one of the many little side streets leading into Washington Square. That part of New York had made a comeback in recent years as a neighborhood for ambitious artists, and of course the rents had shot up rapidly to keep pace with the boom. Amanda had been lucky to find one of the few affordable apartments that wasn't a rat hole.

When Mandy moved to the city, Claire had thought it terrific that her kid sister would be living only a short hop from her, not stuck in Rockwell, the hick town in the heart of Maine where they had grown up. But as she parked in front of Amanda's apartment building, she guiltily recalled how she had hardly found any time during the past year to visit her sister, despite their proximity.

Deadlines, stress, and work had kept her from Amanda, though she was only a twenty-minute subway ride away.

When Amanda first moved away from home, they'd seen each other every couple of days, meeting for lunch, going to the movies together, or shopping. They made up for all the little things they hadn't done much of over the last few years, things they'd usually reserved for holidays and long weekends.

They'd managed in no time at all to reestablish the old bonds that had been there since childhood, bonds that had made them more than merely sisters—made them also damn good friends.

Best of friends . . .

Blood is thicker than water, Claire had thought back then and was delighted to have Amanda constantly around her. And although this was a very casual conclusion, she'd had no reason to doubt its validity. She'd in fact become dedicated to the hope that everything would stay in the future exactly as it was now.

But it wasn't long before this fervent wish turned out to be a pipe dream. And by the time Claire's career really got going, the end of their chummy togetherness was already looming. Their regular rendezvous gave way to phone calls, and in the end Claire simply didn't have the time. They completely lost sight of each other in spite of their good intentions. And she knew all too well that it was mainly her own fault. If she'd just eased up on her job a bit, then things definitely wouldn't have gone that far.

Definitely not . . .

"Now's not the right time to go blaming yourself," Claire muttered, turning off the motor. "Get to work."

She got out of the car and stopped in front of Amanda's five-story brick apartment building. She took the key out of her purse and opened the door to the dingy lobby. The elevator went to the fifth floor, where there were only two other apartments besides Amanda's. Claire unlocked the door and went into the small hallway.

The first thing she noticed was a strong, nauseating smell. It took her a moment to identify it. She took a few deep breaths. When she realized what it was, her heart skipped a beat: *garlic.*

Amanda's apartment reeked of garlic.

It didn't just smell—it stank, disgustingly. The odor was so strong, Claire's stomach was not far from heaving. She made herself breathe through her mouth—firmly determined to keep her breakfast down.

After a few breaths, the obnoxious aroma was scratching her throat, like a harbinger of a bad cold. Some more inhaling, and the feeling subsided. She breathed normally again.

But the garlic stench wasn't the only thing that struck her as odd. After closing the door and thus blocking the light from the corridor, she was in almost total darkness. Her sister's apartment had a southern exposure, so at this time of day it should have been flooded with light and very bright. But the very opposite was true: It was pitch black and stuffy, like a fox's den. Claire could make out some thin strips of light in the living room, which divided the dark space into geometrical patterns. Dust churned in the rays of light, and Claire could hazard a guess about the outlines of furniture in the dark, but everything else was obscured by the darkness.

From the entrance, Claire turned on the hallway and living room lights. She saw that all the window blinds had been lowered. She pulled one of them up, opened the window, and let fresh air and sunshine into the room. The curtains stretched and billowed out in the wind like sails. The scratchiness in her throat eased, as did a bit of the tension that had persistently followed her around like her own shadow.

Only then did she take a look around the room. Couch, table, chairs, TV—everything seemed normal at first glance. The room was tidy and looked cozy.

But this appearance in no way matched Amanda's present state of mind. Claire still didn't really know what she expected to gain from going to her sister's apartment, but she was sure that a little messiness would be more fitting for a woman now tied to a bed in a psychiatric hospital. No, messiness wasn't the right word, Claire thought. After seeing Mandy's state, she'd actually expected to find utter chaos. Chaos of biblical proportions—with dried-out leftovers on the furniture and garbage piled six feet high.

Instead, the space reminded her of a furniture-store showroom. Everything was clean, organized, and sterile. Her impression that something was wrong gradually grew stronger. She dropped her purse on the sofa and took off her coat. Since her first impression of the place didn't make any sense to her, she had to examine the rest of the apartment more carefully. As so often, reason took a backseat to intuition.

You've got to find something! Something to help you understand what's happened to Mandy.

She went into the kitchen, turned on the light, and immediately located the source of the apartment's nauseating smell. The counter was piled high with garlic, most of it still in bags from the market, though a considerable amount on the counter and dish rack was unpacked and peeled.

When Claire took a closer look at the stove, she found several open preserving jars filled to the brim with crushed garlic. That was probably the main source of the repulsive smell, Claire concluded, grimacing in disgust. She closed all the jars and opened the small kitchen window. She tried to raise the blind but couldn't. It seemed to be broken, but she could feel at least a little fresh air getting in around the edges.

Better than nothing.

Though she'd discovered why the apartment smelled, she hadn't gotten one step farther in her search for what was responsible for Amanda's condition. There *had* to be a trigger, she felt.

Nobody turns overnight into a nervous wreck like her sister had. This garlic business wasn't a hot clue—but still, it was a clue.

No woman in her mid-twenties would live with such a stink of her own free will. And certainly not Amanda, who couldn't stand garlic since she was a child.

Claire leaned against the counter and poured herself a glass of water. She scanned the kitchen as she sipped. She didn't find anything unusual here either; except for the garlic, everything in the room was in its proper place. But her gaze fell on the garbage pail in front of the table.

She knew from her job as a reporter that a person's garbage could sometimes tell a lot more about him or her than a credit card bill and a browser history put together.

Though Claire now interviewed politicians, sports heroes, and big shots in show biz, she'd started small—very small, actually. As a girl from the sticks without money or the necessary contacts to realize her dreams, she'd had a choice after college: She could either clear the tables in a fast-food joint and wait for a miracle, or start working for any old newspaper that paid minimum wage but at least offered benefits.

Claire chose the second option and began as a reporter for the *New York City Herald*. The semiweekly was mainly concerned with who was bedding whom and who was in rehab (although said stars generally claimed to be on a professional hiatus).

During that time at the *Herald*, Claire had rooted around for evidence in more than one garbage can and unearthed some amazing things—which is why she in no way felt timid or disgusted when she took the lid off her sister's garbage and sorted through the contents on the floor.

The first thing that struck her was the many empty medicine bottles. Claire liberated one of them from a dried banana peel so she could read the label: Valium—a prescription drug you couldn't simply pick up over the counter.

No doctor nowadays would be so naïve as to prescribe so many doses of Valium at one time, she thought, especially given the recent highly publicized dangers of Valium addiction and overdose.

She counted them: eight. All empty. All that had once contained Valium. She lined them up on the counter. She'd barely glanced at the labels before she'd solved the riddle of Amanda's ability to obtain so much.

Each bottle had a different name in the place for the prescribing doctor. Amanda must have traipsed all over town to accumulate such a supply without arousing any pharmacist's suspicion.

Claire went to the living room to get her notebook out of her purse. Back in the kitchen she wrote down the names of the doctors who'd given Amanda the prescriptions. Of course she knew about patient confidentiality, that none of the doctors was obliged to give her the information she needed. At the same time, she knew from experience that a doctor's duty to keep silent was often merely rhetorical and that you could readily get the information you wanted most of the time.

Moreover, a journalist didn't have to reveal his sources— even if they often leaked very confidential information. In Claire's experience, information would come out eventually. The public knew in no time if a prominent personality was in an addiction clinic or suffered from AIDS, so the sources had to be a closely guarded secret.

After listing all the names, Claire wrote the dates from every bottle to note when the medication was dispensed. She saw at once that there were never more than five days between her sister's prescriptions. Since there were sixty tablets in each bottle, Amanda must have been taking twelve pills every day.

Claire suspected that a daily dose of almost fifty milligrams of Valium would have been enough to knock a bear out of action.

What could have unhinged Amanda to such an extent that she needed so many tranquilizers? And how the hell could she even be alive now if she had actually taken dosages that high?

Claire couldn't figure it out, and that's what scared her.

CHAPTER 4

CLAIRE RETURNED TO THE LIVING ROOM, sat down at the desk, and opened Mandy's laptop.

She knew her sister's password was "CLAIRE" because she'd given her the laptop as a birthday present two years ago. She'd teased Mandy by entering her own name as the password first. Mandy had turned up her nose, claiming that Claire wanted to rub it in that she'd given her the laptop so that *Mandy* would remember to give Claire the most awesome birthday present in return. But it was just a little joke between sisters; Mandy hadn't changed her password.

Claire opened the browser. She typed the name of the doctor who'd most recently prescribed Mandy's Valium into the search box: Dr. Arnold James. Then she hit ENTER.

The search engine spewed out results in less than a second. Claire clicked on the first hit, called up the home page for a New York–based Dr. Arnold James, and there was his phone number.

She took a cell phone out of her purse, the one that she used for the politically charged phone calls that occasionally came with her job. This work phone was prepaid and untraceable, with automatic call blocking so she couldn't be contacted. An enormous advantage, of course, if she had to quiz sources in dicey cases to get critical secrets. That phone had kept her out of the line of fire more than a few times.

Maybe, Claire hoped, she'd be lucky and a few nice words would be enough to get Dr. James to cough up all the information he had about Amanda. She could of course explain her situation and trust he wouldn't be a stickler for confidentiality. *After all, he wouldn't be the first . . .*

Nevertheless, she decided it was better to be safe than sorry. She wanted to find out fast *why* all that Valium without giving him the whole megillah about how she and Amanda were related.

Claire dialed the doctor's office number.

"Dr. James's office," a woman's voice said. "This is Cathy. How may I help you?"

"Hello, Cathy," Claire said brusquely. "This is Officer Susan Richards from the Twenty-third Precinct, NYPD. This is a business call. It's very important for me to talk to Dr. James at once."

Claire spoke quickly and without emotion to give the impression that this was all routine. She knew it was a federal offense to impersonate a police officer, but she felt the odds of being caught were extremely low.

"Dr. James is fully booked today," Cathy said. "It would be better if you tried again just before five. Hopefully he can spare a minute at the end of office hours. Would you like to leave your number so he can get back to you?"

Claire glanced at her watch and saw it was just after eleven. If she waited all day, it would drive her nuts. But that wasn't the only reason she didn't want to wait. Back in the darkest recesses of her mind, she felt that every minute taken finding out what happened to her sister could be critical.

So she decided to go all in.

"I can't wait that long," Claire blustered in an annoyed voice. "Let me suggest, Cathy, that either you get Dr. James on the phone in five minutes, or I'll see that a squad car brings him to the station pronto for questioning."

"You can't do that," Cathy said. "It's high-volume time in the office."

Claire sensed she had her on the hook. Now it was just a matter of gingerly getting her into the boat.

"Are you telling me what I can and cannot do? I didn't catch your last name, Cathy. If this turns into a case of obstructing a police investigation, I'd better know your last name, don't you think?"

Silence for a moment at the other end of the line. Then Cathy broke it.

"I'll see what I can do."

A metallic click was followed promptly by on-hold music. Claire was confident it wouldn't take even five minutes for the doctor to come to the phone. She watched the second hand of her watch go around twice. Just after two minutes a male voice came on the line. "Dr. Arnold James here. How may I be of assistance?"

"Hello, Dr. James," Claire said. "This is Susan Richards with the Twenty-third Precinct. My colleagues and I are investigating a case of illegally prescribed medications. I have some questions about one of your patients who is the alleged ringleader."

Claire could hear a sigh on the phone. She sensed a police investigation was probably the last thing Dr. James wanted on a Friday afternoon. Most of the Manhattan doctors she knew came to work on Fridays with their golf shoes in the car. But even if Dr. James wasn't a golfer, he was probably already more than ready for the weekend.

"Who is the patient concerned, officer?" he asked. His voice sounded soft and weak on the phone.

"Amanda Hagen."

"I hope you are aware that I am not obligated to give information about my patients without a court order?"

Claire sensed that this threat was a last little attempt at rebellion. Soon, she thought, he'd crack and tell her everything she wanted. So she held on.

"Of course you don't *have* to give me any information. I can definitely understand that you'd rather I'd obtain a search warrant for your office. Then I won't have to put up with your excuses, but I can get the information I need directly from your files. So, Dr. James, it's your call."

Her voice was irritated, every word dripping with authority. Claire knew the doctor would probably do anything to shake her off as quickly as he could. To hell with patient confidentiality.

"OK, OK," he responded. "What was that patient's name again?"

"Hagen, Amanda."

"Just a minute, please," James said. Claire could hear the phone being put down and the immediate, rhythmic tapping of a busy computer keyboard.

"You still there, officer?"

"Shoot," Claire said, flipping her notebook open.

"The patient was in my office a week ago complaining of anxiety."

"What was the cause?"

"She didn't want to tell me at first, Officer Richards. So I explained that I'm not allowed to prescribe medications without a good reason. Certainly not such a high dosage."

"And?"

"Then she told me she was scared of . . . how shall I put it? She claimed she is afraid of a . . ."

"Of a what?"

"A vampire. She actually said it was after her . . ."

Vampire. Claire's heart skipped a beat.

". . . or something like that. She confessed that was why she needed a tranquilizer, so she wouldn't completely lose it. Of course I told her she should see a psychiatrist, but she wouldn't hear of it. And like an idiot I let her talk me into prescribing her Valium. These junkies—they always dream up something new to get the stuff. Hello? Are you still on the line? Hello? Officer?"

Claire had heard enough. She couldn't think of anything else to ask. Besides, she couldn't bear to hear Amanda called a junkie. She took the cell from her ear, turned it off, and stowed it in her purse.

Vampire.

Claire chose to save herself the trouble of calling the other doctors on her list. What Dr. Harris said agreed with what Dr. James told her.

Amanda was afraid of vampires. A fear that made her travel all around town to get a cache of tranquilizers. Over and above that, her paranoia had made her live for days in that ghastly garlic stink because of the misguided belief that it would free her from whatever demons haunted her.

Claire had of course seen the connection between garlic and vampires the minute she walked into Amanda's apartment. But she resisted accepting that her sister's delusions were that far advanced. Her mind balked at the admission, like a horse before a steep cliff.

A wave of pity swept through Claire, bringing tears to her eyes. Along with the pity, self-reproach came flooding back. She felt responsible for Amanda's condition.

*How could things get this far? You should have been there for her.
You're her sister and should have been watching out for her!*

A lone teardrop trickled down Claire's cheek and got
trapped in the corner of her mouth. Then the more rational part
of her mind took the reins again and told her that it was absolutely unreasonable to cry now. Instead, she had to track down
the cause of Amanda's delusions as fast as possible.

She considered whether there might have been a case of
insanity in the family. But she couldn't think of any. The Hagens
were descended from Germans who had come to the U.S. in the
first great wave of immigrants in the twentieth century. Claire's
grandmother Heidi had told funny stories about relatives with
tics and eccentricities of every kind—but there was nobody who
could be regarded as clinically insane.

Claire knew of course that mental illness wasn't inevitably
handed down in a family, like bad manners or bad teeth. And
she didn't believe that a mental illness would have manifested
itself so suddenly and powerfully. She knew from her college
lectures that disorders of this kind usually began with mild
symptoms and gradually worsened.

Since she felt she could exclude mental illness as a cause
of Amanda's condition, her mind pulled another one out of
the hat.

Drugs.

Abuse of illegal drugs had occurred to her. But that could
also be eliminated as a cause: Claire knew that Dr. Harris had
ordered blood and urine tests. If drugs besides Valium had actually been a factor, then he'd have found out by now and told her.
No, her sister wasn't a junkie.

What other causes could there be? No matter how hard
Claire tried, she couldn't think of any. Her thoughts went
around in circles, like a roulette ball.

Maybe it didn't pay to keep banging her head against the wall, she conceded as she closed the laptop. After all, Amanda had good care. Dr. Harris would probably find the cause. He would begin treatment, and Amanda would improve in no time, she thought. As naïve as the idea of Mandy's miraculous cure might seem, at least it made Claire feel better and more relaxed for a while.

She was just on her way to the kitchen to make coffee when there was a ringing in her purse. It was a ring tone she didn't recognize.

Amanda's cell, Claire concluded as she went over to the desk. She took the phone out and looked at the display: UNKNOWN CALLER. She hesitated a second, then took the call.

"Hello?"

"Hello," a man answered in a voice as rough as sandpaper. He spoke with an accent that she couldn't identify.

"Who is this?"

For a moment all was silent. Then Claire heard the caller enjoying a long drag on a cigarette and blowing smoke before replying, "You're Mandy87, right? The Mandy87 who wrote something on vampires in the Mystery Forum three days ago? Do I have the right number?"

Claire had to digest all the information that was bombarding her. But as odd as the call was, she caught on fast.

"Yes," she responded a moment later, "yes, it's me."

"Well then, do you want to find out something about vampires, or don't you? Your post sounded pretty serious to me."

"Yes, that's exactly what I want. What can you tell me?" She paused, then added, "About vampires, I mean?" She was surprised at how easily such an arcane word came from her lips.

Vampires!

Cynical laughter was heard from the other end, followed by a coughing fit, probably thanks to the cigarette.

"My dear," the voice continued, "I'm rather loath to talk about such things over the phone. I think we should meet somewhere. Today, if that works."

"OK," Claire agreed, somewhat hesitantly. Amanda's madness took on a whole new aspect with this unknown caller. Claire feared the madness would keep expanding in larger and larger circles in her otherwise quiet and organized life. But she persuaded herself quickly that it was better to follow up on every available clue, no matter how banal or nutty it might appear at first blush. In the end, it would be of little use if she simply folded her hands in her lap and waited for everything to get back on an even keel by itself.

"Where should we meet?" Claire inquired, imagining herself waiting under a highway bridge at midnight, somewhere outside the city where nasty things happened to young women at night, the kinds of things that had given her nightmares during her stint at the *New York CityHerald*.

She was all the more surprised, then, at the place and time the stranger came up with. She wrote the details down, and he gave her a description of his appearance. He hung up before she could say good-bye.

Claire looked at her watch and saw she had about two hours to get ready.

She put on her coat, closed the windows, and hurried out of the apartment.

CHAPTER 5

CLAIRE GLANCED AT HER WATCH as she made her way out of the city. She still had twenty minutes to the rendezvous. But her GPS showed it would take more than half an hour to get there.

She sped up to eighty-five instead of the permitted sixty-five mph, hoping that some overambitious traffic cop wouldn't wreck her plans. If nothing interfered, she'd make it.

She had spent the last hour and a half returning to her East Side apartment to pick up her recording device, a small digital instrument about the size of a cigarette lighter. If she made it there before the stranger, she could hide the device someplace where the recording quality would be good.

But if the unknown caller got there first, then she'd leave it in her breast coat pocket, as in previous interviews. In those cases the quality hadn't been exactly mind-blowing, but with modern audio software even a lousy recording would be perfectly useful.

Useful for what? For a lead story on vampires for the News Review?

Maybe not that, Claire thought. But even so, she'd have evidence to back up her opinion, something to help her understand what had happened to Amanda. After all, the whole world couldn't have gone crazy.

Still, some doubts gnawed away at her as she neared her destination. The unknown caller might well have been a nutcase pulling her leg, somebody who'd lost touch with reality long ago and who was living in a dream world crawling with vampires, werewolves, and bottled-up genies. Claire dismissed the thought and focused on her driving.

Two minutes later she took the first exit to her destination: John F. Kennedy International Airport.

CHAPTER 6

JFK WAS THE LARGEST AIRPORT in New York City, with myriad counters, gates, and terminals. For that reason Claire was grateful that the caller had specified their meeting place so clearly:

"We'll meet in Terminal Four, Gate A-Three, in the coffee shop right behind Customs. I'll be wearing a gray suit and a red silk scarf."

Claire was there now. Her press card got her into the security area without a plane ticket. She'd feigned an interview with a foreign businessman, and the TSA screeners had no reason to doubt her. She'd gone through security quickly since she carried only her purse. Those formalities behind her, she entered the coffee shop, looking for a man fitting the caller's description.

Gray suit, red silk scarf.

It wasn't exactly rush hour in the little shop, and it didn't take long to discover he wasn't there yet. *If he's going to show up at all*, Claire admitted to herself.

She cast her doubts aside and sat down at a table near a large window looking out at the panorama of runways. She ordered a cappuccino and set about looking for a place for her recorder.

It would have been simplest, she thought, to hide the device inside a newspaper and put it right on the table, but that would be too easy to spot.

So she decided on the napkin holder in the middle of the table. She took out about a third of the napkins, placed the recorder in the empty space, and pushed the RECORD button. She hid the extra napkins in her purse and replaced the napkin holder. The waiter brought her cappuccino a minute later.

Claire took a sip while keeping an eye on the entrance. Just then, a man in a gray suit and a red silk scarf came in, stood in the doorway, and scanned the coffee shop.

Unlike Claire, he had no description of the person he was going to meet, so he relied on her to recognize him. This gave her a little time to satisfy herself that the unknown man was not a madman—a potentially dangerous madman. The fact that she was in an airport security area also reassured her. Even if he *was* crazy, at least she could be sure he didn't have a gun. She took a minute to size him up carefully.

He was about five-seven and slightly built, with thin black hair. His olive complexion hinted at a tropical or Mediterranean origin, but Claire excluded Mexico or Latin America; she would have recognized those accents on the phone. As to his age, she could also hazard only a guess: maybe in his fifties, perhaps older.

While she scrutinized him over the rim of her cappuccino cup, the man surveyed the customers. When he glanced at Claire, she raised her hand to signal that she was the right one.

A fleeting smile passed over the man's face before he moved toward her.

"I wasn't sure you'd even come," he said.

"I can say the same thing," Claire countered, offering him a seat.

"Thank you," he said as he sat down.

"I think we should introduce ourselves first," suggested Claire. She wanted to get his name on the recorder in case he had something to do with Amanda's condition.

"Pardon me for being impolite, but I'd prefer we not reveal our true names," the stranger responded with a smile. "I propose I simply call you Mandy."

"Fine," Claire said. "And what will I call you?"

"John. It's as good a name as any." He offered her his hand, which she shook briefly. His handshake was weak and tentative, reminding her of an old woman's. His hands were soft and manicured, leading Claire to believe he didn't do any physical labor. Her nose picked up a sweetish fragrance that quickly dissipated before she could pin it down.

"Pleased to meet you, John. So let's get to the real reason we're meeting."

"You want to know something about . . ." John stopped for a moment and spied around the shop, his eyes skipping from one customer to the next, like a flat stone over the water. When he continued, his voice was muted, scarcely more than a whisper:

". . . about vampires, if I understood you correctly."

"And you know something about vampires?" Claire asked, automatically lowering her voice.

"I know plenty about vampires. Just saw one of those bastards last week. Excuse my language—but since then I've been scared out of my wits."

"You saw a vampire last week? Here, in New York? Did I hear you right?"

"Yes, here in New York. A goddamn vampire."

With every passing second it seemed to Claire that she was trapped in a bizarre dream that she'd wake up from at any moment.

Or maybe she was on one of those TV shows where somebody was playing a really bad joke on her. Because here she was, asking a stranger what he knew about vampires instead of interviewing the mayor that day. *Life sure takes some funny twists and turns*, she observed.

"Tell me about it," Claire prompted. At this point she was leaning toward the conclusion that this rendezvous was a mistake.

John leaned over and folded his hands on the table. His face was about six inches from the napkin holder, and Claire was confident that the recorder would deliver some viable results.

"If you're a cop, you've got to tell me here and now before you accuse me of a criminal offense, right?" John asked.

At first Claire didn't know what he was aiming at. But she still let herself go with the flow of the situation—as absurd as it perhaps was.

Damn absurd . . . no question about it . . .

But she played along in spite of her growing concern—what else could she do at that moment?

"Don't worry," she replied. "I'm not a cop."

"Honest?"

"Scout's honor," she said, raising her right hand as if swearing an oath.

John's eyes didn't leave her for an instant, and he didn't start talking until he seemed to be confident that Claire was telling the truth.

"Do you know what a *lopov* is, Mandy?"

"No."

"Where I come from, a *lopov* is someone who earns a living by stealing and lying. Here in America they're called thieves or con men."

"What are you getting at?"

John fished a cigarette out of his jacket pocket. He rolled it between his thumb and forefinger, and his face had a momentary spark of wistfulness. He continued to play with the unlit cigarette as he spoke.

"*I* am a *lopov*. I earn my livelihood by robbing rich people. I sneak into their houses and steal their valuables."

Once again Claire was glad she was in safe surroundings right then and not under a highway bridge in the middle of the night.

At least relatively safe, my dear . . .

John's confession took her heartbeat up a notch for a minute, but on the whole her curiosity got the best of her, wanting to see how his words connected with what had happened to her sister.

And that's the problem right there, she thought.

She did *not* see any connection with her sister. Or with what John claimed to know about vampires. Nevertheless she let him go on, hoping it would lead to something about Amanda.

"My preferred clientele is in Tarrytown. Most people there have one thing in common: They have lots of money and aren't home during the day. There are lots of lawyers and stockbrokers, and their wives are always either at the spa or club. No one's at home during the day, and because they live outside the heart of the city behind fences and hedges, most are so complacent they forget to turn on the alarm until they lock themselves in at night. So the threat of being caught during a burglary is minimal in Tarrytown. The houses are on private properties, large compared to New York. A good *lopov* can make a mint in that neighborhood."

John paused long enough to stick the unlit cigarette between his lips, and then quickly removed it. A fleeting smile danced around the corners of his mouth—a smile Claire felt spoke a completely different language than his eyes did. It was not until that moment that she noticed the fear in his eyes: They were restless, flitting around the room as if seeking out an invisible danger.

"Last Wednesday my partner and I were on our way through Tarrytown. The house we'd cased was on a large lot. We assumed nobody was living there because nobody had gone in or out for weeks. We'd discovered the house was full of valuables. You must understand—for us the table was set, as they say. We parked our delivery truck in the driveway, broke the garage lock, and got into the house. No alarm system, no watchdogs—nothing. It was child's play."

Claire had finished her cappuccino, and the waiter came and cleared away her empty cup. John quietly tucked the cigarette back in his pocket and ordered a whiskey on the rocks. Claire joined him, although she never drank during the day. Her nerves had been stretched tight for twelve hours, so she hoped the whiskey would help her relax a little. John resumed his story.

"The house was a genuine gold mine. Paintings everywhere, expensive knickknacks, and precious rugs. We could have filled three delivery trucks, no problem. Maybe a large moving van. After about an hour we'd moved everything into the truck that could make us money. My partner . . . call him Jack . . . decided to take one last look in the basement. I urged him to get out. But Jack, poor Jack—he absolutely had to take a look in that damn basement. He finally talked me into it, and I followed him down."

"Then what happened?" Claire asked.

"Jack and I went into that goddamn basement. I could tell even on the stairs that something wasn't right down there. The light didn't work, so we had to use our flashlights. But that wasn't the problem. The basement was a dirty hellhole compared to the rest of the house. The walls weren't sealed, so black gunk dripped through the brick wall into the house. It smelled damp and moldy, and the floor was just tamped-down dirt. It was so dusty that our footsteps left tracks. And there was a stink—airless, like in a crypt that hadn't been opened for a long time. But down we went to look around. We quickly saw there were no prizes to swipe. On the contrary, Jack and I had become prizes without even knowing it."

CHAPTER 7

BISHOP HAD THE TWO SUBJECTS perfectly in sight. He sat a few tables away, pretending to be engrossed in his newspaper. He acted like a bored businessman indulging in a little quiet and coffee. He leafed through the paper halfheartedly, sipped his coffee, and occasionally looked impatiently at his watch. The illusion was perfect. He was just like all the other suits taking refuge in the coffee shop from their stressful routine.

However, his mission was totally different. He didn't have to close some business deal or other in Chicago or fly off to a job interview in Miami. And his concentration wasn't disrupted by a cell phone every couple of minutes. Instead, his total attention was directed to the two subjects' conversation. It turned out that had been a clever move, tapping the phone of that girl in Greenwich Village. At least her posts to the Internet forums had been more specific than all the usual crap he read there. She didn't rave about vampires or have those crazy, romantic ideas. No, quite the opposite. Fear came through in every line she wrote. Pure terror lurked in her words like a snake in tall grass.

Please help me if you know how I can protect myself. It's so awful—I'm so terrified!

She'd pointedly asked for some way of defending herself against the thing that visited her night after night.

Of course Bishop knew right away that the girl probably was beyond help. After only one or two vampire bites, there was a chance she still might have been treated and her immortal soul might have been saved. The accent lay on "might have," because his experience in battles with vampires had taught him that the Devil didn't like to play by the rules. That's why they had to find the vampire that had attacked her. Find him and kill him.

If the girl's condition improved after her master was dead, then everything would be OK and her life could go on as before. If not, then Bishop would kill her—and every other person he suspected of being in league with demons.

That was exactly why he was dying to know what the two subjects were talking about. His team had had enough time after the phone call to get to the appointed rendezvous. He'd stayed in the shop while his men posted themselves at all the strategic points of the airport. Still, his monitoring wasn't proceeding optimally.

The constant background noise in the coffee shop blotted out their conversation, so he couldn't make out a word. Of course, he thought, it wouldn't be any problem at all to listen in with the right equipment. With that, he could have heard them a mile away in the middle of a hurricane. But it was a very arduous task, if not an impossible one, to get the necessary equipment past security.

Since 9/11, the security personnel at airports were specially trained to go over technical devices with a fine-toothed comb to prevent potential terrorist attacks. Passengers' laptops, cameras, or cell phones were usually examined inside and out. It would have been a near miracle for anyone carrying military-grade spy gear to pass through JFK's state-of-the-art screening. Nevertheless Bishop had been able to smuggle a pistol into the security area. It was an Austrian model made completely of ceramics and a composite material, able to pass through any metal detector. It also featured an additional modification: the integrated silencer, allowing one to fire shots as soft as a whisper and not cause a commotion.

He didn't intend to use his pistol for now, but he was greatly reassured to feel its weight in the waistband of his pants. He took another swig of coffee, which was an insult to his refined palate, without letting the two subjects out of his sight.

Even though he couldn't catch a word of what they were saying, it was satisfying for him to know that he was on the trail of the Beast of New York.

He suspected deep down that this demon must be the one that was different, different from all the other vampires he'd hunted down during his career.

CHAPTER 8

"WE WERE COMPLETELY UNPROTECTED down there," John continued, peering into his whiskey glass where the ice cubes had melted. "I was about to go back to the cellar steps when I heard a hiss. It sounded through the whole basement, like a teakettle about to explode. The noise came from the ceiling, and at first I thought it must be a blocked heating pipe. I pointed my flashlight at the basement ceiling, and then I saw it."

As John spoke his voice got softer and softer; some trembling had unobtrusively crept in. Claire felt anxiety and fear emanating from the man in palpable waves. But she tried to persuade herself it was the whiskey and not John's story that brought on those feelings.

"What did you see?"

"The vampire," John said, "the goddamn demon! It was hovering up around the ceiling and watching us. Probably the whole time we were there. His eyes glowed like lumps of burning coal. He was snarling and slobbering with his teeth bared like a dog."

Claire felt like a little girl eavesdropping on a horror story in a tent at summer camp. But she couldn't deny that John's tale was riveting. Even if it turned out to be just the worst kind of sailor's yarn, she thought, she was greatly impressed by his narrative fervor. A cold shudder crept slowly through her limbs, making her shiver.

"Right then Jack looked up and started to scream his lungs out, and I think I screamed too. But the demon just floated down from the ceiling and stood in front of us, grinning. Its eyes bored through mine into my brain, like rusty nails. We were trapped."

The unlit cigarette in John's hand grew soggy, and tobacco crumbs scattered over the table whenever he gesticulated. Claire could see his hands were shaking. Small tremors, but tremors nevertheless.

"How did you know it was a vampire? It could just as well have been a man in a mask," she said, surprised by the expression on John's face as he looked her up and down. It was the sort of look usually reserved for the kind of crackpot who would claim that the moon was made of green cheese.

"A man in a mask doesn't fly around the ceiling. And his eyes were blazing red as well—as red as hellfire itself. But what really convinced me is that even a masked man can't survive three shots in the chest from close range, which is what Jack did to that bastard: He pulled his gun and fired three times. And I'll swear on my mother's grave that every bullet was on target. The reports are still ringing in my ears."

"Then what happened?"

"*Nothing* happened. At least to the vampire. It calmly inspected the holes in its chest and then attacked us. Jack emptied his revolver, and we tore out of the basement. But we couldn't shake the monster off. It followed us up the stairs, snarling and chasing us like a mad dog. We raced through the halls back to the garage and made it through the raised door out to the sunlight and safety."

Claire had a hazy notion about the vampire myth, so she knew about the devastating effect sunlight was supposed to have on the creatures.

"But it was no use—he followed us out of the garage. Into the *sunlight*. Imagine that. A vampire strolling in bright sunlight."

Claire didn't quite know how to respond, so she made a surprised face and gave a bit of a shrug.

"I can't imagine it either, but I didn't have to: I saw it with my own eyes."

John took a deep breath and leaned back in his chair.

"Is that all you wanted to tell me?" Claire said at last.

John squinted at her and studied her every which way, like a jeweler determining whether a precious stone was genuine.

"I knew it," he said finally.

"What do you know?" Claire asked.

"That you're not the person you're pretending to be."

Claire felt she was already in the theater of the absurd anyway and thought briefly about staying with her role. She decided against it, concluding that her true identity didn't make a difference. But she wanted to know how John saw through her impersonation of Amanda.

"What tipped you off?" she asked.

John ground his jaw from side to side as if chewing his words into bite-sized pieces before saying them.

"You don't have a clue about this business. That's what did you in. The person posting to the forum was obviously on the edge of a breakdown. You, on the other hand—you think vampires are a fraud or a crazy myth. I'm wasting my time here, lady."

Though John's words were well chosen, Claire could read a spark of bitterness in his eyes.

"Please forgive me," she said. "I didn't mean to offend you or lie to you. 'Mandy87' is my sister. She's the one who wrote all those posts, and she's claiming a vampire bit her. I'm sorry. I didn't want to waste your time. I just want to find out what happened to my sister."

"To your sister?"

"Yes."

"Where's she now?"

"She's in . . ."

Go on, Claire, tell this stranger where your sister's staying now! Maybe he'll go and see her and perform an exorcism!

". . . in the hospital. She had a nervous collapse or something. She had to be taken to the hospital."

"That's exactly what the doctors told you, right? That it was a nervous collapse, I mean?"

"Yes," Claire said. "They also said she'll get better fast with the proper treatment."

At these words John's eyes turned hard, and all the spirit went out of them. Claire had a vague feeling of dread.

"Your sister is going to die," he stated.

His words came at her out of the blue. They hit her like burning arrows, reigniting the fires of her fear for Amanda. It didn't take long for fear to convert to anger. *How dare this person say such a thing!* Her nostrils quivered, and she could feel the blood rushing to her head. Her cheeks flushed, and her heart hammered against her breastbone. She had to fight hard not to lose control of herself completely.

"Who do you think you are, to talk like that about . . ."

But before she really got going, John lifted his index finger, like a teacher scolding a shiftless schoolgirl. This simple gesture was enough to cut her off. He waited a few moments, apparently wanting her to cool down before he spoke again.

"I've told you the truth. What's the nice way of putting it: Don't shoot the messenger? So please, listen to what I have to say, calmly and quietly. OK?"

Claire's anger subsided. She retreated into the black hole of despair and confusion she'd crawled out of.

"OK," she said.

"Fine. You can still save your sister. As long as she hasn't been transformed, it's not too late. But it won't be easy."

John pulled a silver box out of his inside jacket pocket. It was rectangular, no bigger than a scratchpad. He placed it in the center of the table beside the napkin holder with the tape recorder.

"This will help you save your sister," he said, looking at the box. It reminded Claire of the case her father used to store his cigarettes in.

"What's *that*?" she asked.

Instead of replying, John gave her a smile. Then he pressed a button on one side of the box. The cover popped open to reveal its contents.

CHAPTER 9

BISHOP'S CONVICTION GREW STRONGER when he saw the two subjects exchange an object. It was a silver container, *that* much he could tell. Even though he didn't know what was in it, he could read the reaction on the woman's face: amazement. Her eyes grew bigger, and her face froze in a theatrical expression of disbelief.

Whatever it was, he thought, it must be something of major significance. Possible explanations whirled frantically around in his head until he finally thought he'd got it: It must be a kind of reward. The woman's reward for selling her sister to the vampire.

Bishop had heard many times that vampires reward their lackeys with precious gifts for their services. It was written in ancient books that these were generally gold and jewels, but sometimes they were alleged relics—splinters from the True Cross, bones of the saints, and all sorts of things that the demon's servants believed possessed magical powers. Gifts were usually a pledge to keep the servant happy long enough until his master would bestow on him the ultimate gift: immortality.

Although Bishop knew the relevant literature in the Vatican, he personally had never come across a case of this kind. Still, his interpretation was plausible because the male subject was a gypsy. Bishop didn't attribute any political or spiritual value to the word. He only kept to the facts garnered from his research. And these facts showed that this man was unequivocally one of the Roma.

The man seated at the airport café was Jure Ceres, from the former Yugoslavia. Though he'd lived more than thirty years in the U.S., it was easy to trace him back to the Old World. Bishop had effortlessly discovered his native village, a sleepy place near the Romania-Serbia border. It had only a few houses and a church, but its name turned up relatively frequently in the Vatican annals. Usually in connection with vampires.

Bishop also knew that the Roma were a people who, in spite of their predominantly Christian faith, had various contacts with Balkan mysticism. For many of the people native to this region, vampires and other demons were real. Many so-called superstitious customs were still embedded in their daily lives, rituals that were so old that nobody could say anymore exactly where they came from.

The correlations between the man's origin and the young woman's case were too obvious for Bishop to write off as mere coincidence. That's why he had to assume that this Jure Ceres was something like a vampire's facilitator. As such he posed a far greater threat than Bishop had previously supposed.

But he could worry about that later. The point now was to determine what was in the box the gypsy had delivered to this young woman.

CHAPTER 10

CLAIRE OBSERVED TWO thin glass vials and a little gold chain with one pendant: a crucifix. Neither vial had a label, and nothing else indicated what exactly was the clear liquid they contained. Claire studied the objects for a moment before looking up.

"What's all this?"

"The vials contain two different essences. They are the *only* sure means I know to ward off vampires."

"Then we're talking about garlic, for one," Claire said without dropping her eyes.

"Don't be ridiculous, my dear. That garlic stuff is just an old wives' tale. You can no more stop a vampire with garlic than derail a train by putting a coin on the tracks.

"The vial on the left is concentrate of wild rose oil. On the right, holy water from Saint Peter's in Rome. You can employ them in different ways. It's best to administer them orally to the victim, several drops daily. Both liquids have about the same effect, so you really can't go very wrong when using them. That won't prevent the demon from turning up, but it will keep it from drinking the victim's blood. These substances are pure poison to a vampire. If applied regularly, they'll diminish the vampire's power over his victim, and the victim will recover. But this won't help at all if the victim's already been transformed."

"And the cross?" Claire asked.

"It's not your run-of-the-mill cross. It was blessed by the Pope following a rite that's centuries old. As far as I know, the cross is the most effective protection against vampires, so anybody wearing it doesn't have to be afraid of the demons. Crosses like these were once distributed to exorcists to prevent a demon leaving a body from then taking possession of the exorcist instead. It's best if you wear it yourself when you're with your sister. Better safe than sorry."

John closed the box and pushed it over to Claire's side of the table. She tucked it in her purse without giving it a second thought. She couldn't tell if those mysterious things were a gift or not. She secretly suspected that the conversation with John would now turn to money, money she probably owed him for his valuable services.

A really neat trick. First he spreads fear and terror and afterward cashes a big, fat check for his antidotes.

"Thanks, John. What do I owe you?" she asked.

John gave her a wounded look. His lips pursed as if he'd bitten a lemon, and his eyes shrank to little slits.

"You owe me nothing. These are presents to help you rescue your sister from the clutches of that beast."

Claire hadn't seen this coming.

Whatever he wants, it isn't money!

"Are you serious?"

"Deadly serious," John said as he got up. He buttoned his jacket and took one last frantic look around the room.

"You're going?"

"I've got to. My plane boards in ten minutes."

He pulled a boarding pass out of his side pocket to verify it.

"You're leaving the country?"

"Yes, going back to my homeland. It's not safe for me here anymore after what happened in Tarrytown."

Claire didn't know if his words were a calculated move. One more trick to put the finishing touch on his mixed-up story. Forget the boarding pass—she immediately tried to find a chink in his armor, some tiny inconsistency to help her crack his story. It was a reflex she'd trained herself to have over the past several years.

"And what about your partner? What's with Jack? Is he going, too? I can imagine that it's even dicier for him here than for you. After all, he's the one who shot at the . . . well, you know."

John held out a hand in farewell without answering her question. As she took his hand, Claire could smell the exotic aroma on his fingers, but she still couldn't place it.

Finally John said, "Jack is dead." He let go of Claire's hand. "The doctors say it was a heart attack, but I've seen enough to know better. And anyway, the vampire is probably the least of my problems now. I'm being shadowed—somebody's tracking my every footstep. I don't know who, but I don't feel safe in New York anymore. Take good care, my dear. I hope you can save your sister. Good-bye."

One last smile and he disappeared, leaving her with more questions and doubts than when she came in.

CHAPTER 11

BEHIND THE STEERING WHEEL again, Claire took a mental inventory of the day thus far.

It was just after four in the afternoon, and she'd gone through more extraordinary experiences, even for her, than in a whole month at the *Herald*. But she still wasn't one inch closer to solving Amanda's problem. Her antennae were out in all directions, but instead of discovering anything, she'd come up with only one conclusion—that she was no wiser than at the start of the day.

Inspecting Amanda's apartment, phoning Dr. James, meeting John—all that hadn't changed a thing. In fact, the turmoil of the last few hours left her feeling like she needed even more help facing Amanda's problem. Claire admitted that she had let herself be led on a wild-goose chase to distract her from the fears for her sister that were still circling her head like a flock of vultures. Every clue had led to more confusion, every trail to more puzzlement.

She knew it was time to resign herself to her fate and trust that Amanda would get better with the assistance of Dr. Harris and his colleagues. She should accept that there was nothing she could do to speed up the healing process other than being there for her sister and helping her get her life back on track. Maybe the road would be tough and demand much sacrifice, but she would spare no effort to help Amanda.

This determination revived a spark of hope that her sister would be better soon.

As she started the car, she decided to visit Amanda and have a few words with Dr. Harris.

CHAPTER 12

"GLAD YOU CAUGHT ME," Dr. Harris said, shaking her hand. "I was just on my way home."

Claire would have hardly recognized the doctor without his lab coat. He wore a leather jacket that had seen better days and a French beret pulled down over his forehead. At first glance Claire thought he looked more like one of those street musicians from Tribeca than the head of psychiatry at Hillside Medical Center.

"I didn't mean to keep you, Dr. Harris," Claire said.

"Don't worry, Miss Hagen. As long as I'm still in the building, I'm on the clock—doesn't matter if we're in the office or at the front door."

Claire was getting the hang of the doctor's sense of humor, so she forced a smile.

"That's good. Then it won't bother you if I ask about my sister's condition?"

"No, certainly not," Dr. Harris said. Claire could tell by his tone of voice that his sense of humor had vanished. He fiddled with his glasses as if it were a ploy he'd often used to stall for time, finding moments to choose the right words when dealing with a patient's relatives.

"Your sister's condition has changed, Miss Hagen."

Changed! Hard to be more informative than that!

"Changed? How so? Good or bad?"

"Well, to be honest, I don't know . . . not yet. The psychotic symptoms she presented when she was admitted have turned suddenly into a kind of exaggerated euphoria. I personally think it is caused by the interaction of some sedatives. A colleague believes it might be a result of being hospitalized. We will not know, of course, until we discontinue her current medication."

Dr. Harris's words drifted through her mind like insubstantial patches of fog. As a reporter she'd had many interviews with people who were intent only on saying *anything at all* in response to her questioning besides a direct answer. Most such sessions were with politicians, whose responses sometimes were little more than excuses, verbal blanks fired to rattle the interviewer.

"I don't think I quite follow," Claire said, hoping this gentle hint would push the doctor to give her some straight talk.

"Well, then," Dr. Harris said, "let me put it differently: Your sister's condition has changed, but not necessarily for the better. She is displaying new symptoms that can still be traced back to her original fears. These symptoms prompted me to have her transferred."

"Transferred? To another department?"

"No, no, just to another room."

"Why?"

"Her old room faced south. She claimed that the sunshine would burn her alive. As a result I moved her to a room with northern exposure and blackout curtains to make it dark. Since then she has been a little calmer."

The words hit Claire's brain like insects hit a windshield of a fast-moving car. Though she understood their meaning, her subconscious refused to admit the deeper significance.

John's words immediately resonated in her thoughts: *It was no use—he followed us out of the garage. Into the sunlight . . .*

"What does that mean for Amanda?"

"I cannot tell exactly. But it is possible that it is an outgrowth of the psychosis your sister is suffering from. Of course, you do not have to be a psychiatrist to recognize the connection between vampires and sunlight, Miss Hagen. This sudden aversion to sunlight leads me to believe your sister has begun to think that she herself is a vampire."

The remainder of the conversation consisted of reassuring clichés: *Don't worry, Miss Hagen . . . We're taking care of your sister . . . Everything's going to be all right . . . We're doing our best . . . You've done the right thing . . . She's in safe hands.*

After Dr. Harris felt satisfied that he'd carried out his doctorly duties, he told her where Amanda's room was now, after which he pulled his beret down on his forehead and bade her good-bye.

CHAPTER 13

A NURSE TOOK CLAIRE to Amanda's new room at Hillside Medical Center. It was in a different wing, off one of the many winding corridors on the fourth floor.

When they arrived at the room, the nurse opened the slotted window in the door and peered in nervously. Her movements struck Claire as overly dramatic, but she didn't say anything. Nevertheless, an image came to mind of a zookeeper checking out an animal's cage before entering.

After the nurse was confident that all was well, she took a keychain out of her smock and unlocked the door.

"I'll stay right out here as long as you're inside," she said, smiling at Claire.

"Is that necessary?" Claire asked.

"It's routine," the nurse responded nonchalantly, opening the door. Claire had scarcely gone into the room when the door closed behind her.

The first thing that struck her was how dark the room was. The ceiling light was turned off, and only a feeble shimmer came through the drawn window curtains. Her eyes needed a second to adjust to the darkness and make out Amanda's silhouette. She was sitting on the bed and facing in Claire's direction.

"Hello, Claire," came a voice from the bed. "Nice to see you."

See? I can hardly make out my hand in front of my eyes!

"Yes, pumpkin, and it's so nice to see *you*, too," Claire replied with a cheerfulness she hoped her sister couldn't tell was faked. "Would you mind if I turned on the lights?"

"Go ahead. Make yourself at home," Amanda responded.

Claire groped for the switch beside the door. She felt two and turned them both on, not knowing which one was for the lights. Two fluorescent ceiling lights came on at once, bathing the room in a sickly, sterile hue, a hue Claire forever associated with hospitals. She turned toward Amanda.

Claire first noticed that her sister had wrapped her arms around her upper body in an unnatural way. Even before this impression had reached her consciousness, she realized that her sister was in a straitjacket. It covered Amanda's delicate figure tightly, from her hips to her neck. Each arm was fixed to the opposite side of her body.

Claire could not imagine the reason for such drastic action. She'd believed until this point that straitjackets had long become relics from the past and were no longer used in modern hospitals.

Amanda began to giggle as if she could read Claire's thoughts and said, "Don't worry, hon. This vest is just for my own protection. I won't do anything to you."

Claire could hear the bitter undertone in her sister's voice. Mandy literally forced her words through clenched teeth. Her eyes fixed steadily on Claire, virtually pinning her to the wall.

"No problem," Claire said. "I'm sure it's only temporary."

"Of course it's only *temporary*. I've already been here for the longest time. But as soon as the sun goes down, I'm off and away—you'd better believe it."

Before the sound of her words died away, Claire sensed how gullible she'd been regarding Amanda's condition.

As soon as the sun goes down, I'm off and away!

Before coming to the room, she'd thought Amanda would recover rapidly. She'd hoped her symptoms would fade away with time, as in Dr. Harris's most optimistic prognosis. Instead, she now sensed that she'd been very wrong. Amanda seemed to be slipping even further into her fantasy world and even deeper into her delusions—a realization that brought a stabbing pain to Claire's heart.

"Oh, Mandy," Claire said, "you'll be here nice and quiet until you're better again, that's all."

She forced a smile and walked across the room. Amanda didn't show any reaction to her words. Instead, she just sat there, not taking her eyes off Claire for a second.

"You'll definitely be better soon," Claire continued. "Dr. Harris is very confident. He's really doing everything to help you."

Amanda still hadn't budged from her position on the edge of the bed. Claire figured she'd calmed down a little. She leaned over and patted her on the shoulder. The straitjacket's cotton felt rough, making her fingertips tingle.

"And when this is all over we can go on a nice vacation together. Someplace where the drinks are cheap and the men are luscious, darling. That's a promise."

Amanda kept staring at Claire as if trying to look right through her. She didn't move a muscle, so Claire couldn't tell if a single word had registered with her. It seemed to her that Amanda had suddenly become totally withdrawn, like a snail in its shell. But that didn't sidetrack Claire.

She leaned over a little more toward her sister and ran her fingers through strands of hair on Amanda's forehead. She was hoping that Amanda would react to her caress at least, even if she didn't react to her words anymore.

Amanda definitely *did* react. She first turned her head in the direction of Claire's hand, and then stared at her for a moment. Her whole body seized up. The tendons in her neck swelled and bulged out. She opened her eyes wide and bared her teeth. She emitted a growling noise from her throat, followed immediately by a sharp hiss.

Claire was taken completely by surprise. Before she knew it the smell of burnt hair filled her nostrils. The fingertips that had touched Amanda turned red hot. She pulled her hand back as if she'd accidentally touched a working stove. Amanda jumped up with uncontrollable power.

"Do you want to kill me, you *whore*?" she growled. "Your own *flesh and blood*? Is *that* what you want?"

Her words ricocheted off the walls. Though Claire could understand her perfectly well, she could no longer recognize Amanda's voice. It was a guttural sound like the growling of a large dog.

Like a predator!

Claire pulled back instinctively.

Then she looked at Amanda again and for a second couldn't trust her own senses.

Oh my God, it can't be!

Amanda was no longer standing on the bed; she was hovering over it. Hanging near the wall, weightlessly, like an insect.

Before Claire could comprehend what she saw, her eyes fell on Amanda's face. Or what had once been Mandy's face. It was now a hideous mask bearing no resemblance to her sister. There was no trace of beauty, no shred of humanity, just an expression of pure hatred and boundless rage. It was the visage of a riled-up beast.

The whites of Amanda's eyes had turned red, and her mouth was wide open. Claire's mind suffered a second unexpected blow when she caught sight of Amanda's teeth. They were the teeth of a beast of prey, her eyeteeth pointed, jagged, and unusually long.

Oh my God! What's going on?

Where Claire had touched Amanda, her hair was burned and the skin beneath it charred. Wispy fumes of smoke curled up from the wound. Claire retreated another step and another—until her back was against the door she'd come through into the room.

Oh my God! I'm trapped!

"You tried to kill me, you damn *cunt*," Amanda snarled. She was still drifting along the wall, her head tilted to one side and her teeth bared.

"Who are you in cahoots with, Claire? Why are you trying to kill me?"

The sight of Amanda up in the air was too much for Claire. She felt her strength draining from her body. Black spots began to flicker before her eyes, tiny at first, but with each heartbeat she could perceive a growing darkness that was consuming her.

She heard the key turning in the lock behind her. Then the darkness finally lay upon her like a tombstone, and a feeling of weightlessness overwhelmed her body and her mind.

Unresisting, Claire gradually lost her senses.

CHAPTER 14

WHEN CLAIRE OPENED HER EYES, she was looking into the concerned face of the nurse who'd taken her to Amanda's room.

"Keep lying down until I get a doctor. You've had a serious knock on the head," she said.

Though Claire didn't immediately grasp what the nurse was talking about, her hand instinctively touched the place on her forehead where there was a dull pain. She felt a slight swelling, then saw blood on her fingers after taking her hand away.

"What happened?" Claire asked, pulling herself up.

Her head pounded, and specks of light swirled before her eyes like a furious swarm of fireflies. The memory of what had happened lay deep in her brain. All that came to her mind were mere fragments.

The smell of burnt hair.

Feet floating in midair.

"You were leaning against the door when I unlocked it," the nurse added. "The door opened, and you fell over. Oh my God, I'm so sorry. I didn't know you were right behind the door."

"It's OK. I'm a lot better already," said Claire as she tried to stand up.

She was still dizzy, and the checkerboard pattern on the tile floor swam before her eyes in a confused geometric muddle. When she closed her eyes to stop her vertigo, she saw a new image she didn't know how to interpret.

Fiery red eyes.

She remembered John saying, *"His eyes glowed like lumps of burning coal."*

"Wait, let me help you," the nurse said, lifting Claire by her arms until she could stand on her own two feet. The nurse was stronger than Claire would have thought from her build.

"Can you stand up?" the nurse asked without letting go.

Claire could feel the nurse's grip digging through her coat into her skin.

"Yes, I think so," she answered.

The nurse let her go but didn't move away. Claire thanked her with an embarrassed smile. Then she touched her forehead to explore her wound. She could feel only a few strands of hair sticking to it. When she took her hand away and looked at her fingertips, she saw that the blood was already congealing.

"It's not that bad," the nurse said. "Hardly more than a scratch. Head wounds always look worse than they are. Still, you ought to have that looked at."

Claire's dizziness gradually wore off, and her mind was no longer sidetracked, so she could get herself back on the rails and proceed. She wiped the blood off her coat and suddenly remembered what had just happened in Amanda's room.

Teeth. Long, pointed teeth. The teeth of a beast of prey.

"Oh my God!" she exclaimed and tried to hurry back to the door. Her gait was shaky and hesitant, like a sailor's on a rough sea. The nurse reached to grab hold of her, but Claire shook her off. She made it to the door and quickly slid open its window.

At first, she didn't know what she expected to see. But she was certain it wasn't what she actually did see.

Amanda was sitting on the edge of the bed, rigid and immobile. She watched the door with her mouth twisted into a mocking grin. Otherwise everything appeared to be normal. Claire couldn't see any fiery red eyes or canines. Even the wound on Amanda's temple had disappeared but for a slight redness.

It was all just the way it was when Claire had first come in.

But there was no reason for her to disbelieve what she'd seen. Her senses had not played a trick on her. Everything had actually happened.

What she was looking at now was nothing but a charade. A stage play to wipe away the vestiges of the insanity that had reigned in that room just a few minutes earlier.

"It can't be," Claire whispered. She shut the window and turned toward the nurse.

"What's the matter, miss? Is everything all right?" the nurse inquired, putting her arm around Claire's shoulder. Thoughts rattled through Claire's head, unsteady and labored, like a car with a broken axle.

What should she say to the nurse? That she thought Amanda had turned into a vampire before her very eyes? No, out of the question. If she told them that, they'd probably get the room next to Amanda's ready and keep her here too.

In spite of the confusion raging in her head, she was able to keep herself under control.

"Everything's all right," she said. "It's . . . it's just very painful to see my sister like this, you understand."

"You poor thing," the nurse said, giving her a little hug. "Your sister will definitely be better soon. She's in the most capable hands here."

"Yes, you're probably right. Please excuse me for frightening you. I shouldn't have been leaning against the door."

"Oh, don't worry about that; nothing bad came of it. Come on, I'll take you to the bathroom and help you wash that blood off."

"Thanks. That's very nice of you."

CHAPTER 15

CLAIRE GOT IN HER CAR and drove off. But she didn't know where to go. She simply merged into the traffic crawling and snaking through the canyon of apartment buildings.

Move erratically from one red light to the next. Accelerate, brake, watch out you don't hit a messenger on a bike crisscrossing the blocked lanes of traffic.

Other thoughts chased around Claire's head just as erratically. She thought about Amanda, about John, about Dr. Harris, and the fact she'd witnessed *something* that really ought not to exist. Something supernatural, beyond all the boundaries of her previous life.

With her own eyes she had seen her sister morph into a monster, and she didn't have the foggiest notion how to handle it. She searched for an explanation. But no matter how she tried, she couldn't come up with a reasonable cause for what had just occurred. She also knew it wouldn't be easy to find a solution to Amanda's problem. *What kind of solution could I hope for anyway?* she wondered. Should she go to the police and ask for help?

"Please help me, officer, my sister is a . . . a monster!"

No way.

Or should she look up an exorcist in the Yellow Pages? Was that the answer? Was there any way at all she could help Amanda? And what would happen if she did nothing?

Claire didn't know.

She drove through the increasing darkness, straight ahead for several blocks and then right. And as her car traced bigger and bigger rectangles, the disturbing thoughts made her head spin.

When the warning light came on for the gas gauge, she decided to stop at the next gas station and have a strong coffee. Usually a double espresso would help her pull herself together and calm down. Maybe she'd better have a triple today.

A block later she saw a Shell station. She parked near the diner next door. By the time she turned off the car, darkness had spread over Manhattan. It was nighttime in the city that never sleeps.

When she closed the car door she felt a burning sensation and a pull on the fingertips of her right hand. The hand she'd touched Amanda's temples with before . . . before she was transformed into a *monster*.

Claire inspected her fingers in the glare of the sodium light that flooded the area around her car with a mournful orange color. She didn't like what she saw.

Her fingertips were burned. Large blisters filled with a clear liquid, on her index and middle fingers, that pulsated to the rhythm of her heart. A blister on her ring finger was broken, and she could see raw flesh under it. The wound was pink and weeping but not painful.

Claire thought the shock must have kept her from feeling the wounds. She opened the trunk and took out the first-aid kit.

After disinfecting her fingers with iodine, she wrapped them in Band-Aids, locked the car, and walked into the diner.

There wasn't much going on. She went to the counter and sat directly in front of the giant TV on the wall. The volume was almost completely turned down, but she could see the evening news.

A waitress, looking very bored, got up from a stool behind the counter and came to her.

"And what would you like, sweetie?"

"A coffee, please."

"Black?"

"As black as a brand-new car tire, if you've got it."

The waitress gave a weary smile and hustled over to the coffeepot.

She brought Claire her coffee with a gentle "There you are." Steam rose from the cup.

"Thanks," Claire said.

"You're welcome, sweetie."

The waitress went back to her seat.

Claire took a sip of coffee. It wasn't anything special, neither good nor bad. But it would do the job, she thought, as she had another sip.

The newscaster was talking about the upcoming mayoral election. When the next report came on, Claire's heart skipped a beat. She grabbed the counter so she wouldn't fall over from shock, but her coffee slopped over the cup, ruining her blouse. She didn't even look at it, even though the silk blouse was one of her favorites. She stared wide-eyed at the picture on the screen.

John was looking at her from the TV. It was an old photograph, but she recognized him at once. The caption read: SMALL-TIME CROOK SHOT AT JFK.

"Quick! Please!" Claire shouted at the waitress. "Turn up the volume!"

The waitress's face didn't move a muscle as she whipped the remote control out of her apron on command. Claire could now hear every word:

". . . the victim was a previously convicted petty criminal known to the police as Jure Ceres, an immigrant from the former Yugoslavia with a long record. Ceres had done time in Rikers and some state prisons. Because of his criminal past, police assume the shooting was related to criminal infighting. Investigations are focused on finding out how the killer was able to smuggle a weapon past airport security . . ."

The news switched to a story of a chambermaid who found $35,000 on the subway. Claire stared at the report but took in very little of it.

Her mouth was dry, and her heart was positively racing.

John was dead. The same John she'd met a few hours ago. Maybe she was the last person to see him alive, besides his killer.

Claire was baffled. Thinking back on John's frightened eyes, she shuddered. She put down her cup so she wouldn't spill any more coffee.

"Are you OK?" the waitress asked without getting up. Claire just looked at her without a reply. She clenched her teeth. She was afraid that if she opened her mouth she would scream.

CHAPTER 16

BISHOP WAS AT THE WHEEL of a black SUV and looking in the rearview mirror. The hard lines in his face made him look like an unfinished sculpture. His eyes were the color of washed-out jeans, and his mouth barely traced a thin line between his nose and his chin.

As he regarded himself, he tried to add up how many people had looked into those eyes as they breathed their last. For how many people had his eyes been the last things they saw in their life? Was it fifty? A hundred? More? He didn't give a damn.

He didn't know. The one thing he did know was that those killings were always justified. The fact that he liked doing it didn't change anything. A true master always takes pleasure in what he does.

"What's this? A staring contest with yourself?"

The voice coming from the passenger seat snapped Bishop out of his reverie. He turned to the man beside him and gave him a disparaging look. It was Whitman, Bishop's partner for the past two months.

In all the years Bishop had been in the Organization, he'd never had a partner. Not only that, he'd never even needed one. The only thing he'd needed was a handful of men who took orders and didn't ask questions. That's all. For that very reason he'd felt insulted and humiliated when he'd been assigned a partner.

And to top it all, what a self-important young whippersnapper!

"Mind your own fucking business!" Bishop said, his eyes gleaming like stars on a bitter cold night.

"Take it easy, chief," Whitman said. "For all I care you can spend all frigging night staring in the mirror. I just wanted to get a bit of conversation going before my balls fall off from boredom."

"If you don't shut up, worse things are going to happen to your balls."

Whitman managed a grin.

"Is that a come-on, you old queer? I should have known you were one of *them*. I'll have to take a pass, my good man. I don't have the hots for old geezers like you."

Bishop looked away and gritted his teeth. He didn't feel like getting into a fight with this kid. He turned the radio on instead to cut off the conversation. The soothing sound of classical music restored his calm. He stared into the night, and his thoughts took on a life of their own. In his mind's eye he could see Jure Ceres's face. Memories of the events at the airport stirred in his thoughts.

He saw everything so precisely that he could relive every moment.

CHAPTER 17

WHEN THE MEETING between the woman and Ceres was over, Bishop had to decide which one to follow.

Though men were posted at the exits, he didn't want to delegate anything that he could do better. In his view, if your hands leave the wheel, then you've lost control. And that's exactly what to avoid, always.

While Bishop was mulling this over, Ceres pulled an airline ticket out of his pocket and showed it to the woman. The target didn't know it, but that made up Bishop's mind. He knew exactly what he had to do even before Ceres left the coffee shop: He had to stop the bastard at any cost before he could leave the country and go underground.

That's the reason he decided on Ceres and not the woman. He waited a beat before starting to tail him. He knew from experience that an airport was the ideal place for keeping somebody under surveillance. You could disappear in the seething mass of people—people who were so preoccupied that they wouldn't notice anything. Keeping track of Ceres was a breeze; Bishop just walked a short distance behind him and didn't let him out of his sight. Ceres stepped into a bathroom directly adjacent to the waiting area for Gate A. Bishop took a momentary look around for security personnel then went in after him. He entered just in time to see Ceres going into one of the end stalls.

Bishop knew there was never a more favorable moment to surprise a man than when he's sitting on the toilet with his pants down (except maybe in bed with a woman). He was quite satisfied with the opportunity offered him.

He walked through the bathroom and planted himself at one of the sinks. Washing his hands, he inspected the stalls behind him. He was in luck: He and Ceres were alone. With his hands still wet, he reached for the pistol in his belt. The faucet was controlled with a sensor—and it took several moments until the water turned off. Its splashing noise lasted just enough to cover the sound of Bishop's heels on the tile floor as he hurried to Ceres's stall. Bishop kicked in the door the instant the water stopped.

Ceres sat on the toilet, his pants around his ankles and a lit cigarette between his lips. His eyes opened wide, and his cigarette quivered. When he saw the pistol in Bishop's hand, the cigarette fell out of his mouth and went out in the toilet bowl.

"What the hell's going on?" Ceres screamed, eyes glued to the pistol.

"Who's your master? Where can I find him?" Bishop demanded.

"What the hell? What do you mean?"

"I'll ask only one more time, Jure," Bishop cautioned. *"Where is your master?"*

By then, Bishop knew it would be impossible to get anything out of Ceres. He suspected the vampire had enough control over Ceres to prevent him from betraying him, to protect himself. The ending to this little play was already looming.

"What the hell are you talking about? What master? Who the hell are you?" he shouted.

Bishop lowered his gun and saw Ceres's body instantly relax. He loved these cat-and-mouse games where you made the victim believe in one last ray of hope before you extinguished hope and life in one fell swoop. For him, that element transformed the whole assignment into a kind of classical drama.

"One more thing, Jure," Bishop said, as a grin spread over his thin lips. "There's no smoking in the airport." Then he raised his gun and pulled the trigger three times before Ceres could move. Two bullets in the chest and one in his head, just to be absolutely sure. The silencer made the reports as quiet as a baby's cough. Ceres's body went totally slack, then tipped over to one side and sat there without moving a muscle.

For a moment Bishop considered taking his pulse but decided against it. Miracles happen again and again, he reflected, but still, Ceres would have to be damn lucky to be alive. After all, half his skull was sticking to the wall behind him. And three quarters of his brain.

The man was dead.

Bishop chose not to risk getting caught by taking a pulse. Instead he quickly checked to see whether any of the mess had stuck to his clothing. Once he saw he was clear, he closed the stall door, stuck his pistol back in his belt, and left the bathroom as if nothing had happened.

CHAPTER 18

THE MUSIC FROM the speakers stopped, rousing Bishop from his memories. Turning to Whitman, he saw that he'd just turned the radio off.

"What the hell, Whitman?"

"I don't feel like hearing this classical shit. What are you up to with it anyway? You want to put me in a romantic mood maybe? I'm supposed to open a bottle of red wine and spread a comfy blanket over the backseat? I'm a soldier, for fuck's sake, and if you want to listen to any more of this crappy music, go get earphones, goddammit."

Bishop clenched his teeth one more time instead of responding. The thing he wanted most was to rip out Whitman's throat then and there and watch him suffocate in his own blood. But this impulse died down fast. He'd learned from experience that control is the highest form of discipline. But it was way more than pure discipline in his case. In his opinion, a man without self-control was an unpolished precious stone. That was one of the fundamental principles on which the world was based.

He looked out into the dark, focusing on the door to Claire Hagen's apartment building. It was just after nine, and he calculated it wouldn't be long until she came home. He'd have much more delectation with her than with Ceres, he imagined. Ultimately, he had to discover where the vampire was hiding that he was tracking. He guessed a thorough interrogation might be required to get the desired information. A very intensive interrogation! The mere thought of it gave Bishop an erection, but he didn't let it show.

He stared at the building entrance and scanned every car that went by, on the lookout for the dark green Volvo that Claire's registration stated she owned. But mentally he replayed the scene in the airport, back to the bit where he shot Ceres. Except now he fantasized that it was Whitman instead of Ceres staring at him in disbelief as he blasted him right in the face.

The certainty that he would eventually kill Whitman spread with a languorous warmth throughout his body. At the moment, he didn't know when or how he'd do it. But he believed—no, he hoped—there'd soon be an opening for him to blast that insolent bastard's little brain out.

After all, it was a dangerous business they were in, and Bishop had watched better men than Whitman die over the years. The Organization never once investigated.

In their line of work, it was easier to discard a man than an expired pound of hamburger in a supermarket. And Whitman was right on track to find out that harsh reality.

CHAPTER 19

AFTER HER INITIAL HORROR had receded, Claire got up to go to the bathroom at the diner. She didn't even try to clean the coffee stains off her blouse because she suspected that the soap in the dispenser and paper towels weren't the best tools. She let it go and went into one of the stalls instead.

She felt the blister in her index finger burst when she flushed. The pain was clear and distinct, unlike the earlier blister on her ring finger. It shot from her hand to her elbow and onward, stopping at her shoulder. The Band-Aid on her finger was completely soaked with blood, so she removed it and threw it in the toilet. She inspected her finger again, holding it close to her face to see what she could by the low light in the stall.

The blister was torn open, loose skin dangling from her last finger joint like a burst balloon caught in a picket fence. The wound seeped a little, but Claire didn't think it would get infected. As she began to lower her hand, a familiar smell suddenly reached her nose, weak and barely perceptible. She brought her hand directly under her nose to identify the scent.

It was sweet and strong—she recognized immediately that it wasn't a fragrance from her lotions and creams. But she knew she had smelled it before. *And not so long ago!*

She sniffed her finger again, and suddenly the memory surfaced in her brain: *John!* It was the sweetish scent he gave off when they shook hands. She'd smelled it twice, once when he arrived and again when they said good-bye.

It was probably only an extravagant hand lotion for men, Claire guessed. But her mind wasn't satisfied with such an easy explanation. It tried to undermine her power of reasoning, like a badly trained dog digging under the fence of a neighbor's yard.

In the course of a single day the solid structure of her life had begun to wobble. No, not just wobble: It had completely shattered. Not one stone was left standing on another, and Claire had the feeling it would take a damn long time for her to believe in anything again. *Nothing* was as it seemed at first glance.

She had discovered her sister was a . . . *vampire* . . . a monster. The only person she'd told anything about it was dead, and she was on the verge of a nervous collapse herself.

That smell must have some deeper significance. But just what, she couldn't decipher. It didn't matter how hard she tried to put the pieces of the puzzle together—she couldn't see how they fit. Every thought spawned new questions, and they were all dead ends.

Who murdered John?

What happened to Amanda?

Will it all turn out OK?

The answer to every question was the same:

I don't know!

That she had to admit she was helpless right now was a bitter pill to swallow.

She finally left the stall, carefully washed her hands, and looked in the mirror over the sink. The day had left its traces behind in her face: Her skin was ashen, and there were dark bags under her eyes.

Nothing a good night's beauty sleep can't fix!

But Claire didn't think she would get any shut-eye that night. Moreover, she bet she couldn't sleep for quite a while unless the bedside light was on.

She left the bathroom, paid for the coffee, and returned to her car. When she turned the ignition key, the fuel light lit up again.

She'd forgotten to get gas.

She drove several feet to the self-serve pump and got out. She inserted her credit card, stuck in the nozzle, and heard the pump humming.

A cold east wind blew through the parking lot, making her shiver. She buttoned up her coat and held her arms to her chest, stamping her feet to keep warm. Her eyes fell on a black SUV parked not far from the pumps. Two men sat in the front seats. Claire noticed out of the corner of her eye that they were looking in her direction. But when she focused on them directly, they quickly turned away and looked off into the dark. They didn't talk or do anything, but seemed somehow intent solely on looking inconspicuous.

Claire's whole body shivered again. But this time it wasn't because of the wind sweeping through the parking lot.

CHAPTER 20

"GHOST ONE TO GHOST LEADER, come in, please. Over."

The static from the CB radio mounted on the dashboard turned into irregular clicks. The last words were as garbled to Bishop's ears as if they'd gone through a meat grinder. He was about to reach for the handset when Whitman beat him to it.

"Ghost Leader here. What's up, Ghost One?" he asked.

"I think there's been a leak. We'll abort tailing the subject. Over."

Bishop knew that voice. It was Morales, one of his best men.

"Give me that!" Bishop growled, grabbing the handset out of Whitman's hand.

"Can't you guys even tail a normal woman?" he scolded. Although his guts were churning, his voice sounded calm and composed. He knew it would be counterproductive to chew out Morales and the other man over the radio. That could wait for another time.

"Nothing we can do, sir. The subject spotted us. Sorry, sir. Should we resume tailing her? Over."

Bishop thought for a moment.

"Did you put the transponder on her car?"

"Yes sir," Morales replied. "We checked it. Works like a charm. Over."

While Morales was talking, Whitman got out his computer from under his seat, opened it up, and started running a program. Soon a satellite view of New York appeared on the screen, with a small green dot in the middle moving east. Whitman nodded at Bishop. Bishop acknowledged him and returned to Morales on the radio.

"Well done, Ghost One. We're receiving the signal strong and clear. Do not resume monitoring. Step down."

"Got it, Ghost Leader. Ghost One, over and out."

Bishop put the handset back in its mount. Turning to Whitman he asked, "Where's she going?"

Whitman opened a submenu and added the places they knew the subject usually frequented. A second dot popped up immediately on the satellite image, blinking red.

"She's coming at us. But she's hopping around like a bunny rabbit," Whitman said without taking his eyes off the screen. Its pale glow gave his face a greenish cast. "So we guessed right. We could have done without the damn transponder."

"ETA?"

"If nothing intervenes, she'll be here in twenty minutes."

"Excellent."

Bishop took out a pair of black leather gloves from his jacket. The grin on his face grew broader and broader as he slipped them on.

CHAPTER 21

CLAIRE COULDN'T TAKE her eyes off the rearview mirror. Every couple of seconds her eyes darted to it, looking for the black SUV from the gas station.

It had grown completely dark in the meantime. And to make it worse, giant SUVs were the latest rage. Every other car she saw looked better suited for a deserted gravel road in the Rockies than for the flat, narrow streets of New York City.

Claire was puzzled. She didn't know if she was being followed. She couldn't feel safe for a second.

She kept changing her route and sticking to small side streets. For a moment, she wondered whether it would be helpful to turn off her lights. But then she told herself to be reasonable: She was in New York City, and it didn't matter whether she had the lights on or not—anybody following would see her all the same. And she didn't want to be responsible for causing any accidents.

After a quarter of an hour she finally turned onto the street where she lived, and the tension gradually let up. A last look in the rearview mirror reassured her that no one was following.

She parked the car, got out, and ran to the doorway of her building.

CHAPTER 22

CLAIRE SHUT THE APARTMENT door behind her, locked it, and slid on the chain. She couldn't remember when she'd last closed the curtains, but at the moment it seemed the right thing to do. She even thought about putting a chair under the doorknob, but decided against it.

Don't be ridiculous! That only works in the movies.

Without undressing or turning on the light, she went back across the living room to the window to peek down on the street. She pushed the curtain a bit to one side and searched quickly for the dark SUV from the gas station.

Her eyes flitting up and down the street couldn't spot anything unusual. She was unable to stay calm. Claire stepped quickly into her bedroom directly off the living room.

She knelt to the right of her double bed, feeling around under it in the dark with both hands. In a second she found what she was looking for: a small, crude plastic box. She pulled it out and put it on the bed, opened the lock, and took out its contents.

The steel gun felt cold and unfriendly. But the weapon felt familiar in her hand. Even more, it calmed her down to know that in an emergency she could defend herself.

The gun was a Ruger model P90, the same pistol her father had taught her to shoot in the Rockwell woods. Though the gun wasn't very large, it was very accurate and had great penetrating power.

Because her father didn't have a son, he always took Claire and Amanda along on hunting trips. This could seem odd to urbane New Yorkers, a father training his daughters how to handle weapons. But in the backwoods of Rockwell, it wasn't unusual for children to learn how to shoot.

Claire clicked on the table lamp beside the bed and studied the pistol, which gave off the sweetish smell of gun oil. She pulled back the slide and loaded a bullet into the chamber. She switched the safety off. The magazine held eight rounds altogether—enough to blow a black bear's ass off if you had to, as Claire's father often said.

Claire laid the gun on the bed and pulled out two spare loaded magazines and a box of nine-millimeter shells from the plastic box. Then she stowed the little box under the bed again. As she stood up, she started in terror. A scream escaped her throat, and all the energy drained from her body.

A strange man stood in the doorway, staring at her.

CHAPTER 23

"THAT WENT OFF BEAUTIFULLY, chief," Whitman said, screwing a silencer onto his pistol.

"For sure," Bishop acknowledged. Since the young woman came home, his eyes had been glued to her apartment window. The SUV was parked in an unlighted side street kitty-corner from the apartment building. Bishop had a perfect view of Claire's apartment without running the risk of her seeing him. At first he thought she'd gone out the back door of the building, because the windows were still dark. But scarcely five minutes later a faint glow came from behind one of the windows; she was indeed in the apartment.

Everything was going according to plan.

"So what now?" Whitman inquired.

"Now we can take our time. She's in the trap. The building has two exits, and she can't escape through either one. The boys are posted at the rear exit."

"Shouldn't we just grab her?"

"No, we'll wait a little," Bishop cautioned. "Maybe we'll get lucky and her master will pay her a visit. Then we could save ourselves a lot of shit and get them both right then and there. Besides, most of the people in the building are awake. If we go in and make a racket, we'll have more problems than we'd like. That's why I think it best to keep it low-key for now. The woman is the only solid clue we've turned up that points to the monster in New York. We've got to take it one step at a time."

"Good, then wake me up for the kickoff," Whitman said.

He reclined his seat all the way and closed his eyes, but didn't take the gun from his hand.

CHAPTER 24

CLAIRE CRINGED AND couldn't breathe. But her instincts were on full alert. Without even thinking she grabbed the pistol on the bed and a second later pointed it at the stranger. A searching glance over the figure in the doorway told her he was unarmed. Nevertheless, the barrel of her gun shook in her hands.

"Who are you? What do you want?" she shouted.

By way of an answer, the stranger slowly raised his hands and showed them to her. Claire's first impression was right: He was unarmed.

Maybe, maybe not! Maybe he just wants to distract you?

"I asked you a question," Claire hissed, raising the gun and aiming it at the stranger's chest. The distance between them was less than fifteen feet. In spite of her excitement, she knew she couldn't miss at that distance. Any unexpected move and she'd shoot him.

You'll blow his ass off—just like Daddy showed you!

"Are you deaf, goddammit?"

"Calm down," the stranger said. "I won't do anything to you. I just want to talk."

His voice sounded too composed for a man faced with the possibility of being shot dead at any minute.

Much too calm!

"You want to talk? Then say something. But keep your hands where I can damn well see them!"

The stranger responded with a grin. He stared at Claire over the gun, looking her straight in the eye. He didn't seem any more threatened by her gun than by a child's water pistol.

"Why are you following me?" he asked at last. The grin was still plastered to his face, but his eyes grew dark.

"You're all confused, pal," Claire said with as much composure as she could muster in the situation. "I haven't a damn clue who you are."

"Oh, really?"

"Yes, for Chrissake!"

"You were with an older man today. At the airport, remember?"

"With John?"

"Was that his name? John?"

"What are you getting at?" Claire shouted. Her hands on the gun handle were growing tense, and all the blood in her fingers drained away. She heard her father's voice in her head again:

You gotta pull the trigger, baby. Pull it gently, and don't YANK IT!

"What did he tell you about me, this guy John?" the stranger asked. The smile completely left his lips, and his eyebrows knitted together. His eyes suddenly were piercing and displeasing. Claire squinted without taking her eyes off the gun sights.

"What the hell do you mean? Who are you, and what are you doing in my apartment?" Claire screamed. The muscles in her forearms had clamped up completely, and her hands were bathed in sweat. She could feel the gun getting more and more slippery.

"This 'John.' Did he give you a scoop? Are you looking for a good story? About the horror lurking in the basements of New York?"

The questions pounded in her brain.

John actually *had* talked about a basement. The basement in Tarrytown. In the house in which he'd found the . . .

VAMPIRE!

The stranger seemed to know her. Maybe not personally, she thought, but he knew she was a reporter.

What else does he know?

Before Claire could think this through, things started happening fast and furious.

The stranger's face began to change.

The eyes dwindled down to two fiery red dots, and his nose puckered up suddenly into deep folds like a dog's muzzle. But the worst was his mouth. His lips pulled back from his teeth and gums, exposing the pointed teeth of a beast.

"What did he tell you?" the creature snarled in such a deep voice that it seemed to penetrate Claire's entire body like the bass in a dance club. She could feel a slight dizziness coursing through her brain, just like when she fainted in the hospital. Though she was still unprepared for these horrors, they seemed less threatening this time, thanks to her gun. Not much, but a bit.

Before any thoughts began to take hold in her head, her instinct kicked in. And her instinct knew only two things: She was in danger, and she had to act!

FAST!

As if by reflex, Claire pulled the trigger. The bang was deafening, and the flame from the muzzle blinded her for a split second. But Claire fired once more, and then again right away. She lowered the gun to assess the damage she had caused. The sour smell of gunpowder took her breath away momentarily. But the sight she saw was even worse—it made her heart skip a beat.

The creature was still standing in the doorway. It had three holes in its chest from which thin wisps of smoke emerged. But it seemed completely unfazed. Not a drop of blood flowed from the wounds, as if its body were not a living organism but a shop-window mannequin. The creature stood there as before, its face a mask of pure hate, lips trembling and nostrils quivering. And its eyes . . .

Oh my God, those eyes!

. . . were red-hot lances that stabbed right through her.

Claire raised her gun again and this time aimed at the creature's head. The moment she was about to fire, the figure disappeared. It dissolved into thin air with an alacrity that surpassed her eyes' ability to see.

Claire gave a sigh of relief. Then suddenly something cold closed around her right wrist, gripping hard. The first sensation was cold, but after that she was swept away by a wave of hot and all-consuming pain.

Despite the tears in her eyes, she could see the paw that enclosed her wrist. It had the talons of a giant bird of prey with long leathery fingers that ended in curved black claws. Claire's hand locked up with pain, causing her to pull the trigger and fire another round. She heard something smash into a thousand pieces in the living room. But everything was swept from her mind when the creature seized her arm and bent it backward.

Too far backward.

Claire tried to defend herself but couldn't really fight. She dropped the pistol, which landed with a dull thud on the bedroom carpet. Then her arm was pulled back so far that her hand touched the space between her shoulder blades. A cascade of pain flooded her body.

"You've ruined my best jacket," the creature hissed. Claire could feel its face on the nape of her neck. Her every hair stood on end.

"Please . . . that hurts a lot," she managed to say between pressed lips. The vise-like pressure on her arm relaxed right away. It wasn't much, but the pain reduced instantly. The grip on her arm was still so tight that she had no chance of eluding the creature's grasp.

"And now you'll tell me what this John character told you. And I advise you not to lie to me."

The voice wasn't so much a voice as the sound of someone tearing a cloth in pieces and trying to make consonants and vowels out of them.

She somehow thought that was funny, and in spite of everything—her fear, the pain, and the certainty that she'd soon die—it brought a fleeting grin to her lips.

CHAPTER 25

BISHOP HEARD THREE SHOTS in rapid succession and recognized the flame from a gun muzzle through the apartment's window. Whitman jumped from his nap with a start. In spite of the flurry of activity, it didn't escape Bishop's notice that Whitman was awake immediately, awake and keyed up, like a good soldier should be.

"What the hell's going on?" Whitman asked.

"It's moving," Bishop retorted, grabbing the handset. "Ghost Leader to Ghost Two. Go!"

"Understood, Ghost Leader," came the voice from the radio, as if the other guys had just been waiting for that order.

Bishop put the handset back on the dash and nodded to Whitman.

"Let's smoke her out," he said.

"Will do, chief," Whitman said and turned to go.

The two men dashed out of the car at the same time and went to the back of the SUV, where both reached in—knowing exactly what they were looking for.

Bishop got out his preferred weapon for this kind of operation and released the safety. It was a German MP7 with a silencer and a night sight—a compact gun with very high penetration power, perfect for fighting in buildings. Whitman grabbed a grenade launcher of Russian manufacture. As he loaded, Bishop was already running to the entrance of the woman's building. His silhouette melted into the darkness.

Just as he reached the door, another shot rang out from the apartment.

CHAPTER 26

I'M GOING TO DIE!

Claire was surprised at how indifferent she felt about this thought and the way she accepted it. Her certain, impending death seemed unavoidable, but everybody else on this crazy roller-coaster ride was already dead. John was gone, and his partner, Jack, if John was to be believed. And she'd be the next to go.

That's how simple it was.

Though she could have persuaded herself that she had to rage, scream, and beg for her life, she submitted to her fate and hoped only that it would go quickly.

Please, please, dear God! Let it be over quickly!

"What did he tell you?" the creature hissed, loosening its grip some more.

"Nothing," Claire said. "Just that he'd flushed a vampire in Tarrytown."

"Why did you arrange to meet him?" the creature asked. Its hissing voice did not sound as menacing now, and it loosened its grip on Claire's arm a little more. She could feel that the creature's claw was now almost human. The coldness had left her, but she felt bruised and tender.

Her confidence rose.

"Because of my sister. I met him because of my sister."

"Your sister?" The voice was fully human again.

"Yes, she is . . . well, she's . . ."

"She's what?"

Claire reflected for a second on what to say. The word "vampire" still sounded crazy in spite of the events of the day. At the same time she was aware of the fact that the whole situation was crazy.

The whole damn world has gone nuts!

"She's a vampire," Claire said. "My sister's a vampire."

Total silence but for the furious beating of her heart.

"A vampire?"

"Yes," she said and paused for a moment. "At least, she's like you. She changed too. I saw it with my own eyes. I wanted to help her, and John offered his assistance. Did you kill him?"

"No," the stranger said. "I suspect he was killed by the guys who've been tailing you since the airport."

"In a black SUV?"

"Yes, them."

"Who are they?"

"I suppose they're hunters," the stranger said, releasing her hand. Her fingers had been completely frozen but now tingled as some feeling slowly came back. The stranger's voice wasn't excited or angry. Claire didn't dare turn to face him.

The certainty of her own death had faded, but not completely. The thought was standing at the ready on the border of her subconscious, like a soccer player on the sidelines who could hardly wait to get back in the game.

"Hunters?" Claire asked.

"Yes," the stranger said, "vampire hunters."

CHAPTER 27

IN SPITE OF THE GUNSHOTS, the apartment building appeared to be abandoned. No curious neighbors stuck their heads out into the hallway to see what was going on. Nobody explored the hallways to locate the source of the shots. Instead, the people in the building had crept back into their homes, like frightened mice into their holes. Bishop recognized from his experience an unwritten law of many city dwellers: Stay out of trouble.

But the peace and quiet didn't fool him. He knew patrol cars from the New York police were sure to be on their way. Even though nobody was in the hallways, Bishop assumed that the phones in the nearest police station would be ringing off the hook nevertheless.

So we've got to work fast, he concluded.

Very fast.

When he got to the apartment, Morales and Jones were already there, ready to break into the woman's front door. They'd stormed the rear exit of the building as planned. Morales had attached an explosive device to the doorknob. He and Jones stood on either side of the door, guns at the ready.

Bishop could almost smell the tension the men were under. Their eyes were opened wide, their faces frozen. They'd ducked their heads down to listen intently to the muffled sounds in the apartment. Bishop knew they were waiting for orders—ready to strike and unleash a proper assault if necessary.

Pushing the speaker button on his walkie-talkie, he spoke but a single word.

CHAPTER 28

WHITMAN HAD LOADED the launcher with a stun grenade and flipped up the sights. He placed the barrel on the edge of the SUV's roof to facilitate his aim and reduce the recoil. Then he trained it on the fourth-floor apartment where the shots had come from. He eased the trigger back until he could feel the release point. Then he waited.

Not a minute later Bishop's voice came over the walkie-talkie.

"Fire."

The word had barely sounded in his ears when Whitman pulled the trigger. A single grenade shot out of the barrel, sounding like a champagne cork popping.

PLOP!

The grenade left a sparkling tail behind it, like a shooting star. An instant later it thundered with full force through the window. Pieces of glass rained into the apartment and out into the night.

CHAPTER 29

THE WINDOW TO HER LEFT shattered. Claire cringed away instinctively but too late. Tiny splinters of glass bored into her left side, causing a burning pain. The sudden shock made her forget for a moment the creature standing behind her.

She focused entirely on the thing that had just smashed through the windowpane. Her adrenaline slowed her perception of time. Everything had taken a mere fraction of a second, but Claire's senses stayed razor-sharp.

Out of the corner of her eye she saw the object whir through the window, bang against the opposite wall, and fall to the floor. It was black and round, hardly the size of a cell phone. Claire then heard a buzz coming from the strange object. It emitted a bright glare that instantly expanded. While she was still trying to process that, a flash of light enveloped her, as bright as hundreds of suns. A simultaneous roar like thunder was followed by a blast that knocked her off her feet.

The lightning flash was immense, and the bang beyond anything she could have imagined. She went deaf and blind at a single stroke. Her perception was totally extinguished in a split second. She fell, believing she was dead.

Dead! Oh my God, I'm dead!

Robbed of her key senses, all she could feel was a hot pain in her side and her heart beating frantically. As she fell to the floor, she hit her head against the wall and became disoriented. The rusty taste of blood was in her mouth, and she smelled the stink of burned hair. She could also feel her clothing sticking warmly to her left side. *Blood*, she thought, *a lot of blood*.

Claire did not give up. In spite of her helplessness and panic, a germ of certainty took root: the certainty that she was still alive. Pain brought her back to reality.

Dead people don't feel any pain, kiddo!

Claire reacted quickly. Her hands searched hurriedly over the bedroom carpet until she felt the cold steel of her gun. She wrapped her fingers around the handle and trigger, then began to crawl toward the bed to hide under it. That probably wouldn't work, she realized, but at least she had some idea of where she was. Whoever had done this would probably come after her. And if he did, and tried to grab her, she'd simply fire at him. She'd empty the clip and hope he wasn't lead-proof like the unknown interloper. She knew there were still five cartridges in the gun. That should last until the police came . . .

Or I'm dead!

. . . she reasoned as she crawled farther along. It was an act of pure desperation, but she couldn't worry about that now. It was the only thing to do. The alternative was to yield to her fate without a struggle, and that was out of the question. She crept toward the bed as quickly as her pain allowed.

Keep going! Just don't stop! You'll make it!

The very moment she touched the edge of the bed, an arm came around from behind her and yanked her by the chest onto her feet. The irrepressible strength of it took Claire's breath away. Then someone . . .

Or SOMETHING!

. . . ripped the gun out of her hand, robbing her of her only means of self-defense.

CHAPTER 30

A CONFUSION OF VARIOUS sounds came through the door and into the hallway: the shattering of window glass, the dull thud of the grenade hitting the wall, and the explosion afterward. Bishop delayed a few seconds before ordering Morales to trigger the explosive.

Morales and Jones pressed themselves against the wall to avoid the blast. Bishop stood several yards behind them, out of the danger zone. All he did was shield his eyes from stray splinters or ricochets. Morales heard the command and hit the button to explode the device. The blast ripped the door off its hinges and blew it across the room. The door hit the wall at full tilt and splintered into tiny pieces. The blast blew out all the remaining windows. The curtains wafted out into the night, tattered and torn like the sails of a ghost ship.

Everything now went at top speed. Morales entered the room, then Jones. In a matter of seconds they'd whipped their weapons around the room, ready to shoot anything that moved.

"Clear," Morales yelled.

"Clear," Jones confirmed.

The coast *was* clear. Bishop came in with his gun at the ready. He turned left—toward the room the shots had come from minutes ago.

His night-vision device made everything swim in a medley of slightly contrasting green tones. He found the bedroom door half-open, revealing dark shapes moving around. Bishop recognized the woman, and behind her he saw . . .

"Contact. FIRE!"

. . . her *master*. The monster was transformed and stared at him as ferociously as the Devil himself. Then it turned to the woman and pushed her out the shattered window. Bishop saw her feet disappear from view.

The moment seemed to be suspended in midair, as if time had stopped. Then Morales's and Jones's automatics rang out behind him. Bishop fired two short rounds himself through the crack in the door directly into the demon's chest. They were fatal hits—after all, every bullet had been blessed and treated with holy essences, specially prepared for hunting vampires.

The demon lurched back a step but caught himself. What happened next Bishop hadn't foreseen. Instead of falling down dead, the creature raised its right arm. Before Bishop knew it, he saw a flash of lightning.

An invisible fist banged the side of his head, throwing him backward. That's when he finally heard the report.

He staggered backward as more shots came from the bedroom. Bullets hissed by him like an angry swarm of hornets.

He eventually lost his balance and tumbled sideways. Out of the monster's line of fire. He was lucky. Not one more bullet hit him.

CHAPTER 31

CLAIRE'S SENSES REVIVED sluggishly. First she heard noises. They were faint, as if her ears were plugged with wax. She thought she heard a bang. *Maybe it's just my imagination*, she reflected, and listened again. Before she could hear a sound, someone grabbed her and pushed her out the broken window. Her legs got crossed, knocking her off balance and making her lurch forward.

For a second she envisioned herself falling headfirst four floors down until she hit the sidewalk in front of the building.

But no. Her chest banged against the fire escape railing instead, right in front of her bedroom window. She clutched it instinctively, just to be sure. The cold autumn wind caused her to shiver, but for the moment it swept away all fear. Whatever had happened, she thought, she had survived it.

Almost! You're not safe yet!

Fear returned promptly with the dull rattle of gunfire in the bedroom. Claire knew it wasn't her imagination this time: All kinds of guns were going off behind her.

She didn't know if she was being shot at, but she had no desire to find out. She let go of the railing and crouched down against the brick wall. The howl of police sirens was getting nearer, but she couldn't estimate when she might be rescued. Her hearing returned slowly and not fully.

With bullets flying nearby, instead of waiting for the knights in blue armor, she elected to climb down to the sidewalk.

She still couldn't see but was confident she could make it with mental concentration and focus. Staying tight against the wall, her right hand groped for the lever to lower the ladder. Her other hand clutched her purse, which was hanging from her left shoulder and banging against her right hip. A voice deep within her warned her not to lose it. She obeyed, even though she couldn't place the voice or where it came from.

She worked her way forward, bit by bit, feeling for the lever. Just as her fingertips felt it, an arm once again wrapped itself around her chest.

"Don't be afraid," said a voice that Claire thought she recognized.

What followed felt as if she were shot out of a cannon. She had a flying feeling at once liberating and thrilling. Then she blacked out.

CHAPTER 32

BISHOP LAY MOTIONLESS on the floor for a moment, expecting more shots. None came, so he got up and looked sideways. A familiar pair of eyes looked at him, expressing sheer terror. It was Morales. He lay on his side next to Bishop. By the light of the streetlamps shining through the window, Bishop could see every detail of the scene even without his night-vision device.

There was a silver-dollar-sized crater in Morales's forehead, and Bishop could see right inside his skull.

Morales's pupils were dilated as if he had tried to drink in his last sight and preserve it for all eternity. Bishop had seen enough. He turned around and looked at the bedroom, which was empty.

"What the hell is going on up there, dammit?" Whitman shouted over the walkie-talkie.

But it barely registered in Bishop's consciousness. Instead of answering, he touched where the first bullet had hit him. He could feel the blood running over his fingers, even through his glove, following the rhythm of his pulse. When he probed it further, he realized that half his left ear was missing. Its loose edges were completely frayed. Tatters of flesh squished through the fingers of his gloved hand.

But it didn't end there. The skin on his head had been ripped open, from his temple to the back of his head. If there was such a thing as good luck, Bishop thought, then he'd used up a lifetime supply in those minutes. Or at least one hell of a lot of it. The round had hit him at a favorable angle, skirting his skull but not penetrating it. But still, it left a devastating cut on the left side of his face, a deep wound that radiated pulsating pain, growing greater with every second and taking his breath away.

The sound of approaching police sirens snapped Bishop back to reality. He saw that Jones was inspecting the bedroom. The faint glow of his night-vision goggles produced green shapes on his face.

"The beast is gone. Dove out the window," Jones said.

"And the woman?" Bishop asked, trying to stand up straight.

"She's gone too."

Jones came over, took him by the collar, and helped him to his feet.

The sirens got louder and louder.

"We've got to get out of here, boss," Jones said.

"Get going. Pull out," Whitman urged.

"What about Morales?"

Bishop took one last look at the body at his feet. He had been one of his best men, maybe even something of a friend.

Then he turned to go.

"Let the dead bury their dead," he commented as he rushed out of the apartment.

CHAPTER 33

DARKNESS.

Claire's mind sank into darkness. Her unconsciousness had blanketed her mind like a shroud.

Her thoughts flickered, meaningless and disconnected, like fireflies on a sultry summer's night. Mental images spun around far too rapidly to be recognized, barely more than splashes of color.

But all that dissolved.

When she opened her eyes, she was in the middle of a forest. She felt the soil under her feet and breathed in the earthy scent she recalled from childhood.

Giant pines were tightly packed together, with their knotty trunks and intertwined roots. Scattered among them were stunted spruce trees, their bony black branches looking like the bones of long-forgotten nightmares.

It was deathly silent.

The only sound Claire heard was the dull beating of her heart in her breast. She looked around for help orienting herself. But she didn't recognize the area or find anything to help her get her bearings. Then all of a sudden she knew exactly where she was.

This certain knowledge came like an inspiration.

You're in Rockwell Heights!

Claire was sure. She really was in Rockwell Heights, a lonely stretch of land between the town of Rockwell and the Canadian border. It was an untouched region, no streets or settlements. A place free of intruding pulp mills or sawmills.

There weren't many people familiar with this neck of the woods. Only a few locals from Rockwell and the surrounding area went there in the autumn to hunt. Virtually all the tourists stayed away. The trip in was too onerous. The highway stopped seventeen miles before the Heights. After that you had to rely on hidden footpaths the smugglers had used to bring whiskey over the border during Prohibition.

But the paths weren't passable in the spring months immediately after snowmelt. And all summer long, swarms of mosquitoes attacked every living thing with a drop of blood left in its body.

But Claire knew the area. Her memory was of course somewhat rusty, but the longer she took in the forest air, the clearer her recollections became. The cool breezes of the woods swept away the dust of forgetfulness.

She'd hunted with her father around here when she was young. She'd learned to shoot on this very stretch of land. She'd caught her first raccoon in these woods and shot her first deer.

With Daddy.

A feeling of happiness suddenly flowed through her body and mind. But it dissipated as quickly as it had come. Then another thought crowded into her mind.

You've got to get to the cabin before dark! It's dangerous in the woods at night!

The voice in her dream vision now sounded frightened and worried. Uneasiness stirred in Claire. She was about to look at her wrist to see the time when she realized she couldn't move her arm. She looked at herself and discovered she was in a strait-jacket. Her arms were lashed around her body, unable to move even a fraction of an inch. Claire pulled and shook at it but couldn't free herself.

Once again there was the voice in her head.

You've got to get to the cabin! It's not safe in the woods in the dark!

Quick!

Claire's anxiety escalated with every word. She knew she had to make it to the cabin, but she had no idea where the cabin was. Her recollections started to grow dim, and the woods suddenly became unfamiliar. It was getting darker and darker. Claire didn't know how soon it would be completely dark. She looked up at the sky to orient herself by the sun. That instant she was paralyzed, unable to believe her eyes.

The sky was . . .

Oh God!

. . . a surging sea of blood. Giant breakers crashed over one other, leaving rusty red whitecaps. Mountainous waves rose and toppled over with a crack of thunder that shook the ground underfoot.

It took a great effort to turn away from the sight. Claire drew some deep breaths and discovered that the forest scent was gone. Now her nose sensed the odor from a newly dug grave. The more she breathed it in, the stronger the feeling of panic seized her. Claire began to run, slowly at first, then faster and faster, jumping over tree roots and cutting through the under-brush. The farther she ran, the more closely the trees closed in. Thorns dug into her legs, tearing open her skin, cutting them to shreds. She pressed on, running farther and farther, searching for her father's log cabin. But the more she ran, the more alien the forest became.

The sea of blood surged and seethed overhead. A storm was brewing, she realized, so she upped her pace. There was rustling in the underbrush behind her, but she didn't dare turn around.

Keep going, keep going . . . you're gonna make it!

Then she heard laughter to her right, a high, sharp sound that cut right through her.

Claire increased her pace, though she knew she couldn't keep it up for very long. Since she couldn't move her arms, she had to run bolt upright, the only way she could keep her balance. But it was exhausting to keep moving that way. She had a stitch in her side like a knife that gradually slowed her breathing. She felt nauseous and started to gag. A bitter taste was in her mouth. Her tongue was numb, stuck to her palate. She was on the point of jumping over a tangle of roots when her strength sagged. She came up short, and her right ankle got caught in the roots. Losing her balance, she fell down headfirst, landing with her face on the ground.

Another laugh resounded behind her, somewhat nearer than last time.

Claire climbed to her feet, tried to stand, but failed because her bound arms couldn't support her. She rolled from one side to the other like a beetle flipped over on its back. Her feet dug into the forest floor but couldn't get any purchase. She was about to try it a second time when a figure emerged from behind a spruce—a silhouette, barely more than a shadow.

"Hello, Claire," the figure said in a woman's voice.

Though Claire couldn't see her, she knew at once who it was. *Amanda.*

"What are you doing here in the woods all by yourself, sister dear?" Amanda asked, coming a bit closer to Claire without leaving the shadow of the trees. The whole world seemed to Claire nothing but shadows. Only a weak, reddish shimmer lent things some shape. A lightning bolt from the bloody sky above her was followed by a thunderclap that made the whole world tremble.

"Have you gotten lost, you poor thing?" Amanda asked, coming closer. In spite of the dark, Claire could see that her feet didn't touch the ground.

Oh my God. She's floating on air again!

Claire's chest was seized by panic, making it hard to breathe. She fought for air like a fish on dry land. When she looked up at the figure, she saw two fiery red dots where eyes should have been.

"Wait, I'll help you," Amanda said, stepping out of the shadows so that Claire could clearly recognize her.

Claire looked into her sister's eyes. They glowed like embers.

Her thin lips formed an ugly grin. Her teeth were jagged like a rusty bear trap, long and bent inward.

Another lightning bolt flashed across the bloody sky, bathing Amanda's face in a brief, bright glare. The entire world turned pale for a split second, but her eyes glowed all the more.

"Come on, get up," Amanda said. Her face was nothing but eyes and teeth. Thick saliva bubbled from between her teeth and ran down her chin.

She leaned over Claire and raised her hand. It was a paw with long, black claws. Her fingers looked like dried-out twigs. Her skin was clear, almost completely white. Another flash of lightning, and it became virtually transparent. A tangle of black veins showed where blood had stopped flowing.

Claire's feet were still scrabbling over the forest floor, unable to find firm footing. The paw grabbed her by the shoulder and lifted her off her feet. Claire stood directly facing the creature that had once been her sister.

"I told you I'd help you," Amanda said.

Before Claire could respond, a second paw grabbed the back of her head, burying itself in her hair and then pulling her head backward.

She tried to defend herself. She was cramping up all over her body. She tried to kick at the creature, tried to elude her grip, tried . . .

. . . anything at all.

But nothing worked.

Instead of breaking loose, she only stared with wide-open eyes up at the sea of blood undulating in the sky.

"I'll help you, sister dear," the creature said, its voice no more than a growl. Then it leaned down and buried its teeth in Claire's neck.

Although it was a dream . . .

Oh, please, dear God, please just let it be a dream!

. . . Claire could sense every detail with the utmost precision.

She felt the cold the creature emitted. Felt its teeth boring into her skin. She could even feel the blood flowing in warm waves out of her neck in the rhythm of her heartbeat—straight into the sucking and slurping creature's gorge.

But that wasn't the whole story. There was a sensation that was much worse than all the others combined. A feeling far away from her neck, in the center of her . . .

. . . female areas . . .

. . . a euphemism her grandmother had always used. It was an increasingly powerful tingling that streamed through her body in warm waves.

Claire gave in to the feeling, stopped fighting the creature, and closed her eyes.

Her body tensed up, then every muscle went limp.

CHAPTER 34

"THIS IS GOING TO HURT a helluva lot, boss," Jones said.

He held a surgical clamp in his left hand and a scalpel in his right. His hands looked huge, as if the disposable gloves were at least two sizes too small. But Bishop had no choice: He could either have Jones sew him up or bleed to death.

There was no way they could go to an emergency room after the shootout because all hospitals in New York State were required by law to report every gunshot injury to the police.

So he had to be content with what he had, and what he had was Jones—a former French Foreign Legionnaire with special training as a medical orderly. And instead of a sterile operating theater, he had a double room in a rundown motel in the Bronx with wallpaper hanging like tinsel in the corners and a carpet that looked as if someone had recently driven a herd of cattle through.

Still, Bishop knew he should consider himself lucky. While he was still in a dense fog from shock, Jones had sized up at once the seriousness of the situation. He'd closed the wound temporarily with instant adhesive back in the car, and then with a pressure bandage. If he hadn't, Bishop would probably have bled to death in the backseat. After the steady flow of blood had finally stopped, only then did Jones give Bishop something for his infernal pain. Bishop's head began to feel like it was stuffed with cotton batting, and he could clearly feel the painkiller clouding his thinking like a fog bank. But those were the only drops of wormwood in the giant ocean of alleviating balm.

"Hurry up. I haven't got all night," Bishop growled, clenching his teeth. His jaw muscles bulged, and another gush of blood spurted from his ear. Or rather from the tattered remains of it.

Jones proceeded. First he clamped the remains of the ear as best he could; then he cut off all the tissue he knew couldn't be saved. The longer Jones was busy with his scalpel, the more tissue fell victim to his efforts.

Bishop kept a stoic face through it all. He stared at a grease spot on the wall over the dusty television while the pain suddenly ate its way through his mind like a swarm of termites on a rotten door frame. The painkillers didn't seem to be up to his pain level anymore; the medicine's effects vanished, and Bishop was once again completely abandoned to the terrible torture racking his entire body.

It wasn't long before the worst was behind him. After Jones finally removed his hands from his head, Bishop could take in the full extent of the amputation: Almost the entire ear was dangling between Jones's forefinger and thumb.

"Hurt much?" Jones asked.

"Like my prick was torn off," Bishop replied.

Jones wrapped up the piece of ear in a gauze bandage and threw it into the wastebasket beside the bed. Looking back at Bishop, he could really see the scope of the wound. When he'd verified that the amputation was good enough, he sat down on the edge of the bed and took out the sewing equipment from the first-aid kit.

"Now I'm going to sew up your ear and your head wound," Jones told him.

"You don't have to talk," Bishop got out between clenched teeth. "Just do it!"

"OK, boss," Jones acquiesced. He did the first suture. Compared to the pain of the amputation, the stitches were a pure blessing—Bishop hardly felt a single suture. His thinking cleared, and some questions popped up that he hadn't considered since the shootout.

While Jones was carefully putting in one suture after another, Bishop's eyes drifted over to Whitman, who was on a chair beside the door to the room with a gun and silencer in his hand.

Better safe than sorry.

All kinds of thoughts buzzed through Bishop's head as he studied his partner, thoughts as clear and distinct as gravel on a crystal-clear mountain lake floor. And every idea generated new questions that simply wouldn't leave Bishop in peace.

"Did you see the woman when she was on the fire escape?" he asked.

"You talking to me, chief?" Whitman asked.

"Yes, dammit! Just answer the question."

"Take it easy," Whitman said, getting up and going to stand beside Jones. "Yes, I *did* see the woman," he admitted.

"Why didn't you take a shot at her? You had a clear field of fire," Bishop asked.

"Clear field of fire? You're getting it confused, chief. You, Morales, and Jones were the storm troops. It was *your* job to nab the woman and the vampire. I was your cover, just like the other guys at the back door."

"Cover or no cover—you could have fired," Bishop snarled, looking at Whitman with daggers in his eyes. "But you didn't, and I want to know why."

"Keep still, boss, or you'll tear the stitches out," Jones spoke up.

"Why? I'll tell you why," Whitman said. "The woman was right in front of the window. I could hear shots coming from the apartment behind her, and the only gun I had was the one I have in my hand now. A nine millimeter."

"What are you getting at?"

"I'm getting at this: You can't take a precise shot with a gun of this caliber at that distance. I could have missed the woman and hit you or one of the other guys. The risk was too great. *That's* why I didn't shoot. I didn't want to kill my own men. It was simply a precautionary measure."

Bishop didn't respond. He didn't know what to make of Whitman's words. Of course he was right as far as the gun's caliber and the distance was concerned. But nevertheless he wasn't happy with the answer. The operation hadn't gone as planned. One man was dead, he was wounded, and the vampire and that little bitch were still on the loose. Upon sober reflection, the operation was a total fuck-up.

"Why didn't you get the rifle?" he quizzed Whitman further.

Jones had given up trying to make Bishop keep still. So he went on sewing as if nothing was happening.

"Of course I was going for the rifle, chief. But I'd barely turned around when the show was over. The woman and the beast had taken off."

"Did you see the vampire?"

"Yes, a damn ugly son of a bitch. He grabbed the woman and with one jump was on the roof and out of sight before I could get the rifle ready."

Jones pulled the thread tight, made a knot, and cut the thread. He peeled off his rubber gloves and tossed them into the wastebasket. He looked at Bishop and then Whitman and then turned back and forth.

"Something wrong, Jonesey?" Whitman asked.

"Well," Jones said, "maybe, maybe not!"

"Out with it," Whitman replied.

"Well, there's one thing that I can't get out of my head."

"What could that be?"

"Morales is dead, the boss is wounded, and I was probably real lucky that the beast's clip was empty or it would have got me too. Still, the operation went like clockwork, if you ask me."

"Like clockwork?" Bishop growled. "We lost one of our best men. Nothing went like clockwork over there! Absolutely nothing!"

Jones kept looking from Bishop to Whitman and back again. His lower jaw was grinding the words on his tongue as if trying to make them so small that they'd do the least damage.

"I must contradict you, sir," he said. "The attack was carried out perfectly. We utilized the moment of surprise optimally. We had the greater numbers and reacted quickly and properly."

"Get to the point, Jonesey," Whitman said.

"OK," Jones said. "Everything went very fast, and the light was anything but good. But I could swear on my mother's grave that I hit the demon fatally. Morales hit him too, and the boss did. We all hit him. But he still waltzed out of the apartment completely unharmed. And I don't think the bastard was wearing a bulletproof vest. What do you think, boss?"

"No," Bishop said, "no way."

Of course he knew he'd hit the demon, that they'd all hit him. In spite of his shock, the wound, and the pain, he could still remember that bullet-ridden chest.

But he'd rather have kept those facts to himself, at least until all the contingencies had been cleared up. Because in his business it was precisely those contingencies that could sometimes get your ass in a sling.

That was why he had to examine the cartridges still in the weapons. Even if you're going to war on the Vatican's side, you aren't immune to mistakes.

Maybe they hadn't been shooting with the cartridges prepared for fighting vampires at all. Maybe there was a fuck-up and a cardinal or a drunken Swiss Guard shipped an untreated box to the U.S. instead of sending treated ammo.

Those possibilities would of course explain why the shots had no effect on the demon. Not until the two options had been cleared up and eliminated could he address the last possibility left—that the vampire in the apartment was a hybrid, a bastard that the Organization had been hunting for more than fifty years, which could help root out the plague of vampires once and for all.

For some reason this suspicion had already crept into his mind at the airport, that this particular demon was very special. The idea had been germinating for a while and now branched out in all directions. After the shootout, he had to seriously consider it.

"What do you say to this, chief?" Whitman asked. "Are we dealing with one of those Nazi lab rats here?"

Bishop was surprised that it seemed Whitman had read his mind. He looked at him without batting an eyelash.

"That's very unlikely," he lied. "Very, very unlikely. After all, that's nothing but a myth. We'd better check the ammo instead of running after fairy tales."

He stopped for a minute to get his thoughts in order. Then he continued.

"I think the Organization made a mistake. File an immediate request for new ammunition for all weapons."

Bishop could see Whitman's face twitch a little, and briefly. A tiny crack in his otherwise very cool, impassive, indifferent mask. But he was absolutely sure: Disbelief had flashed over Whitman's face. Whitman did not believe him. And that wasn't the whole story. Maybe he had something up his sleeve, Bishop considered, warning himself to proceed with caution.

For a second their eyes met, like dueling swords. Then Whitman spun away and went back to his post on the chair by the door.

Bishop recalled the events at the airport and the moment when he blew Ceres away. And once again it didn't take long for his imagination to replace Ceres's face with Whitman's. The very thought of killing Whitman sent a feverish shudder right through him.

All the same, he had to take it one step at a time and wait for a favorable opportunity. And the way things were going, Bishop guessed that his chance would probably come soon.

CHAPTER 35

AN ORGASM SWEPT THROUGH Claire's body. That feeling, so intense and sublime, washed away all thoughts from her mind. And all her fears along with them.

The moment the sensation hit her consciousness, the surging sea above her began to change, starting with little cracks that quickly expanded. The colors paled with her every heartbeat. The phenomenon turned translucent, then disappeared completely.

The first thing she became conscious of was that she was in bed, covered by a sheet. A second thought flashed through her mind, filling her with joy.

I can see! Oh my God, I can see again!

Whatever had robbed her of her eyesight in her apartment hadn't done so permanently. It still felt as if she was looking at the world through a milky veil, but she hoped that would soon pass.

She sat up and surveyed the room. It was dark and had a dusty smell. There were no windows and no clues where she was. A naked bulb dangling by a cord from the ceiling was the only source of light. Claire looked around some more and found there was only one door to the room.

Her initial joy at her revived eyesight gave way to the fear that she was being held against her will. In a strange place. By someone who wasn't particularly inclined to like her, in view of the events of the past night.

You've got to try and get away!

That motivated her anew. She *had* to make a getaway, and that meant inspecting the room as fast as possible to find something to help her, because whoever was keeping her would probably be coming back soon.

So better not to be empty-handed, she thought. She had to find a way to defend herself.

Claire was about to get up when the sheet slid off her body to reveal that she was completely naked. The whole left side of her body was riddled with wounds. Cuts, scratches, and scrapes covered her side, and she could tell that her arm was hurt the worst. But she felt no pain—not the slightest ache or twitch—though the wounds looked very fresh. They had been cleaned, and the larger wounds were dressed.

Examining her arm more closely, she discovered that some cuts had been stitched together. Expertly and very precisely. The sutures were neat and properly executed, the ends professionally knotted . . .

"Don't worry," a man's voice sounded. "They won't leave any scars."

Claire cringed and instinctively drew the sheet up over her nakedness. Only then did she see where the voice had come from. A stranger had entered the windowless room. But the longer she studied him, the more she believed she'd seen that face before. The seconds ticked by . . .

Think hard! Think hard! . . . and then it all came back.

In your apartment! It's the stranger from the apartment!

"What do you want from me?" Claire asked, her usual self-assurance completely gone from her voice. She was on the brink of tears.

"I was bringing you breakfast," the stranger said, raising his arms. Claire then noticed he was carrying a full tray.

Without waiting for her to act, he crossed the room and put the tray on the night table beside the bed—a carafe of orange juice, fresh rolls, and fried eggs and bacon. Cutlery was wrapped in a napkin beside the plate. Claire eyed the blade of the bread knife and wondered if it might make a good weapon.

Better than nothing!

"You *are* hungry, aren't you?" the stranger asked with a smile.

"But you might want to get dressed first," he went on. "Your clothes couldn't be salvaged, but I've put out some clean things on the dresser. I hope they fit. Things went so fast I didn't have any time to get your sizes. Still, I think these will fit reasonably well."

He pointed to the dresser against the wall on the other side of the bed. Claire took a quick look, and there really was an ironed stack of clothing, her purse, and maybe the most important thing of all . . .

Thank God!

. . . her pistol.

Instinct led her hand out from under the sheet and wrapped it around the pistol grip. A split second later she pointed the gun at the stranger's head. He didn't show any emotion but simply watched her.

But scarcely did Claire have him in her sights when she remembered what had happened the previous night. She had fired at him several times, and it got her nowhere, absolutely nowhere.

Instead . . .

. . . he changed into a goddamn monster!

Claire lowered the pistol and laid it beside her on the bed. It took no small effort to drop the weapon. But she guessed it couldn't make her situation any better. Needlessly annoying the stranger, on the other hand, would definitely not make it better.

Into a goddamn monster!

"Please excuse me," she said, her voice composed. "I forgot you're bulletproof."

The stranger smiled again as he folded his arms over his chest.

"Actually not bulletproof," he said. "It almost always tickles a bit and ruins my wardrobe."

Claire forced a smile as well.

"I'll leave you to yourself now," he added. "Get dressed and have a bite. We've got a few things to talk about."

Claire was surprised at the ease with which he spoke to her. It seemed for a moment that she was not being kept in a dungeon. Instead, it rather reminded her of visiting friends who always fussed over her, friends who were always careful to do everything right by her and to pick up even her tiniest wish just from reading her eyes. And though her present situation was actually more than absurd, Claire's feelings at that moment stood in stark contrast to all that. It felt damn good right then to be cared for and fussed over. That was also a luxury, Claire realized, that she'd experienced all too rarely in recent years.

Work, always work . . . day in . . . day out . . .

"Oh, please excuse my rudeness," the stranger said, bowing to Claire and interrupting her thoughts. "My name is George. George Powell."

He offered Claire his hand. She paused for a moment and looked at it. After she'd assured herself that it wasn't about to transform into a claw, she took it.

"Claire," she said. "Claire Hagen."

"I know," he said. "I read your column."

Without a word he turned around and left the room. He closed the door behind him, but Claire didn't hear a key turning in the lock. The only noise she heard was the soft click of his heels walking away from the door.

CHAPTER 36

"WELL?" BISHOP INQUIRED.

His voice sounded tired. He hadn't slept a wink that night, just laid on the double bed staring at the wall and mulling everything over. The loss of blood made him constantly thirsty and unable to relax. That was nothing new for Bishop; he'd been shot several times before and knew that the body tried to keep its fluids in proper balance.

"Nothing," Whitman said.

"Nothing at all?"

"Well, OK, at least we know the direction in which the woman escaped. Our informant at AT&T gave me the statements for all her calls for metropolitan New York. You can see where her cell was used and when. Besides, I used a master password to get into the central server. From now on we'll get every signal in real time."

"Did she ever use it?" Bishop asked, propping himself up in the bed. "I mean her cell."

"No, she didn't make any calls, if that's what you mean, chief."

"But?"

"But the active recording of calls is only one record a cell phone provider temporarily stores," Whitman explained. "They also keep records of the broadcasting towers the cell phone connects to. So you can reconstruct a pattern of movement."

"With date and time?" Bishop asked.

"Yes, everything to the precise second with exact GPS data."

A smile scooted over Bishop's lips in spite of his fatigue.

"Where's the woman now?" he asked, getting out of bed. He crossed the room and stood beside Whitman at the desk. Then he cast a fleeting glance at the screen of Whitman's laptop. Closely aligned columns of numbers flew across the screen, but Bishop couldn't discern any pattern. He stood up straight.

"That I can't tell exactly, chief. We can see that she's moving north. Her cell coverage was sporadic at first and connected with different towers. She was following an almost straight line on the map."

The grin on Bishop's face got broader and broader.

"They flew over the rooftops," he said.

Although he had to worm every bit of information out of Whitman, Bishop kept his resentment in check. In the meantime a budding certainty came to dominate his thinking, the certainty that they'd picked up the trail again. Maybe only a faint trail, but what the hell.

"I see it the same way," Whitman said, "but they didn't do that for long. About three minutes later, they must have taken off in a vehicle. The pattern of movement is more or less a checkerboard, like highway maps."

"Got it," Bishop acknowledged. "How long were they on the road?"

"About half an hour."

"And then?"

"Yeah," Whitman said with a sigh. "Then the signal was dropped. From one second to the next."

"She turned off her cell?" Bishop suggested.

"No, I don't think so. A cell phone that's switched off still sends one last signal to the tower it's on. Imagine it's more or less like a worker who goes for a quick piss and tells his superiors he's going. But that wasn't the case here. The signal was simply cut off."

"What does that mean?"

"It could mean one of two things," Whitman responded. "Either she destroyed the cell phone, or she entered a building with no reception."

Bishop walked away and folded his hands behind his head. Countless thoughts were spinning through his head. He knew the trail wasn't very promising; the woman could have gone over the hills and far away. The vampire too. Nonetheless, they couldn't give up, he concluded. There was too much at stake.

Bishop went to the window, pushed the curtains aside, and took a look down. Two black SUVs were parked on the far side of the street. Four people lolled around in front of them, smoking and chatting. One of the men was Jones. He'd gone to see the other guys and to stretch his legs a bit. He kept looking up at the window of their room as if making sure that everything was OK. When he saw Bishop at the window, he nodded. Bishop nodded back to show that everything was all right.

But everything was not all right, Bishop thought as he left the window. Morales was dead, he was wounded, and the woman and the vampire had slipped through their fingers. They had to act quickly before this minimal clue was completely useless.

"What do we do now?" Whitman asked.

"How big an area do these towers cover?"

"A tower has a range of one hundred-plus yards on average. In remote areas it's bigger, of course. But since we are actually in the center of the free world, there's hardly a street in New York that doesn't have at least one tower."

"Do you know the last tower they were on?"

"Yes, a tower to the north of the city, past the Tappan Zee Bridge."

"Tarrytown?"

Whitman cast an eye on his screen with the New York street plan on it.

"Yes, Tarrytown."

CHAPTER 37

CLAIRE'S HUNGER WASN'T AROUSED until her first bite into the fried eggs. It flashed through her mind that the meal might have been poisoned. She paused momentarily—her mouth full of egg, and a roll in her hand. Then she resumed her munching.

Why would the stranger . . . *George* . . . have gone to the trouble of treating her injuries if he intended to poison her anyway?

It made no sense!

That sounded plausible even to the frightened woman that she was. She swallowed everything down while hardly chewing. She'd survived the past few days on coffee and chewing gum, and it was damn good to feel something warm in her mouth.

When she'd finished off the last piece of bread, she drank the orange juice in one gulp. Then she treated herself to another glass and drank half of it. She put the tray back on the night table, slipped out from under the sheets, went over to the clothes on the dresser, and started to get dressed.

George didn't know her sizes, but the things fit rather well. Even the panties and the bra. She put on the jeans, a T-shirt, and a man's flannel shirt over that. The shirt was a little too large so she didn't button it up, and she rolled up her sleeves so they wouldn't get in the way. Then she picked up her purse and looked at her cell. She didn't have any reception, so she put it back. Her hand grazed something cool. She took it out and saw the silver box John had given her. The very thought of what had happened to John made her heart skip a beat, and she felt a dull twinge in the pit of her stomach.

Claire pressed the button on the side of the box, and the lid sprang open to reveal the two vials and the golden chain and crucifix. At the same time John's voice slowly came to mind. She could distinctly hear him as if talking with him face to face:

They are the only sure means I know to ward off vampires . . . The vial on the left is concentrate of wild rose oil. On the right, holy water from Saint Peter's in Rome . . .

Claire still didn't know what to make of it, but the contents of the box suddenly intrigued her, the golden chain even more than the vials. She wrapped the end of the chain around her forefinger and lifted it carefully out of the box. Then she dangled the crucifix before her eyes for several seconds. At first glance the chain didn't seem to be anything special. It was an everyday necklace with an equally everyday pendant. There must be millions of them, she mused. Once again John's voice sounded, as if to set Claire straight.

. . . as far as I know the cross is the most effective protection against vampires . . .

It was just a recollection—but its intensity was disconcerting. Claire shuddered, and the hair on the back of her neck stood on end. She was petrified for a minute, the crucifix swinging before her face like a soothsayer's pendulum. A soft glow came over the Savior's face, and she felt a sudden impulse.

Claire followed the impulse. She took the chain off her finger, opened the clasp, and put it around her neck. When the clasp snapped shut, she hid the crucifix underneath her T-shirt. The metal felt cold on her skin but warmed up so fast that soon she could hardly feel it. Then she shut the silver box and stowed it back in her purse.

At that very moment the door opened and George entered.

CHAPTER 38

BISHOP WAS IN THE PASSENGER SEAT, Jones was at the wheel, and Whitman navigated from the backseat.

It was just after nine a.m., and traffic was gradually beginning to thin out. But the trip was still going slowly.

"Isn't there another road we can take?" Bishop said, looking back at Whitman.

"Sure there is," Whitman said, "but there's an accident on the highway, and traffic's backed up all the way to downtown. Can't go any faster, chief."

Bishop looked through the windshield at the bustling street. Honking echoed through the canyon of buildings, bicycle messengers weaved in and out among the vehicles, and a never-ending stream of pedestrians spilled over the sidewalks and crosswalks.

He couldn't understand why in the world so many people absolutely wanted to live in this Moloch, this dirty, stinking concrete wilderness. New York City always reminded him of an ugly woman wearing too much makeup to try to hide her flaws.

To him, the flashing lights, the showy glass towers, and the high-end boutiques were merely a mask behind which the disgusting face of this pulsating monstrosity tried to hide.

His head was spinning, which made the world swim before his eyes for a moment. He knew it was a side effect of the painkillers and not physical symptoms of his disgust with the city. He shut his eyes briefly, waiting for the confusion in his head to subside. He blotted out his surroundings, slamming the door on the world.

"Think we've got a problem, chief," Whitman said.

"What's up?" Bishop asked, keeping his eyes shut.

"You've gotta see for yourself!"

Bishop hesitated before opening his eyes. The dizziness in his head had gone, so he turned to Whitman and his laptop. The screen was pointed toward him.

The first thing Bishop saw was a newspaper headline: "Suspect in Airport Murder Caught on Surveillance Camera." And the next thing was his own face, captured in a grainy still from a videotape. Though the tape quality wasn't exactly the best, Bishop was still pretty easy to recognize; he calculated it might be enough to get him arrested.

Maybe even indicted, who knows?

But then he thought it was still too early to agonize over it. He took another look at the picture, trying to figure out exactly when and where it was taken.

He recognized the bathroom door behind him, so the picture must have been taken immediately after he'd bumped Ceres off.

Bishop looked from the screen to Whitman.

"What did you find out?" he asked.

"Not much," Whitman replied. "Except for this picture, they've nothing to go on. Our mission isn't threatened, if that's what you're getting at. But from now on we should keep as low a profile as possible."

"Good," Bishop affirmed as he turned around. "Actually, it's very good." He'd secretly expected his face would be linked to the crime. After all, airports in the U.S. were under very heavy surveillance. There was hardly an inch that wasn't covered by cameras, so it was only reasonable that he'd been caught on film leaving the bathroom.

Probably before and *after, for sure.*

But he persuaded himself that he'd had no choice. After all, Ceres was trying to take off, and arresting him was out of the question, given the location. He'd done the only correct thing, he concluded.

The ONLY correct thing, goddammit!

That thought swept all doubts from his mind and made him relax.

"How much farther?" he asked, closing his eyes again and leaning back in his seat.

"Depends on traffic," Whitman replied. "Shouldn't be much longer than half an hour."

"Excellent," Bishop said.

CHAPTER 39

"HAVE A SEAT," George said. He motioned to a chair at a small table in the kitchen.

They had left the room where Claire had been sleeping. George went first with Claire following, somewhat hesitantly. They crossed a sunny hallway to this room with windows looking out on a huge piece of land surrounded by high trees.

How do you like it?" George asked, taking her out of her thoughts. She'd sat down at the round kitchen table, where she folded her arms.

"I beg your pardon?" she asked.

"How do you like your coffee?" George repeated, as he crossed to the gurgling coffee machine.

"Black," Claire said with a forced smile.

George nodded, then waited.

Meanwhile Claire scanned the room. Everything she saw spoke of an exquisite taste. The appliances were expensive, imported models; the counters appeared to be black marble, and the grain of the cabinetry was a special kind of wood she couldn't quite recall.

No, not mahogany . . . maybe teak?

But in spite of all the beautiful, expensive objects, Claire knew at once there was something not quite right. For instance, the wall opposite the dining table featured rectangular patches in a color that didn't quite match the rest of the decor. The sections were brighter, with a nail at the top of each patch.

Her insight was spontaneous. She knew for certain where she was.

Tarrytown!

She was in the house in Tarrytown, the very one John had burglarized. The brighter rectangles marked where the pictures were that he and his partner had lifted. John's voice tiptoed into her consciousness again:

. . . the house was a genuine gold mine. Paintings everywhere, expensive knickknacks, and precious rugs . . .

But that wasn't all. A second look told her that some appliances were missing. There was a gaping black hole where the microwave should have been. A cord dangled there, like a tongue out of a toothless mouth.

She *was* in the house John had told her about. Claire was positive. In the house of the . . .

. . . vampire!

The coffee machine stopped gurgling. George poured two cups and sat down at the table.

"Thanks," Claire said.

"You're welcome," George replied.

They sat there for a few minutes, staring silently into their cups. Finally Claire looked up. George likewise. Their eyes met.

"We've got to talk," she said.

"Absolutely," George responded.

Claire took a first sip, peering at her host over the edge of her cup. For the first time, she viewed him as a real person. And not as the . . .

. . . monster . . .

. . . stranger who'd attacked her in her apartment.

The first thing that struck her was how difficult it was to judge his age. At first glance, he looked about mid-thirties. But on closer inspection that couldn't be. His skin was too smooth, his eyes too lively. She could hardly find a wrinkle in spite of his three days' growth of beard. Not around his mouth, not on his forehead. No crow's feet. Thick hair. Perfect teeth. She was none the wiser for all her scrutiny. His face seemed like an optical illusion—a sight that baffled her vision and her reason.

"What is it you want to know?" George asked, his eyes fixed again on his coffee, or rather on the steam rising from it, as if trying to interpret a secret message there accessible only to him.

Claire hesitated as she tried to get her thoughts in order. When she realized she couldn't, she put the very first question to him that came to mind.

"Who are you?"

"George Powell."

"I'm not in the mood for joking, Mr. Powell."

"Me neither—you have my word on that."

"Well, then . . . ," she pushed ahead after a moment's pause, "*what* are you?"

George heaved a sigh as he folded his arms across his chest.

"I am . . . ," he said. "You must know it's complicated."

"Go on, Mr. Powell. I seem to have plenty of time."

George looked deep into her eyes as if trying to read her mind.

"I was once a human," he finally confessed, "then I turned into a vampire, and now I'm a freak of nature, if you will. I'm sort of a cross—a zoologist would call it a hybrid life form. I think that scientific definition applies very well to what I am."

"Then you're something like a mule? Am I hearing you right?"

No way did he miss the sarcasm in Claire's question. A grin opened up on his face, flashing his impeccable teeth. They were human teeth, those of a person who seemed to care a lot about his appearance. Nevertheless, Claire could remember all too well what those teeth looked like after his transformation.

Like a rusty bear trap!

The memory of it made her limbs shudder and shiver.

"Yes, in principle I'm something like a mule," George continued, "and the only difference is that's not how I came into this world. I was born a normal human being. Later events made me into what I am today."

Claire had another sip while she let his words sink in. Deep down she could hear a soft voice she'd never heard before. It sounded from the depths of her subconscious and rose up into her conscious thoughts bit by bit.

The whole world's gone crazy, Claire! The whole goddamn world!

But in spite of her doubts, she kept trying to concentrate on the conversation. Trying to figure out what lay hidden beneath George's words.

"Are you serious?" she asked. "That you're a vampire, I mean."

"Of course," George replied, "and I wonder how long you'll keep denying that there are things in this world you didn't have any idea about a short while ago. Terrible things, hushed up for centuries by people, nations, and religions."

Claire was excited about the abrupt turn the conversation had taken. She secretly regretted that her voice recorder wasn't handy. If luck was with her, Claire thought, then it was still in her purse down in the basement. If she'd had it with her at this moment, tabloids all over the country would probably have killed to get a copy of this kooky conversation.

"So you expect me to believe you're a vampire and one of many like you?"

"I don't expect you to believe it, my dear. You know what happened in your apartment. You saw it all! How would you explain that?"

"No idea. Maybe you had a mask on and a bulletproof vest. And my brain made up the rest under stress."

Even before she'd finished talking, it felt like she was lying. Like erecting a barrier piecemeal to shield herself from what her reason had long found obvious. She was intent on seeing how George would counter her words. But instead of responding, he just stared at her while his hands slowly began to unbutton his shirt, one button after the other. When it was completely undone, he pulled the shirt open, exposing his naked torso.

"Does this look to you like I was wearing a bulletproof vest?" he asked.

Claire stared at his chest, which was riddled with a dozen bullet holes, each one about finger-wide with black, scabby edges. She could see raw flesh through them. The wounds were large, but not a single drop of blood could be seen.

The sight hit her with the force of an earthquake. The mental barriers she'd constructed collapsed in an instant. The unshakable evidence was there: The man sitting across the table from her *really wasn't human.*

She immediately thought of her sister. Her anxiety about Amanda had been suppressed during all the excitement, but it was smoldering deep down in her subconscious, secretly hidden away. The fierceness of the memory took Claire's breath away, and her throat tightened. She pictured again how Amanda had turned into a monster. She saw her ferocious, hate-filled eyes, and the greedy maw that had once been her mouth.

Amanda, oh my God! I've got to help her!

CHAPTER 40

"PRETTY PART OF THE COUNTRY," Jones said.

He parked the SUV on the shoulder and turned off the motor. Whitman looked up from his laptop to the imposing buildings and manicured front yards, then back to the screen.

"Not bad," Whitman said, hammering away. "I could retire here."

Bishop had no feel for the splendor and beauty around him. It was a secluded neighborhood, with the properties spaced widely apart. Almost every house had the same Victorian pastel colors and resembled the bleached bones of an era that had had its day.

Every house might be the demon's hideout.

Every window with a view of the street was a possible lookout where the beast might be spying on them. There wasn't a light to be seen, and no other signs of life either. The darkened windows were like the eye sockets of a skull, showing no expression, no life.

"Are you getting a signal?" Bishop asked without looking at Whitman.

"No," he answered, "but her cell was last detected around here."

"Can you find out the house she's in?"

"No, not a hope. I can say only that it must be a house within a hundred-yard radius."

"How many houses in all?"

"More than twenty."

Bishop thought hard. His deliberations circled systematically around the remaining possibilities, like a good sheepdog around an anxious flock. The circles grew tighter and tighter as he filtered through the options, one after another, weighing the odds of their success. This game involved more luck than brains in many ways, but it hit the mark amazingly often.

"What about the tax records? Find out who owns the houses. Maybe there's an irregularity that can help us."

Furious typing in the backseat.

"Not possible either," Whitman said after a while. "Most of the homes belong to offshore companies. The Caymans, Monte Carlo, Hong Kong. All the moneybags in this area are probably avoiding taxes by registering their properties from shell companies all over the world."

Bishop wasn't happy with that. But he sensed the trail was still warm. Maybe they'd gotten a little bit lost, he conceded, but they were on the right track. His boundless confidence had always been the driving force behind his actions. That's why he hoped for success this time.

"What do you suggest, chief?" Whitman asked.

Bishop pondered. But only briefly.

"We'll wait it out," he announced. "After all, they can't lie low forever. Besides, the element of surprise is on our side. I think Miss Hagen hasn't got a clue how closely we're trailing her. They'll come crawling out of their hiding place sooner or later, and a cell signal will betray them. Then we pounce and nab them."

He'd hardly finished when a burst of static sounded from the CB—followed by the voice of one of the men from the other SUV who'd gone to the cargo terminal for new ammunition.

"Ghost One to Ghost Leader. Come in, please."

Bishop picked up the radio.

"Ghost Leader here. What's up, Ghost One?"

"We've got the ammo crates. The customs guys turned a blind eye, as always. It was child's play. Request further instructions, Ghost Leader."

Bishop reflected for a minute whether it would be useful to have the other men take part in the operation. He decided against it, even though he might need their cover and very likely their firepower. For one thing, two black SUVs in a peaceful residential area would be too conspicuous. And for another, he urgently needed a few men to return to base and prepare for the interrogation of the woman. No matter how it turned out, there wouldn't be much time to pry the necessary information out of her.

Besides, the woman wasn't all that important anymore, Bishop reasoned. The highest priority was to seize the vampire. If he'd guessed right, then they really were dealing with one of the experimental Nazi rats. And if so, this mission might be one of the most crucial he'd ever had. Moreover, it could be the most important mission in the Organization's entire history. Because if the vampire really was a hybrid . . .

"Ghost Leader, are you there? Come in, please."

"Ghost Leader here." Bishop recovered. "Withdraw to Ghost House. Make preparations. We'll probably bring guests. Code Blue!"

"Understood, Ghost Leader. Over and out."

Then things started happening quickly.

A penetrating beeping sound came from Whitman's computer. Bishop and Jones whirled around.

"What is it?" Bishop wanted to know.

Whitman's head snapped up with a broad grin on his face. "Jackpot!" he exclaimed.

"Jackpot? What the hell does that mean?" Bishop grunted.

"I've got a signal."

Bishop's eyes opened wide. Even though he was confident he would catch the woman, he hadn't dreamed things would move so fast.

"Where's it coming from?"

"From that house up ahead," Whitman replied, pointing to a house about fifty feet away on the other side of the street. The yard was bordered by tall cypresses, so only the front gable was visible.

"It's 80 Hawthorne Street," Whitman said. "She's in the house. She's dialing a city number, if I'm interpreting the signature right."

"What'll we do?" Jones asked, looking back and forth between the other two as if he didn't know who was calling the shots. They were both his superiors and held the same rank in the Organization.

"We'll go get her," Bishop stated.

He reached under his seat for his automatic and released the safety. Whitman did the same. He closed the laptop, reached behind him into the cargo area, and picked up his rifle. Jones just sat there doing nothing except clutching the wheel.

"Go!" Bishop ordered. "We're raiding the joint."

"Yes, sir!" Jones shouted back. He started the SUV and stepped on the gas so hard that the tires squealed.

CHAPTER 41

BEFORE GEORGE COULD make a move, Claire jumped up and raced down the hallway—back to the room she'd come from. It was unpremeditated, just intuition. An instinct that she had the element of surprise.

She made it to the room, grabbed her purse off the bureau, and immediately retraced her steps into the hallway, closer to the windows. She called the Hillside Medical Center where Amanda was. The ringing at the other end told her she had reception again.

She felt a wave of relief when a woman's voice answered, "Hillside Medical Center, Information. How may I assist you?"

Claire was about to ask for Dr. Harris when suddenly a hand clutched the arm holding her cell.

She turned and saw George's glowering face. His angry eyes glinted like two drops of oil on wet asphalt. He squeezed her hard before she could say anything, so hard that a burning pain ran down her arm. It wasn't as intense as on the previous night but still strong enough to interrupt her phone call.

"Ow! That hurts, dammit!"

"Gimme that!" George shouted, trying to grab the cell. But Claire fought back. She struggled to elude his grasp, hit him on the chest, and kicked his shins, all moves she'd learned in a self-defense course. All moves that now had one thing in common—they were totally ineffective.

"You don't get it," she exclaimed. "It's my sister. I have to help her."

"*You* don't get it," George shouted. "The people after me are probably monitoring your cell. They'll find us!"

That very moment he wrenched the phone from her hand and made a fist before she could act. When he opened his hand the remains of the cell rattled loudly onto the floor. He had completely destroyed it.

Claire could feel anger mounting inside her. She was about to rip into him and ask why the hell he did that. Her lips were forming to shout the words that were on the tip of her tongue . . .

You fucking asshole . . .

. . . when they heard a high-pitched noise outside. Almost like a bark or a shout.

They froze as their brains processed the noise. Then they identified the sound: the squeal of spinning automobile tires.

Somebody's in a damn big hurry.

While looking up at George, who had also pricked up his ears, she could hear the clear and distinct roar of a motor. The noise grew louder by the second.

George ran to the kitchen and looked out the window to the street. Claire was right behind him. The sound got louder and louder. It was menacing, like the roar of a low-flying bomber.

Claire looked through the window, past the yard and down the street. A black SUV came into view. Then another squeal of tires. The brakes locked, the car slowed, pointing toward them, and came to a halt at the curb.

Claire didn't move, fascinated by the sight. She was watching the doors opening when George seized her arm and pulled her away. She didn't want to leave the window before seeing who was getting out. But the window rapidly disappeared from her sight.

George pulled and twisted and piloted her through the kitchen. He opened a door, and Claire found herself in the garage, where two cars were parked.

"C'mon, get in!" George urged, pointing to the car on the left, a black Audi sedan. He got in the driver's seat, closed the door, and started the motor.

"Who are those people?" Claire asked. She looked at him with frightened eyes. George paid no heed. Instead, he took a remote from the console and pressed the sole button on it. The garage door began to rise.

"Let's go! Buckle up!" he commanded, revving the motor. "And keep your head down!"

The garage door was a third of the way up. Claire could see most of the driveway, the lawn, and the SUV's grille at the curb.

"Who are these people, for Chrissake?" she repeated while buckling up.

"I'll explain later. Now we've got to make ourselves scarce."

Her seat belt clicked as George stepped on the gas. The car moved with the force of a racehorse out of the gate at the Kentucky Derby. Claire's upper body was jerked backward and pushed into her seat. She was pumped up with adrenaline, and her heart raced. In all the excitement she could nevertheless see that the garage door was only half open and that it would be impossible for a car to slide under it undamaged.

Oh my God, we're going to ram it!

That was her last clear thought. She screamed and covered her face with her arms as the car barreled toward the door.

CHAPTER 42

WHEN THE SUV screeched to a stop, Bishop tore open the door and hit the street, followed by Whitman and Jones. They hid behind the open doors until they were sure there was no immediate danger. They scanned the property from one end to the other.

"I can't see anything," Whitman ventured.

"Good," Bishop said. His automatic was at the ready, set to fire if anything moved in the windows. But the house looked empty, with no lights in the windows and nothing moving anywhere.

"Jones," Bishop ordered, "you go to the right. I'm going through the front door."

"What about me, chief?" Whitman spoke up without lowering his rifle.

"You stay here and give us cover. And don't mess up the way you did last time."

"Aye, aye, Captain." Whitman's voice had an undertone of mockery.

"Let's go," Bishop ordered and moved off. Jones did the same. They ran over the curb and the front yard, heads down and guns at the ready. Bishop was halfway to the house when he saw the garage door moving out of the corner of his eye. Then he picked up the sound of rusty hinges that hadn't been oiled for a long time.

He stopped and looked over at Jones, who looked at him with raised eyebrows, as if not knowing his next move. The parameters for the attack had just changed, and he was waiting for his superior's instructions. Bishop could tell by his face what his question was. When Jones got no new orders, he kept going to the right side of the house.

Jones was just crossing the driveway when the garage door was ripped off its rails with a terrific crash. The door bulged and billowed out like a sail in a stiff breeze, then crumpled. A black car shot out and raced toward Jones.

Bishop was about to shout for him to take cover. But everything happened too fast. He could only look on helplessly.

By the time Jones saw the danger it was too late. The car hit him at full tilt, cutting his legs out from under him. The force of the impact tossed him high in the air and spun him around. He accidentally fired a round that whizzed over Bishop's head into the autumn sky. Then Jones's head hit the windshield with an ugly, hollow sound that resounded over the yard.

The car kept going. Jones's lifeless body flew over the roof of the car and landed in the driveway. He didn't move. Bishop could see a pool of blood spreading out from under the man's body.

Bishop snapped out of it, raised his automatic, and instantly pulled the trigger. His weapon jerked and hissed, and a constant rain of ejected shells fluttered to the ground. The first salvo riddled the entire side of the sedan and shot out the back window on the passenger's side. A spray of broken glass whirled through the air, sparkling in the noonday sun. The car kept going. Bishop had to act fast.

He took aim once more and pulled the trigger the same instant the Audi turned out of the driveway and into the street. The rear tire on the passenger's side exploded in all directions, amorphous and black, like a swarm of bats. But the sedan still didn't slow down. It shot off to the left and sped up.

At that moment, Whitman's rifle rang out. It was a high-caliber, semiautomatic carbine. His shots came at regular intervals. Deafening, like heavy thunderclaps. Bishop saw that all of his partner's shots were on target. The first two bullets hit the rear window. The first smashed through the glass, creating a spiderweb pattern. The second shattered it to bits and hit the front windshield. The sedan kept moving, but Bishop couldn't see anybody in it. *They must have ducked*, he thought as he put in a new clip. Whitman was focused and kept up his fire. One bullet after another hit right under the trunk, making huge holes. Bishop could see them from fifty yards off, and he knew what Whitman had in mind.

He was trying to hit the gas tank. The SUV wouldn't burst into flames—that only happens in the movies. But still, most vehicles react very badly if the tank gets shot to pieces by a high-caliber bullet. The lightning-quick drop in pressure in the gas lines usually meant that the motor would cough and die.

Whitman kept firing, one shot after the other, preventing anyone in the vehicle from returning his fire. The street was too narrow for the car to swing back and forth to dodge the shots. So the driver bet on speed to get out of the hairy situation.

Bishop was ready to start pumping lead into the car's rear end too, when the vehicle veered to the right with squealing tires and vanished from sight.

He lowered his gun and looked over at Whitman.

"We've got to get out of here," he shouted. With a few steps, he was across the yard and on the driveway where Jones's twisted torso lay, his gun on the ground, the barrel directed at Bishop.

"Is he still alive?" Whitman shouted.

Bishop didn't know yet. He leaned over Jones, lifted him by the collar, and turned him on his back. That's when he discovered the full extent of his injuries.

Jones's forehead was completely bashed in. Bone splinters jutted forth and parts of his brain were pushed out, with his left eye dangling from its socket.

Can't do anything more for him, Bishop concluded as he turned to go. But just then Jones called out in a whisper.

"Help."

Bishop turned and looked down at the ground. Jones's intact eye was wide open and staring at him. That first word was followed by a rasping "Please!"

Jones kept staring at him, his body battered and twisted. Bishop met his man's gaze as he mulled it over. He knew it was already too late to help Jones. Even if a doctor with all his equipment were on this spot at this moment, he probably couldn't do anything for him. Just hold his hand and wait for the end. What the hell more could he do anyway?

While they looked into each other's eyes, the seconds were ticking away.

Bishop finally reached a decision. He leaned down to Jones once again.

"Jonesey, can you hear me?"

"Yes. Please. Help," Jones sighed. A gush of blood shot out of his mouth, stifling his voice.

"Can you move your right arm, buddy?" Bishop asked.

Bishop had seen right off the bat that Jones couldn't move his left one. It was broken in several places and stuck out at a weird angle.

"Yeah, think so," Jones said.

As if to demonstrate, he moved his arm bit by bit, lifting it up toward Bishop. It was a gesture filled with pain. But Bishop suspected that would do for what he'd decided.

"Help," Jones uttered one last time, making a fist with his raised hand that fell open again.

"Help yourself," Bishop said. He took the pistol lying beside Jones and pressed it into his hand. He granted him one last look, then turned and walked back to the SUV.

"Help. Please," Jones cried. His voice was a mere sob. Again and again and again he repeated his plea.

"Please, boss. Help. Please, please, please."

But Bishop never wavered. He reached the SUV, got in, and closed the door behind him. Whitman was at the wheel and had already turned on the ignition.

"I think he's had it," Bishop said.

"How bad is he?" Whitman asked, stepping on the accelerator. The SUV jerked into motion.

"Couldn't do anything more," Bishop added.

"Is he dead?"

A single shot rang out from the driveway behind them. Then silence.

CHAPTER 43

CLAIRE'S SENSES FELT dulled by the intense action around her. Bullets whistled around her ears, ricochets zipped by the car, and glass showered down on her like sharp hailstones.

She cringed time and again, expecting a searing pain to burn her body somewhere. A pain to show she'd been hit. It was only a question of time, she feared, before a bullet shattered her spine or shredded a lung.

She bent forward at the first reports of gunfire, burying her head between her knees. She pushed down low on her seat and clenched her teeth. But she didn't think this would help her survive unscathed. The powerful certainty of her imminent death seized her heart with fear.

This is it! I'm gonna die!

She tried not to imagine the awful pain, tried not to wonder whether she'd die on the spot or slowly bleed to death. Any thought for her future was nipped in the bud. Instead, she gritted her teeth more tightly and listened to her inner voice.

Her brain was momentarily in neutral, and her thoughts stilled.

Then images suddenly began to swirl through her mind, like colorful leaves in an autumn storm. Images from childhood, images from college—images of Amanda.

Who'll take care of Amanda if I die? she wondered. *Who will help her . . . ?*

Oh please, God, no!

Tears welled up, running down her nose onto the rubber mat at her feet. She was choked up with despair and struggled for air.

She waited and waited, unable to move. Expecting to be hit.

Bullets hit the car every second, like dull blows from invisible fists.

Seconds passed.

But nothing happened.

The car ate up the road, accelerating foot by foot. Claire could hear the motor revving, could feel the increasing speed. And every inch away from the danger zone diminished the thunder of the rifle reports.

One last shot. Another bullet zinged into the rear of the car. George turned the wheel sharply to the right. The tires squealed, and Claire was slung against her seat belt.

"You can sit up now," George said, his eyes glued to the road. "We've shaken them off for the time being."

CHAPTER 44

BISHOP KNEW A CAR chase was a nonstarter. His photo was in an all-points bulletin, and the last thing he needed was an arrest for careless driving. In that case even the Organization couldn't do a thing for him. They'd simply hang him out to dry, deny ever knowing him, and mark time until he was found dead in his cell. The supreme order for agents taken prisoner crossed Bishop's mind.

Suicide!

Therefore his top priority was to get away from the scene of the shooting as fast as he could and go underground.

That's exactly what they did. Whitman headed back to the city so they could melt into the seemingly endless stream of vehicles clogging the roads and polluting the air.

No way. Don't even dream of chasing them!

But Bishop wasn't satisfied with this reasonable argument. Rather, his brain was actively processing what had just happened.

That they'd failed was perfectly obvious. In a single day they had lost two men, and by a whisker he'd missed being killed, thanks only to an enormous piece of luck.

A whole damn truckload of luck.

As if that wasn't enough, once again they were left empty-handed. The woman was gone; the vampire, too. They'd nothing to show for it but two complete flops and a screwed-up liquidation at the airport.

Bishop was aware that failures like those would have consequences for him personally. He surreptitiously kept eyeing the radio, as if expecting some high-ranking superior to call at any moment and read him the riot act.

The radio was linked to a satellite so it could be reached from anywhere on the globe. He tried to calculate what time it was in the Vatican. He scrapped the effort when he remembered that the time didn't matter. Operations Command worked around the clock, so they didn't care if it was four a.m. or p.m. If they wanted to hand him his ass on a platter, they'd do it at any time of day or night. The worst-case scenario would be getting yanked off this operation.

But something else was bugging him, apart from the danger of having to quit the field and being replaced by Whitman. Something that was tugging at his power of reason like a vicious dog on a chain.

When the car hurtled out of the garage, he'd had a split-second opportunity to look inside it. And what he saw preyed on his mind.

It was obvious that the woman was in the car—no doubt about it. She was in the passenger seat covering her face with her hands. That wasn't what he was brooding over. It was the fact that the vampire was driving the car.

Admittedly, he'd only seen him once before—when the bastard was transformed. But the worst transformation couldn't render demons completely unrecognizable. Their faces indeed had bestial traits, but the human being behind them was ordinarily easy to identify.

And Bishop recognized the man behind the wheel, which explains why he was absolutely certain that it was the same monster from the woman's apartment. The monster that had shot Morales and wounded Bishop himself. And that hadn't given him a moment's peace.

When the car had raced out of the garage, it was in broad daylight, and the sun was shining. Your run-of-the-mill vampire would've burst into flames in a few seconds.

He would've caught fire like a torch, dammit.

But this one didn't, Bishop reconfirmed. The bastard had floored it and took off. As if sunlight didn't bother his ass.

The closer the SUV came to the Bronx hideout, the more Bishop's thinking crystallized. What was merely a bold theory until then now took on palpable shape, so much so that it couldn't be ignored.

That vampire was one of the hybrids.

A goddamn Nazi lab rat.

The tension in his shoulders dissipated, and waves of anxiety subsided.

If his assumption was correct, there was a good chance the mission could be salvaged. Even more, if he wasn't mistaken, it could mean ultimate victory over the demons. A victory so great that it would go down in the chronicles for all time.

For all time!

There was a grin on Bishop's face and a glint in his eye.

CHAPTER 45

THE USED-CAR SALESMAN didn't ask any questions. All he was intent upon was getting Claire's credit card. He examined it and swiped it. Then he graced Claire with a fake friendly smile while waiting for the OK from the credit card company. The wait took longer and longer, causing her more embarrassment with every passing second.

"The card has a twenty-thousand-dollar limit," she said. "Trust me."

Though the shooting and the getaway lay many hours behind, the shock was still profound. Her heart rattled like an old sewing machine, and one shiver after another ran through her. She tried not to let on so as not to create suspicion, but he probably didn't trust her anyway, she admitted. Who else would buy a used car so quickly without insisting on a test drive? Who'd fork over seven thousand dollars without turning on the motor at least once?

"Trust is good," the dealer said, as if expecting his cue, "but checking is better."

"You're the first used-car dealer I've ever met who quoted Lenin," George offered.

"Lenin? You mean Mark Lenin who played for the Mavericks last year?"

"Oh, forget it," George said, leaning back in his chair and folding his arms over his chest.

Some beeps sounded from the credit card machine, and the display blinked. Claire looked at the dealer expectantly.

"So? It went through OK?"

"Everything's hunky-dory."

"I told you," she said.

"Yes, sweetheart, but do you know how often people try to cheat me? If I weren't so suspicious, my kids would go to school in potato sacks. And my wife would probably have to sell a kidney to pay for all her expensive creams.

"OK, Miss Hagen," he said, after printing the required paperwork on his ancient dot-matrix printer, "we'll just set you up with some temporary plates, and you'll be good to go."

Ten minutes later it was a done deal, and they were on their way out of town, George at the wheel of a sky-blue Subaru SUV, Claire in the passenger seat.

"Good idea to leave the other car in a parking garage," she said. "It might be days before it's noticed."

"I hope so," George added. "The longer it takes, the better for us. It might buy us some more time."

The decisiveness with which George handled everything impressed Claire immensely. While she was still coping with shock and fear, he'd already hatched a plan. He'd managed to make the car with the bullet holes disappear and arrange for a new one right away. The ease he'd done it with looked almost routine, as if the man beside her had planned his escape long ago.

"Have you done this before? Escaped like this, I mean?" she asked, trying to confirm her suspicion.

"No, not like this. Didn't have to until now," George said. He took his eyes off the road for a moment to give her a reproachful look.

"I'm very sorry," Claire said eventually.

"What for?"

"Everything that's happened. I want you to know that I absolutely cannot do anything about it. I don't know who those people are and why they're out to get me."

A moment of silence followed. George was watching the traffic and seemed to be pondering something.

"You don't have to feel sorry," he said after a while. "I know their methods and all that can happen if you mess with them."

"But *I* didn't pick a fight with them," she said. "I don't even know who they are."

"I've told you already. They're hunters."

"Vampire hunters?"

"Yes, vampire hunters. They're with a religious cult that has sworn to hunt down vampires ever since the Middle Ages. They operate worldwide, as far as I know. But what I don't understand is where you come in."

Claire hesitated a beat and pondered how much she should tell him. After all, the man at the wheel was still a complete stranger. She didn't know who or what he was. Or what he intended to do.

Fate had chained them together like two galley slaves. They were rowing in the same direction, but that didn't mean they were both thinking the same thing. Strictly speaking . . . *it didn't mean anything at all.*

Before her doubts could gain the upper hand, she remembered that George had probably saved her life that day. And also the night before, when those armed men crashed into her apartment and opened fire. As if that weren't enough, he'd treated her wounds and made breakfast for her. He'd done pretty well for an absolute stranger, Claire decided.

Though that was only one side of the coin. No matter how much she had to thank George for at this moment, the man hadn't given a damn about making a first impression.

Quite the contrary . . .

Not only had he tailed her at the airport—he'd gone so far as to break into her apartment, scare the hell out of her, and quickly cause her physical pain. From that angle, Claire thought, she had every reason to still be suspicious of him.

But she'd barely come to that conclusion when she remembered again that George had saved her life.

And twice, at that . . .

This simple, reassuring fact promptly allayed her doubts.

Feelings of guilt began to gnaw at her—rat's teeth chewing their way up from her subconscious. She began to believe that she had nothing to fear from George, stranger or not. This insight loosened her tongue and alleviated her anxiety more.

"I think it's because of my sister," she said. "My sister is a vampire. I think she's the key to this whole mess." To her amazement the words had lost a bit of their craziness.

Vampire.

The word tripped so easily off her tongue that it was scary. She wondered if that meant the whole world hadn't gone crazy—just her! The very thought reignited her fears, making her shiver.

"How do you know your sister's a vampire?" George asked, keeping an eye on the traffic.

"She transformed yesterday evening when I visited her in the hospital. She looked like a monster and floated around on the ceiling for several seconds."

"Maybe she did. But I don't think she's a vampire. Not yet, at any rate."

"But I saw it with my own eyes! She turned into a monster."

Claire didn't reflect for long before deciding to tell George what had happened to her sister. She began with the two policemen who'd woken her up to tell her that Amanda was in the hospital and ended by recounting the events in Amanda's hospital room before she'd blacked out. She omitted the episode with John because she suspected that George wouldn't be favorably disposed toward him anyway. She concentrated instead on the things she'd discovered in her sister's apartment and described Amanda's transformation in detail.

It took about half an hour for her to get through the whole story. All that time George watched the road and listened.

It seemed to Claire that he *knew* it would be a relief to her to finally get everything off her chest. But even if he didn't know, she thought, it did her good to talk to someone about those things. She felt with every word that the events of the past day were shedding some of their terror. Her agitation settled down, and her anxiety crept back into the dark hole in her psyche from which it had crawled out.

When she'd finished, George was silent at first. It looked to Claire as if he was pondering her story before forming his opinion.

"So? What do you think?" she asked, breaking the silence.

"I still take the same position," George said. "I don't think your sister's a vampire. Maybe she was bitten and infected, but my experience tells me that the process is not completed yet. You want to know why?"

She searched for the right reply for a minute. But she hadn't the foggiest notion what George was getting at. So she gave up.

"Beats me. Why don't you tell me?"

"Well, if the transformation were over, your sister would have been long gone. You can't hold a vampire. Your sister would have broken out and vanished in a flash by now if she were a vampire. That's one reason I believe she's still not completely lost."

"And the second reason?" Claire wanted to know.

"The second is . . ." George stopped. He took a quick look at her, and their eyes met. The expression in his eyes stimulated her fears once more.

"C'mon, out with it!" she said.

"The other reason is that you wouldn't be alive if your sister were a vampire. After a complete transformation, she'd kill you at once, without fail. You and anybody else who came too close."

CHAPTER 46

"HOW'S IT LOOK?" Bishop asked.

He was sitting on a double bed in a rundown hotel and cleaning his gun. It never took longer than half an hour, even if he took his time about it.

But this time he'd been at it for over two hours, cleaning and oiling every single component. He had to kill time, and he knew that working at a monotonous job was the best way. Otherwise he'd have to sit idly on the sidelines while Whitman tried to trace the woman and the vampire, and that would drive him nuts.

"I think we've got a lead," Whitman exclaimed.

"Can you be a little more specific?"

"A credit card payment, almost seven thousand dollars."

"Where?"

"A used-car dealer in the north end of town. Looks like they've swapped cars."

"When?"

"About three hours after they escaped. We could send two men there. Maybe the dealer knows where they went."

"Pure waste of time," Bishop said. "I don't think they told him. And if they did, then it's probably misinformation to throw us off track."

Whitman got up, stretched, and walked around the room a couple of times. Then he stopped beside the bed, concentrating.

"So we can't do anything except wait for her to use her credit card or cell again," he said.

"That's not quite right," Bishop responded. "We know that they plan to leave town. Or else why the hurry to buy a car?"

"We could at least try to find out the make and model—"

"Why bother?" Bishop interrupted. "To go looking for a needle in a haystack? Is that what you want?"

Whitman had no answer.

Bishop went back to his gun and put the last pin in the cover. Then he repeated the operation several times to ensure that no part would get stuck. He put in a new clip and set the gun down on the bureau beside the bed. He looked up at Whitman, who was still standing there with arms folded.

"I've got an idea," Bishop said, getting up from the bed. The room reeked of gun oil and the stink of cigarette smoke that had accumulated in the furniture over the years.

"I need two men," he said, "and we've got to get cracking. You stay here and keep checking the credit cards and the cell towers. And try to find out who owns that house in Tarrytown. Maybe that'll help us."

He put on his coat and put the gun in his shoulder holster.

"No problem, chief. But what the hell are you up to?" Whitman asked.

Bishop grinned at him without a word and went to leave. Opening the door, he turned around and said:

"Let it be a surprise."

Then he popped out of sight.

CHAPTER 47

THE CITY'S OCTOPUS-LIKE tentacles extended into the hinter-
land. But George and Claire left the metropolis's reach farther
behind hour by hour.

The towns got smaller, the streets narrower. The buildings
didn't loom as high in the pale autumn sky, and country scents
crept into the car through the heating vents.

George had rejected the idea of taking the thruway, saying
he didn't want to get pulled over. So they drove the secondary
roads, through anonymous towns and villages. They repeatedly
turned off to skirt major population centers in order to confuse
their invisible pursuers, slowing down their progress inland.
Not until dawn did they cross the border into Massachusetts.
They could make out the Berkshires and the higher Appala-
chians on the horizon, like black giants beneath towering
clouds.

Claire's mind had been muddled during the whole trip and
didn't give her any respite. One question plagued her: Was there
any possibility of rescuing Amanda? There must be, she prayed.

There's always a possibility somewhere!

But the thought was unpromising. Guilty feelings crowded into her mind again and sent hot, stabbing pains into her heart and soul.

She'd abandoned her sister to save herself. Simply up and left her while she was most helpless and alone.

You're Mandy's older sister, and it was your responsibility to look out for her!

Her father's voice rang out in her mind once more, tearing open childhood wounds. His voice was a suffocating blanket in her thoughts and smothered every spark of hope.

But there was another voice. A voice on the margin of her perception. Croaking in a foreign accent.

John! It was John's voice!

It sounded like background noise in Claire's mind, like an atmospheric disturbance. She concentrated, trying to understand what the voice was constantly repeating.

She listened deep within her, blocked out the surrounding noise, and listened carefully to John's words to her:

These substances are pure poison to a vampire. If applied regularly, they'll diminish the vampire's power over his victim, and the victim will recover . . .

She suddenly remembered the silver box he'd given her. But fear gripped her at the same moment. Fear that she'd lost the box during their escape. It might have slipped out of her purse unnoticed in the confusion.

Please, no, please, please, please . . .

She grabbed her purse from the dashboard at once, opening the zipper and rooting around furiously in the mess inside. Her fingers eventually found the smooth surface of the box, and her agitation died. She gave a sigh of relief before leaning back in her seat.

"Everything OK?" George asked, looking over at her. The car's instruments wrapped his face in a bluish glimmer.

"I think so," she replied, meeting his gaze. "I've got one more question."

One more question?

No, Claire thought instantly; she had a million questions. She wanted to know who George was, what was his usual business, and how exactly he was involved in all the things that had burst into her life during the last day or so. But in spite of the burning curiosity eating her, there was something that was even more important at this very second.

Infinitely more important . . .

"Shoot!" George said, snapping her out of her thoughts.

"You said Amanda hasn't been transformed yet."

"Yes, that's what I said. And?"

"How sure are you?"

George looked back at the road and thought for a minute.

"Very sure," he said. "Where are you going with this?"

"I'm thinking it might not be too late to save her. What do you think? Is it still possible to stop the process? Could we maybe even reverse it somehow?" Claire asked in a voice no more than a whisper.

"In some circumstances, it might be possible," George replied. "You have to isolate her and take care that the vampire that bit her doesn't get too close again. That could restore her health. But it would still be risky."

"But it *might* be possible?"

"Yes, absolutely," he answered, "but you must know there's no guarantee she'll be herself again."

"I don't need any guarantees. All I need is the glimmer of a chance."

"What are you thinking of doing?"

"I've got to get back to New York and help her. I've got to get her out of that hospital and lie low with her until this is all finished."

"No way! The hunters will be keeping a close watch around the clock. If you show up at the hospital, you're toast."

"But what else can I do, dammit?" Claire cried.

"We..."

Pausing for a moment, George ventured, "We have to disappear as fast as we can and wait until this blows over. Anything else would be suicide, pure and simple."

CHAPTER 48

WHEN BISHOP GOT BACK to his hotel room, he was a changed man. The worry lines on his forehead were smoothed away, and his face was relaxed. His pale blue eyes twinkled like highly polished opals, and even a tiny smile graced his mouth.

"Where the hell have you been?" Whitman asked as he got up from his chair.

Bishop strode across the room as if he hadn't heard the question and started packing the gear that was scattered over the bed. He jammed one piece after another into a black sports bag and didn't pay the slightest attention to his partner watching from just two steps away.

Things had gone better than planned, and now was the time for him to enjoy the happy feelings that came with success, he thought.

"I'm still waiting for an answer," Whitman persisted.

Bishop stared at him with shining eyes. He could tell with one look how ruffled Whitman was.

The bastard doesn't like it if he's not in on everything, he thought, and that turned his smile into a broad grin.

"I settled a few things that had to be settled. And you? Did you find out who owns the house in Tarrytown?"

Whitman went back to the desk, typed a few commands, and a man's picture popped up on the screen. Bishop recognized him in an instant. It was the man . . .

. . . the monster . . .

. . . who shot Morales and ran over Jones. No doubt about it.

"What did you find out?" he asked. The smile had vanished from his face, and his eyes didn't have the same glint as before.

"The man is one George Powell," Whitman said, "who was licensed as a general practitioner in New York. Official documents indicate that he hasn't been practicing for years. In fact, his Social Security information shows that he's been retired for fifteen years."

"*Retired?*" Bishop exclaimed, again studying the features of the man looking at him from the screen. At first glance, he'd have guessed Powell was in his thirties. Early forties at most, he thought, and looked quizzically back at Whitman.

"I know what you're thinking, chief." Whitman nodded. "I thought the same thing. Right after seeing his picture I asked myself, how in hell could somebody his age be retired?"

"Well? What did you find out?" Bishop said, though he knew the answer already.

"OK," Whitman went on. "Mr. Powell is in amazing shape if you consider the date on his driver's license. Mind you, he turned ninety-one last month. Don't you think that's astounding?"

"Yeah," Bishop said, "really astounding." He was glassy-eyed, and his voice was weak.

"You know what that means?"

"Yeah," Bishop said. "We're up against a fucking hybrid."

Bishop saw no sense anymore in not sharing his hunch with Whitman. Even if he couldn't stand the guy and was biding his time for an opportunity to get rid of him once and for all, he knew Whitman was no dummy. Bishop had studied the files and discovered that the son of a bitch wasn't anybody's fool. If Whitman hadn't detoured into the Marines on his way to college, he'd probably have become a brilliant scientist. But he became one of the best engineers in the military instead and had quickly climbed the career ladder. The Organization subsequently sniffed out his potential and recruited him the way they did all their agents. With a few exceptions, all their personnel were formerly in the military, a motley crew of specialists cobbled together from all corners of the earth.

No, Bishop confessed, he mustn't keep anything else from Whitman unless he wanted to get himself in trouble. After all, his partner was a young whippersnapper who'd throw him to the wolves without giving it a second thought if it helped him lick his superiors' boots better.

"Bingo!" Whitman shouted. "We did indeed smoke a hybrid out of his hidey hole. Now we've got to find him and catch him. You know what that means?"

"It means we've got a hell of a lot of work to do," Bishop said.

"And without so much as a whiff of a lead. Not on him, not on the woman."

With that, Bishop took his bag off the bed and made for the door.

"Where are you going?" Whitman queried.

"Come on, move it," Bishop urged. "I've got a little surprise for you."

CHAPTER 49

THE FUEL GAUGE LIT UP. They were running low on gas. So George took the next exit and pulled over at a station. The neon sign on the roof promised hot food and good service around the clock.

"Do you want a bite?" George asked after filling the tank. He stood beside the passenger door, still looking as if all the strain of the past day hadn't left a trace on him.

Claire thought for a moment and then agreed. She wasn't hungry but wanted a strong cup of coffee. Besides, she wanted to stretch her legs—after more than four and a half hours in the car, she was virtually numb from the hips down. Her feet were swollen, her legs tingly.

Meanwhile the sun had set, and an icy wind swept over the land. Claire felt exhausted and worn out although it was only ten. All she longed for was to pull a blanket over her head and to block out the whole world for a number of hours. The world, and with it all the terrors that had just come into her life—terrors that made her previous worries and fears look like wretched playthings. She tried briefly to search her mind for something from her life that had caused her anywhere near as big a headache as the events of the past hours. These thoughts whirled around in her head for a while without crystallizing into anything.

Completely hopeless . . .

She couldn't come up with anything close to the consternation and fears that had entered her life in a flash and turned it upside down.

The only thing she could think of that had unhinged her recently had been the ugly separation from Keith, her fiancé.

That goddamn piece of shit . . .

When Claire recalled that period in her life, it almost seemed to her that she was gingerly feeling a scar that could break open at any moment. Obviously she knew she'd been in love with him, and after she'd discovered that he'd been playing fast and loose with fidelity, her heart wasn't merely broken—no, it had been shattered to bits. She'd thrown herself into her work all the more—to distract herself from the gnawing pain that was reducing her life to rubble. And if you came right down to it, Claire admitted, her enormous, angry commitment to overwork might well have been the reason for her gradually losing sight of Amanda. Her efforts to patch her life together again had torn it open at another spot—like a moth-eaten piece of clothing that was beyond repair.

The cold wind picked up, and an unexpected gust made her stumble. At the same time she banished her unpleasant memories from her mind. Her thoughts broke off like a fishing line that had made a futile attempt to haul a giant monster out of the depths of her unconscious—a monster, she felt, that was still circling around in absolute darkness and would remind her later of all the pain and agony she'd suffered.

Claire took several deep breaths, then dissipated her tension with a sigh. Turning around to look for George, she saw he'd parked the car in the meantime. He came up to her at a good clip, and an indescribable easy manner radiated from his movements and his face. It almost seemed to Claire that he was the calm central point around which the total madness of the past day had pivoted. And although she still didn't have a clue who or *what* the guy was, it just felt good right then that she knew he was by her side.

Damn good, actually . . .

And this feeling of security was enough to bring a broad, instant smile to Claire's lips. Not *too* broad, but a smile neverthe-less. George responded to it at once, and they went into the res-taurant together.

It was adjacent to the gas station and exuded the enticing smells of bacon and fresh coffee. They sat down at a table at the back and ordered java from a waitress so friendly that she did the roof sign credit.

Soon they were left alone. Nobody was at the nearby tables. A few truck drivers sat at the counter, busy eating dinner and watching the news on the little TV mounted on the wall. Nobody could eavesdrop on them.

"Where are we going, anyway?" Claire asked, after her first sip of coffee.

"I don't know yet," George said. "I thought of Mexico. Somewhere on the Pacific Coast where people don't ask too many question as long as you wave dollar bills around. But the way things have gone, that would probably be too risky."

"How so?"

"Well, OK," George said, looking at his coffee. "You paid for the car and the gas, so I don't want you to misunderstand: I'm very grateful for that. I'd probably be stuck in New York if you hadn't helped. But I think we're going to have problems pretty quick if you keep using your credit card."

"But that's the only money we've got for now."

"That may be. Nevertheless, we've got to expect it to reveal our whereabouts anytime now to the guys chasing us. They've got connections to all kinds of companies and institutions, access to all kinds of information. They're not to be trifled with."

"What do you expect to do?" Claire asked. "Flush the card down the toilet and get a job here washing dishes?"

She surprised herself by the edge to her voice. It sank in just that minute how tired she was and how much she longed to pull the covers over her head and sleep.

"Sorry about that," she apologized. "This is the first time ever that I've had to lie low, and I'm still a bit jumpy, it seems."

George burst into a smile, and Claire couldn't help doing the same and giggling as well, though it made her feel so silly. She didn't forget how serious their situation was, in spite of the brief moment of levity.

"Why don't we just go to the cops?" she asked.

George looked up from his cup and stared at her.

"And *then* what?" he asked.

"Then we tell them what really happened in my apartment and your house and ask for protection until they grab the characters behind us."

She sensed that George was against the idea even before she finished her sentence. He was scowling, and his eyes appeared to convey a silent accusation.

"Not a chance," he countered. "The cops won't believe us. If we roll out the whole story, the odds are very good that they'll have us committed on the spot."

"We could at least try," Claire argued. "We could get a lawyer ahead of time to make sure that wouldn't happen."

"A lawyer might keep us out of an asylum. But who's going to protect us from the guys chasing us?"

Before Claire could answer, he continued.

"I'll tell you who: *nobody!* As soon as they know where we are, we're in hot water. Those guys have contacts who can open a lot of doors for them. We'd be very naïve to believe the cops could defend us against them."

"So what do you think we should do?" Claire asked. "Where do we go?"

"We've got to go somewhere we can stay and not be bothered for a few weeks. A place where we're by ourselves and don't make any waves. At least until things in New York have calmed down a bit."

"Sounds to me like you want to go to Las Vegas," Claire teased. Her mood had improved a little, thanks to the coffee. Her tiredness seemed to have been swept away.

The waitress came back, poured a second cup, and asked if they wanted to order anything to eat. They said no, so she spun on her heel and disappeared behind the counter.

Claire almost never had more than one coffee. But this time, she reasoned, she could easily make an exception. She had the feeling that a long, stressful night lay ahead of her.

With her next sip, an inspiration flashed through her mind with the force of a thunderbolt. Fragments of her dream the previous night brought goose bumps to her arms. And in the space of a second she knew where they could hide. She knew a place that was safe and remote, where they could lie low until things cooled off. She put her cup down and turned around to reassure herself that nobody was close enough to hear her.

"What's the matter?" George asked, noticing her immediate excitement.

"I've got it," Claire said. Her lips barely moved as she spoke, and her voice was a whisper.

"What is it?"

"I think I know the perfect place for us to hide."

CHAPTER 50

"HOW THE FUCK did you do that?" Whitman blurted out. He was at the rear of the SUV and gawking into the cargo area with eyes wide open.

"For a man working for the Catholic Church, you swear one helluva lot," Bishop said.

Bishop also had trouble for a moment taking his eyes off what was in the back of the car. But he was more amused by the expression on Whitman's face. He looked like he couldn't believe his own eyes.

Whitman resembled a fat kid touring a chocolate factory. His mouth hung open, and his eyes bulged at the sight. It wouldn't have taken much for him to start drooling, Bishop guessed.

He wondered if the same look of amazement would flit over Whitman's face just before he blew him away. Bishop fervently hoped so, even if he didn't know for sure.

"That doesn't answer my question," Whitman insisted. "*How* the fuck did you manage it?"

"I won't bore you with the details," Bishop riposted, "but I *would* say that you can learn a lot from me."

Stringing Whitman along and just leaving him standing there like an idiot delighted him. That was the reason Bishop kept mum about the details of his exploit. It was like a magic trick: If you explained every detail to the audience at the outset, then the most outlandish trick would lose all its appeal. So he simply said nothing and enjoyed his partner's expression of disbelief.

When he felt that Whitman had had enough of the load in the back of the car, he banged the hatch shut.

"C'mon," Whitman kept pushing. "Out with it—how did you manage to pull it off?"

Bishop didn't field the question but walked around to the car and got into the driver's seat. Whitman followed him and sat down beside him.

"You can go ahead and tell me, chief," he persisted. "I won't argue when you take credit for it. I'll even mention your exceptional achievement in my final report."

Bishop flung him a cynical look. He raised his eyebrows and forced a smile. Though he couldn't see himself, he felt he succeeded very well in hiding his hatred for Whitman behind this mask.

"Let's nail the woman and the vampire first," he said, "then I'll let you in on everything you'd like to know."

Bishop paid close attention to his partner's reaction and saw at once this wasn't the answer that the bastard expected. Whitman had an angry gleam in his eye, and he pressed his lips together until all the blood drained out of them.

Bishop was so tickled by the sight that he burned it into his memory for all time.

Then he looked ahead, started the motor, and drove off into the gathering darkness.

CHAPTER 51

"ROCKWELL?" George asked.

"Yes, Rockwell," Claire said, "but as a stopover. We'll be there by tomorrow morning if we switch drivers."

"And then?"

"Then we stock up and vanish into the forest. Dad's cabin is about thirty miles north, near the Canadian border."

George looked skeptical, as if it went against the grain for him to hand over the reins and hope her plan would work. His face grew dark and turned to stone.

Claire judged from his past behavior that he was a man who relied on nobody but himself.

"And you're sure somebody won't connect this hunting cabin with you?" George asked.

"One hundred percent sure," she said. "The cabin was a smugglers' hideout during Prohibition. It's not on the map, and only a handful of people besides me know that it even exists."

"Sounds good," George conceded, though his voice was uncertain and hesitant. "And how about the car? Can we get there by car?"

"No way," Claire answered. "We have to bushwhack for the last couple of miles. I think we can make it in a day carrying all our gear. Maybe less."

"But somebody's going to find the car sooner or later and get suspicious, a hunter or a hiker or who the hell knows who'll be going through those woods."

"The car's the least of our problems. There are a lot of lakes in the area. Some so deep that it'd be easy to dump it. We can do that before taking off for the cabin. Nobody will suspect a thing. It's dead up there this time of year."

George didn't say anything but was thinking hard. He frowned and examined his banged-up spoon.

Claire sensed he needed time to warm up to her plan. Meanwhile she could take care of what had been plaguing her since their hasty escape. She had to call Hillside to see how Amanda was doing.

"I'll be right back," she said, getting up to go to the restroom. Her agitation increased with every step.

She went into a stall, locked the door, and took her cell out of her purse—the untraceable one.

She called Information because she hadn't memorized Hillside's number.

The operator gave her the number. She entered it, and the hospital's on-hold music kicked in almost immediately. About a minute later Claire heard a click. A woman's voice answered.

"Hillside Medical Center. How shall I direct your call?"

"This is Claire Hagen. I'd like to speak to Dr. Harris."

"One moment please," the voice said. Another click, and then Dr. Harris was on the line.

"This is Dr. Harris. What can I do for you?"

"Hello, Dr. Harris," Claire replied. "I hope I'm not catching you on your way home again. This is Claire Hagen. I'd like to know to how my sister is."

Total silence at the other end. Claire's heart skipped a beat.

"Miss Hagen, thank God you're all right!" the doctor exclaimed. His voice sounded alarmed and nervous. The words poured out of him so fast that she had trouble following. "The police were here today asking about you. They told me what happened at your place. I hope you're well and not hurt."

"Don't worry, Dr. Harris," Claire reassured him. "I'm fine."

"What happened at your apartment? One of the policemen said you'd been abducted. Are you sure everything's *really* all right? Should I inform the police? Do you need any help?"

"I told you I am fine. Unfortunately I don't have time for details. I just wanted to find out how Amanda's doing."

More silence.

Claire's heart sped up, and her strength drained from her legs. She suddenly felt, that the doctor had bad news. Her throat tightened, and her breathing stopped from fear Amanda might be worse. She leaned against the wall and shut her eyes.

Please, please, please, let her be OK!

"Are you still there, Doctor?"

"Yes, I am, Miss Hagen."

"Well, then, how is Amanda?"

"Amanda is gone," he said.

Gone!

The word was like a slap in the face. She winced and ducked her head as Amanda's voice invaded her mind:

As soon as the sun goes down, I'm off and away.

"Gone?"

"Yes, gone."

"How? When?" she implored. Her voice almost gurgled, and she felt suffocated.

Oh God, Mandy!

"I cannot tell exactly, Miss Hagen," Harris said. "By the time I went on my last rounds two hours ago, she had disappeared. Her room was locked from the outside, and there were no signs of a breakout. I cannot explain what could have happened, not for the life of me. In all my time here I have never had a patient . . ."

Claire had heard enough.

She took the cell away from her ear and hung up. Tears welled up and ran down her cheeks. A pained, weak sob escaped her throat, like a pup's whimper. She wished she could fully vent, cry until her tears dried up and her eyes were red and swollen. She wanted to finally get out all the things she'd kept bottled inside for the last two days. All the fear, impotence, madness . . .

But she did not give in, though she was burning to. The desire to break down was eating her up, yet she didn't let go, because if she did, she'd be of no use to anybody.

Not to herself, not to George, not to Amanda.

Least of all Mandy . . .

She wiped the tears from her cheeks and blew her nose on some toilet paper. A few deep breaths calmed her down, and her anxiety gradually eased. Her heartbeat steadied, and her thoughts regrouped. Reason once more gained control over the madness and fear churning inside her.

That's better. She sighed. Then she flushed, and the bubbling water took away the toilet paper along with her tears.

She was about to go back to the restaurant when a new, urgent idea struck her. All of a sudden she knew what she should have been doing all that time.

She grabbed her cell again and called the only number in her contacts. It was Arthur Flynn's private line—her boss at the

News Review. While the phone was ringing, she wondered whether he already knew what had happened. Then she realized who she was calling: Arthur Flynn, the head of one of the largest-circulation newspapers in New York, with connections that were the envy of his peers. He probably knew more than the cops, Claire figured.

I'll bet he does!

"Arthur Flynn here. Who's interrupting me during an important meeting?"

"Hello, Art," Claire responded.

Then a moment of perfect silence at the other end.

"Claire? Oh my God, are you OK, hon? Where are you? What's happened? I've tried a million times to reach you! I've been worried half to death!"

The barrage of words tumbled out of him, making him hard to understand. But she couldn't miss the concerned undertone in his voice. She'd never heard him so upset in all her years at the paper.

She was touched by his concern, but knew it wasn't good for his heart to be *that* agitated. After all, Arthur Flynn was a sixty-year-old, very overweight chain-smoker with two heart attacks and at least as many open-heart surgeries behind him.

So she hoped the excitement wouldn't be too much for him. She'd gladly have reassured him that everything was A-OK, but there was no time to waste. She came straight to the point. "Listen, Art. I'm fine. But I don't have time to explain. Please don't worry your head about me. But I do need your help."

Art's first response was a long sigh of relief. Then he spoke up.

"Thank God you're OK. What can I do for you, Claire?"

"Here's the situation . . . ," she said and spelled out the essentials. She knew she shouldn't tell him too much so he wouldn't get any funny ideas about her mental state. She left out everything about vampires or Amanda, and said less than nothing about George.

She focused instead on the fact she knew who shot the man at the airport the day before. She knew Art would prick up his ears if he thought a good story might be in there somewhere. And what better story, she reasoned, than exposing a secret organization that plotted murders and also randomly killed innocent people around the city?

Exposés like this would sometimes vault even tiny newspapers up to the Olympian heights of journalism, often to a Pulitzer Prize. And Claire knew Art would rather die than let a good story slip through his fingers, reason enough for her to feel more optimistic while talking to him. Her confidence grew.

Arthur Flynn listened without interrupting. She concluded with a request. He agreed without a moment's hesitation.

"Consider it done, kiddo," he said.

"Thanks, Art."

"Don't mention it. And take care of yourself, Claire."

"I'll do that," she said. She ended the call and stowed the cell back in her purse.

She reviewed what she'd said and decided she'd done the right thing. It was right to let Art in on it, she argued. And she also knew in her heart of hearts that "the right thing" wasn't the point; she was really hoping the information she gave Art was enough to save her skin in an emergency.

She had no idea how influential her pursuers actually were. But she didn't think the network of their connections was so tightly woven that Art Flynn . . .

. . . *that sly old dog* . . .

. . . would *not* be able to slip through.

CHAPTER 52

"YOU'RE RIGHT," Whitman admitted. "They've definitely left town."

Bishop took a look at the laptop and saw a credit card company's logo parading on the screen.

"She used her credit card?" he asked.

"Yes," Whitman replied, "it was posted just this minute. Used it at a gas station in Massachusetts—in the station and the restaurant. And proceeded to withdraw every cent up to her limit at an ATM."

Bishop knew the significance of that: The woman had taken out all the money available in one fell swoop. Which meant she'd guessed her card was being monitored. So she made up her mind to go for it and stop dropping bread crumbs leading to her hideout.

"She's learning," Bishop concluded.

"Yes," Whitman agreed, "that's exactly how I see it. Wouldn't be surprised if she threw in a disguise. You know, wig and all. What do you think, chief? Where's she going?"

Where's she going?

Precisely the question rolling around in Bishop's mind for hours, like a snowball. And just as a snowball gets bigger and bigger, so did the number of possible answers to that question.

Where the hell is she going?

Obviously she wanted to underground. But since they had to deal with having no access to her cell or credit card, they were now looking for a needle in a haystack. Nonetheless, he believed they still stood a good chance of getting her.

Her and the vampire!

His hopes rested primarily on some new, useful data on the woman they'd turned up in the meantime. They'd first limited themselves to Social Security documents, bank withdrawals—what any average cop would have done in his shoes.

He'd poked around in the dark, hoping the solution to the problem would drop into his lap. Maybe he believed that fate would smile on him and put him back on the woman's trail.

But he knew their information couldn't help them construct a solid personality profile. Any institutional information would be too general and unspecific.

Once Whitman realized that, too, he broadened his search. And the more time he spent on his laptop, the more information he dug up on the woman. It was far more vital for their search than her annual income or her favorite restaurants.

They'd assembled the basic data on her life—which led Bishop to conclude that the woman wasn't stupid. Just the opposite, he figured—that little bitch had a pretty little head. She was nobody's fool. Her grades in school and college proved she could have become a rocket scientist without any problem if she'd wanted to.

Of course this information wasn't by itself sufficient to capture her, as Bishop well knew. But he took some comfort in knowing much more about the enemy than the enemy knew about him.

For if the military had taught him anything, it was the irrefutable fact that wars and battles aren't won solely by having superior weapons and braver soldiers. It was by gathering intelligence and exploiting it. And that's exactly what they'd done in this case, he knew.

That wasn't everything, not by a long shot. They still had an ace up their sleeve, and Bishop fully realized the time had come to play it. If it all went according to plan, he hoped this cat-and-mouse game would soon become a thing of the past.

He looked in the rearview mirror at the cargo they were carrying in the back. At that angle he only saw the top edge of the container between the headrest and the rear bench seat. But that sight was enough to fill him with confidence and delight.

The feeling he was still on the right path despite all the setbacks monopolized his thoughts. Bishop conjured up a smile, which lasted on his lips for several minutes.

"Hey, chief? Gone to sleep?" Whitman asked, breaking Bishop's train of thought.

"No," Bishop answered, "I was just wondering where she's gone."

"So?"

"I have absolutely no clue," Bishop stated as he turned to his partner. There was still a grin at the corners of his mouth. A grin that instantly brought a scowl to Whitman's face.

"Considering we've been wasting time for hours, you're in a damn good mood, huh?"

Bishop picked up on Whitman's difficulty in exerting self-control. It amused him almost as much as the notion that they'd soon have this mission behind them.

"I don't believe we're wasting time, my friend. I think we're on the point of making a giant leap forward. We just have to be smart about engineering it."

"*A giant leap forward?* You should hear yourself talk, chief. You sound like Neil Armstrong on a bad trip."

Bishop ignored his snarky comment, partly because he enjoyed watching Whitman frantically trying to keep his cool.

But the main reason was that he knew that only one man in the car was on a bad trip.

That man was Whitman, and at the end of this bad trip, Bishop mused, he'd be staring down the barrel of a pistol, groveling for mercy.

CHAPTER 53

IT WAS GEORGE'S IDEA to withdraw all the cash right then and there instead of taking the risk of having the credit card used to track them. He also advised loading up on chocolate bars and energy drinks to keep them awake during the trip.

Claire was still unnerved by her phone call to Dr. Harris, so she just nodded and obeyed his instructions.

She was glad he'd accepted her proposal to hide out in the Rockwell woods. She was also happy he'd reinforced the decision with renewed vigor and enthusiasm by making plans and taking care of the provisions. Her constant anxiety for Amanda still clouded her mind.

But her worries didn't stop her from asking the gas station cashier for a little favor. She spoke with her while George was loading their purchases into the car.

"I dunno, lady," the cashier said. "What if you're askin' me to do something against the law? I could wind up in court, and you oughta know I'm on parole."

"I *guarantee* there's nothing illegal about this. You just have to send this letter by registered mail to this address. It is *very* important!"

She placed the envelope on the counter. It was thin and looked a little the worse for wear. The cashier was Marcy, to go by her nametag, and she eyed it with suspicion.

Her expression relaxed after Claire laid a hundred-dollar bill on the envelope. The worry lines on her forehead smoothed out, and the corners of her mouth suddenly were at half-mast again.

"Sorry, can't," she said. She folded her arms across her chest as if to lend more weight to her words.

But Claire was undeterred. She saw the cashier's eyes and mouth weren't speaking the same language. Her eyes were positively glued to the bill, and Claire knew she had her on the hook. She reached into her purse again for another hundred-dollar bill and put it on top of the first one.

"How's it looking, Marcy? Can we do business?" she asked. Then she pushed the envelope and the money farther over the counter.

Marcy seemed to consider it for a moment. Suddenly she grabbed the envelope, folded it in half, and stuffed it quickly into the neckline of her uniform. Then she spirited away the two bills with an alacrity that Claire wouldn't have thought her massive figure capable of.

"We can do business, lady,'" Marcy finally said, "but if somethin's fishy about this, you're gonna get your ass out of trouble by yourself. I don't know you, never heard of you."

"No problem," Claire promised. "That'll never happen. But I'm trusting you to do this."

She wheeled around and made for the exit. She wondered whether Marcy would think of opening the envelope to see what could be worth two hundred bucks. That would foil her whole plan, and she'd be left empty-handed in an emergency.

A sudden panic seized her. She was about to reverse her trajectory and run back to the counter to snatch the envelope from Marcy's ample bosom. But she calmed down quickly because she reasoned that Marcy would only be puzzled by the envelope's contents. She'd find nothing but an object a bit larger than a postage stamp.

The automatic doors were opening for Claire's exit when Marcy's excited voice rang out between the shelves of potato chips and window scrapers.

"Thanks again, lady. You can count on me one hundred percent. I'm goin' to the post office right after my shift and mail your letter. Have a good trip."

Claire didn't turn around but just waved good-bye. She hoped that Marcy wasn't on parole because she was also a postal employee who opened customers' letters looking for valuables. The idea struck her as funny and put her in a somewhat better mood.

She walked out into the night and over to the car. She'd barely closed the door when George stepped on the gas and left the station behind.

"What took you so long?" he wanted to know. Claire thought for a moment before deciding he didn't have to know what had gone on. She still didn't trust him fully even though he'd saved her life twice. So she said:

"The cashier asked if I'd like to go with her to a meeting of the Jehovah's Witnesses next Sunday."

"And what did you say?"

"I said what I always say in these situations."

"Which is?"

"I asked what this Jehovah did that was so bad that they're looking for so many witnesses to get him off."

Claire said it as casually as she could, hoping that her words would have the desired effect. Before she could look at him a loud guffaw exploded from the driver's seat.

George turned toward her and they looked each other in the eye for a second. It dawned on Claire that this was the first time he'd laughed since they'd met. It was an infectious, honest laugh, and it wasn't long before Claire joined in.

She giggled nervously at first. But soon she couldn't hold back anymore. She collapsed in her seat and held her stomach as one gale of laughter after another shook her.

It took several minutes to get herself under control, and that was enough to drive away all her worry about Amanda and the things that might happen to her.

She felt fine. The clouds had rolled away.

CHAPTER 54

BISHOP PULLED OFF THE INTERSTATE and parked at a truck stop. He turned off the motor and sat there without saying a word.

"Why the hell are we here?" Whitman inquired, looking around the parking area.

The area formed a large bulge by the side of the road. It was dotted with huge puddles, a pile of garbage, and a horde of used condoms that sparkled in the lamplight like a school of exotic jellyfish.

"Wait a minute," Whitman said. "This place is a secret gay hangout. Is this where you spend your weekends, chief? Surrounded by love-starved truck drivers?"

"Shut your stupid trap and come with me," Bishop said, opening the door.

Whitman followed. They went to the back of the SUV, and Bishop quickly raised the hatch. The sight they saw fascinated Whitman, leaving him speechless.

The second SUV with the other four men turned into the rest area and parked some distance away. The driver's door opened to disgorge a dark figure. Bishop knew the man by his walk, even when he couldn't see his face.

It was Petric, the third man in the chain of command after Morales and Jones were killed. Bishop hadn't worked with him much yet, but the few times he had, he enjoyed it.

Bishop mostly appreciated Petric's professionalism and his commitment. Apart from that, he was one of the few men you could rely on absolutely. He'd brought Petric along for that very reason when picking up the cargo in the SUV instead of Whitman or one of the others. This had been child's play, thanks to Petric's help.

"Everything OK, boss?" Petric inquired. He joined Bishop and Whitman and also stared at the car's contents. His eyes grew clouded, and he gritted his teeth.

"Yes, we're good," Whitman piped up, "except we haven't got the slightest fucking idea where the woman and the vampire are."

Petric dealt Whitman a withering look to let him know that when he'd said "boss," he didn't mean him. Then he looked in the SUV again.

"Man, who gives a shit how long I've been in the Organization," Whitman said. "I'll never get used to the sight of this goddamn thing. Why are we lugging this . . . this *thing* . . . around anyway? Why don't we dump it right here and now?"

"It's very simple," Bishop said. "Because this 'thing' will help us find the woman. And maybe the vampire, too."

"How the hell will it do that?" Petric asked.

Bishop twisted his mouth into a smile before putting on his black gloves.

"This thing," he said after a pause, "is the goddamn sister of the woman we're looking for."

CHAPTER 55

"THERE'S SOMETHING I've got to get off my chest," Claire admitted. "It's been on my mind for hours."

They'd stopped about an hour earlier to stretch their legs and go to the bathroom. Claire took the wheel afterward to spell George. He'd fought the idea, saying he wasn't tired and was easily good for a few more hours. And Claire believed him because he still looked fresh and rested after many hours at the wheel. Nothing in his face or body language betrayed what they'd been through in the last several hours. Nevertheless, she insisted on driving. For one thing, driving took her mind off certain thoughts, and for another, she knew the quickest way to Rockwell.

"And that is?" George asked.

Claire took a deep breath and slowly released it.

"I wanted to thank you," she confessed.

"What for?" he asked. "After all, you've paid for everything so far. If anybody in this car has to thank somebody, it would certainly be me."

"But you saved my life," Claire replied. "Two times."

There was absolute silence in the car for several moments.

"You're welcome," George said. "Glad to be of service."

Claire looked at him and gave him a smile. It was completely dark inside the car, and she imagined he probably wouldn't see it. But she just felt like it at the moment.

She saw the first snowflake flying through the beam of the headlights. Then another, and five minutes later it started to snow in earnest.

And it wouldn't let up.

CHAPTER 56

"ARE YOU SURE this'll do the trick?" Petric asked.

"No," Bishop replied, "but what else can we do?"

It was a rhetorical question, a sort of kick-start for him to get things rolling. He went over to the rear of the SUV and inspected its contents. Meanwhile he was pondering how best to proceed.

Take it one step at a time!

In spite of his long-standing experience with vampires, he found the thing before him both scary and stimulating. Even he rarely had the pleasure of being face to face with a demon.

He had but a glimpse at best of the creatures when he came across them. Usually no more than a few seconds—the seconds he needed to kill them as fast as possible.

Shoot, burn, behead, put them in sunlight . . . and, and, and . . .

And after they're dead, he thought, there wasn't much of them left. Hardly more than a charred skeleton that held no trace of its former horror. Most of the time even that wasn't left. So he enjoyed the sight that this moment offered even more.

The young woman . . . *Amanda* . . . was huddled in the middle of the high-grade steel cage that took up the entire rear of the SUV. Her knees were pulled up to her chest and her face deeply buried in the folds of her straitjacket. Just her eyes peeped out, closely following every movement on the other side of the bars. Except that they weren't eyes anymore, Bishop thought. They were glowing red coals in the semidarkness.

Wherever sunlight had hit her body, she was singed, and the skin was peeling off. Tatters of skin were hanging from her forehead and temples, like torn-off pieces of wallpaper. Red flesh was visible underneath them.

But for Bishop, this sight didn't generate one iota of sympathy for the woman that this thing had been just a short time ago. He knew, of course, that the cage wouldn't have helped much if the creature had been at full strength. It would have slipped through the bars without any problem and slit all their throats in a fraction of a second.

But she's not at full strength. I took care of that!

Right. He'd taken care of that. At least, he'd done his best. He'd rushed into the room in Hillside and given her a tranquilizer shot. A dose that would have felled a racehorse.

She'd raged and thrown herself against the wall. Ultimately she'd keeled over and then lay there motionless. He'd grabbed hold of her and with Petric's help dragged her to the car. The operation lasted five minutes.

It had been perfectly timed, Bishop recalled. Because as long as those bastards weren't entirely transformed, they still possessed a circulatory system in a rudimentary form. A system that allowed the anesthetic to spread throughout the body. If he'd been too late, the dart from the gun would have been completely ineffective, and his only choice would have been to kill her.

"Boss," Petric wondered, snapping Bishop out of his reverie, "what are we going to do?"

Bishop wrenched his eyes from Amanda. He turned to Whitman as the grin on his face widened.

"What's the matter?" Whitman asked.

"I might have a question," Bishop said, his grin growing broader.

"Which is?"

"Are you right- or left-handed?"

Whitman eyebrows came together. His eyes flashed.

"What the hell are you up to?"

"First answer the question, Charles," Bishop dodged a reply.

Charles.

He'd never once called him by his first name. That wasn't the practice within the Organization. Most agents didn't even know their partner's name, and only their superiors had access to personnel files.

"Right-handed. Why?"

"Good," Bishop continued, "then please give me your left hand."

The worry lines on Whitman's face grew deeper.

"You old queer, you're still trying to find ways to hold hands with me."

Whitman held out his left hand in spite of his remark and gave Bishop a quizzical look. Before he could react, Bishop grabbed his wrist. Then he took a knife from his belt, an army knife, eight inches of tempered steel so sharp you could effortlessly slice open a car door.

"What the fuck?" Whitman swore as he tried to free himself from Bishop's grasp. He pulled and tugged, but Bishop's fingers were like a vise around his wrist—it was too late. Bishop struck, sliding the blade over Whitman's wrist quick as a flash.

Nothing to see at first, and it seemed he'd missed. But then a thin cut appeared on Whitman's palm. Some blood flowed slowly, like runoff from a blocked-up gully. In a few seconds his palm was filled with it.

"What the hell?" Whitman shouted, opening his eyes and mouth wide.

"Easy, Charlie," Bishop said to soothe him. "We've got to get this thing to talk while it's able to. And we need some bait."

He looked at Whitman's hand, which was dripping blood onto the ground.

"Why didn't you cut yourself instead, you fucking asshole!" Whitman screamed.

Bishop waved him off. "I got shot last night, dammit. I've already lost enough blood. And now we're going to get some intelligence out of this motherfucker."

"So what am I supposed to do?" Whitman asked.

"Hold your hand up to the cage. Watch that you don't get bitten. She seems to be knocked out OK, but you never know with these bastards."

His words didn't offer any comfort to Whitman, on whose face fear and disbelief fought each other. But Whitman did his duty nevertheless: He stepped up and held his bleeding hand so that the creature couldn't miss it. He moved slowly and tentatively. But it didn't take long for the hoped-for reaction to kick in: The red eyes grew bigger; Amanda raised her head and bared her teeth.

"Amanda?" Bishop quickly asked. "Can you hear me?"

The thing that had been Amanda couldn't take its eyes off the bleeding hand. Fascination filled its eyes with tears. It lusted for every drop of blood as its tongue skipped over its rough lips and saliva drooled out of the corner of its maw.

"Amanda, are you there?" Bishop tried again.

"Yes," Amanda answered in a hiss.

"I want to play a little game with you. The game goes like this: You tell me what I want to know, and my friend will give you a taste of the blood on his hand. What do you think?"

Instead of a reply, Amanda made a quick move for Whitman's hand. She banged her head with all her might on the bars with a hollow clatter. She collapsed and lay motionless on the cage floor. A huge wound in the middle of her forehead dripped thick, black blood.

"Is she dead?" Whitman asked.

"*Dead?*" Bishop retorted. "If these things could be killed this easily we'd all be out of a job, right?"

Whitman didn't have a comeback. He clenched his bleeding fist, and with the other hand he slipped the belt off his pants. He wrapped it around his arm several times and knotted it. The trickle running over the side of his hand suddenly dried up.

"Amanda?" Bishop asked.

"What?" she growled. Her eyes narrowed down to two thin slits, fixing on him.

"Where's Claire? Where's she hiding?"

"Claire?"

"Yes, Claire, your sister. Where is she?"

Bishop talked to her like to a child who had gotten lost, calmly and gently. Trying to reach whatever was still human in Amanda, buried in her demon's body.

"Claire . . ." Amanda growled.

"Yes, Claire," Bishop said. "Where the hell is she?"

Amanda's bloodless lips curled into a smile. But her eyes remained hard. Her whole expression struck Bishop as the desperate imitation of a human being. She looked like a wolf that had squeezed itself into a too-small sheepskin, yet was trying frantically to maintain its disguise.

"I had a dream about Claire," Amanda continued. "We were playing together."

Bishop was puzzled. Experience told him it was not in a vampire's nature to be honest. They were masters of deception. They were liars and tempters.

I had a dream about Claire . . .

In spite of his doubts, he gave Whitman a sign. Whitman caught on immediately and stuck up his hand again toward the cage. His blood had gradually clotted, but the smile on Amanda's face froze at once.

"C'mon, Amanda," Bishop implored, "tell us where she's hiding out, dammit."

Amanda sat up. She tried to get out of the straitjacket, and Bishop guessed she'd probably soon succeed if the transformation kept advancing unchecked.

He knew that the entire operation hung in the balance and depended on chance.

He would not give up now.

CHAPTER 57

"HOW MUCH FARTHER?" George asked.

The question reminded Claire of her childhood vacations. Trips across the country, squeezed into a Ford with a broken exhaust and air conditioning that went on strike every few minutes.

How much farther, Daddy? How much longer?

"About a hundred and twenty miles to go," Claire said, "but if it keeps snowing like this we might need about three hours."

The few flakes had given way to a blizzard, and Claire had to take her foot off the gas. Though she'd been driving on snow-covered roads since she was a teenager, she was glad they had all-wheel drive.

"Are you tired? Want to switch?"

"No, thanks. It's OK. I'll tell you if I get tired."

"Fine," George said. "That's smart. Or at least it's better than waking up in the ditch with two broken legs."

Claire didn't miss the teasing undertone in his voice. But she didn't want to get into it. She didn't feel like kidding around or being merry at that moment.

For one thing, she could blame recent events: Amanda, the shootout, the escape—they all weighed on her mind like the dark shadow of a thundercloud. For another, she had to admit that the man beside her was just as much a stranger now as before. Granted, she reflected, he had twice saved her life. And she had him to thank for getting out of New York. Despite their newfound ease with each other's company, these facts weren't sufficient to clear her mind of doubt. And the longer her doubts plagued her, the more uncertain she was, as far as George was concerned.

What's he planning to do? Who is he, anyway? How'd he get mixed up in this business?

The questions rolled around in her head and wouldn't leave her in peace. But if Claire had learned anything over the past years, it was the art of posing the right questions at the right time. Questions she often used to see behind the front people put up.

And that's exactly what she intended to do now. Use the rest of the trip to get some assurance about George and his motives.

If he could *not* assuage her doubts, she would simply dump him in Rockwell. She'd lure him out of the car and then step on the gas. Though she'd be on her own afterward, that might be a considerably safer choice. At any rate it would be much, much safer, she concluded, than being holed up in the cabin with a total stranger.

"Speak up!" George interrupted, as if reading her thoughts. "There's something on your mind."

Claire looked at him, or rather, his dark silhouette. She preferred to look him straight in the eye when they talked to confirm he was telling the truth. But the darkness made that impossible. The faint light from the dash made his face somewhat visible. But she couldn't make out his eyes.

Claire had reached a decision regardless, and there was no thought of changing it: She had to get George's story before they got to Rockwell.

"I was thinking back on some of the things you told me this morning," Claire replied. She was careful to sound as relaxed and casual as she could.

"What things?"

"For instance, you said you were once a human being and didn't become a vampire until later on."

"Yes, that's what I said. And?"

"Well, now," Claire continued, "I really don't know where to begin, I mean . . ."

He cut her off. "You're interested in how that all happened, I suppose."

"Yes," she said. "After all, the story sounds crazy, don't you think?"

"You bet! Madness might even play the starring role in this story. OK, where do I start?"

"How about at the beginning?" Claire suggested.

"If you like—but I must warn you, it's a hell of a long story."

"So you shouldn't waste any time, don't you think?"

CHAPTER 58

A THIN, CRUSTY SCAB had formed on Whitman's palm. But that didn't seem to faze Amanda. She still lusted after blood, and her eyes blazed more than ever.

"C'mon, goddammit!" Bishop snarled. "Tell me where Claire's hiding. Where is she?"

Amanda turned toward him. She broke into a smile that revealed two rows of pointed teeth.

"Like hell I will, you goddamn motherfucker!" she spat. "That cunt Claire is mine and mine alone. I've got a score to settle with her."

Amanda's smile expanded. It was an expression of sheer scorn for the three men peering into her cage. Whitman appeared particularly unsure of himself. He kept looking over at Bishop as if searching for what he planned to do next.

But Bishop didn't let Amanda's little game rattle him. He knew it was time to get tough. He looked at Petric.

"Hey," he ordered. "Give me the holy water."

Petric reached into a pocket on his army vest and pulled out a thin vial containing a transparent liquid and gave it to Bishop. Bishop flipped off the cork with his thumb and looked again at Amanda, whose face had turned completely dark in the meantime.

Bishop had a momentary feeling that the creature knew the carrot was gone now. *Right*, he exulted, *now it's the* stick's *turn*.

"Amanda, Amanda," he called, leaning toward the cage, "you could have had it so damn easy. But it looks like you've decided to do it the hard way."

"Go to hell!" Amanda hissed. At that very instant Bishop's hand moved with lightning speed and splashed all the liquid on Amanda's face.

At first there was only a hiss—a long, drawn-out high-pitched sound. Amanda's face had become a contorted, even more grotesque mask. Her skin began to glimmer and smoke wherever the holy water landed. Her hair caught fire. First a few flames licked at her temples, and soon half her head was blazing.

She was quickly wrapped up in putting out the fire, throwing herself back and forth and beating her head against the cage floor and bars. The car rocked and squeaked from the force of her struggles. Pungent smells poured from the cage, burned flesh and singed hair by far the strongest.

Amanda finally extinguished the flames. She lay on her side, her head a veritable picture of devastation.

Her hair was almost completely burned away and her scalp charred. Her right eye was dull and black, her nose completely burned.

"*Now* are you ready to talk?" Bishop sneered.

Amanda fixed him with her one remaining eye but said nothing.

"OK, Petric," he said, "I need the second vial." He was about to turn to Petric when a growling sound escaped the cage.

"No!" Amanda snarled. "No, don't! It hurts too much."

"I'm not so sure you *really did* get my message, Amanda. Maybe another dousing with holy water will do you a world of good. What do you think?"

There was a bright glint in his eye. Triumph was written all over his face, like a crude stage mask.

"No," Amanda begged. Her voice almost sounded human again. "I'll tell you what you want to know. But please don't hurt me anymore."

"For the last time, Amanda," Bishop threatened, "where is Claire?"

"She's in Rockwell," Amanda confessed.

Bishop was astonished at how rapidly she answered. He'd been afraid deep down that she'd keep trying to fool him and jerk him around. Maybe she still was, he pondered. But it was very tempting for him right now to trust the words coming from between her charred lips.

"Why Rockwell?" Whitman interjected. "Your parents' house was sold long ago, and there's nobody there she's in regular contact with. We've checked. There's not a single soul in Rockwell she's close to."

Amanda gave him a disparaging look—a monumental achievement, given the circumstances. After all, more than half her face was completely disfigured.

"She won't stay in Rockwell," she growled. "She'll take to the woods, to our dad's cabin. She'll feel safe there."

"How the hell do you know that?" Bishop demanded. He tried to appear skeptical, knowing all the while that she was probably telling the truth. If Claire had indeed fled to her hometown as Amanda said, she would be doing what most frightened people did. *That's what most people do if they're at their wits' end, he repeated to himself, they head for home.*

"I had a dream about it," Amanda replied.

Her lips spread out in a smile, and from her one remaining eye glistened pure hate.

CHAPTER 59

THE BLOWING SNOW had grown heavier, causing Claire to reduce her speed even further. All-wheel drive or not, she could feel the car losing traction on every curve and threatening to skid out. She frequently had to turn the wheel in the opposite direction to keep the rear end in line. On top of that, the wipers were slowly but surely reaching their limit—though they were on high, the gaps only let Claire see ahead for a fraction of a second. All the more reason for her to consider it a blessing when she caught up to a fully loaded logging truck. Since she couldn't go more than forty-five miles an hour, she decided to stay in its slipstream instead of passing.

That meant two things: Visibility improved because most of the snow simply went over the roof, and Claire could relax behind the wheel, since she just had to follow the truck and watch his brake lights. Now she could concentrate better on George's mesmerizing story.

"I was born in 1846, in a small fishing village in Greece, two days' journey from the port of Patras," he began.

Then he paused to let his words sink in. It was as if he was expecting a critical remark. The seconds ticked by, and when none came, he continued.

He first described the time when he was still a human being. He was a shepherd, he said, and lived with his family in a little fishing village. Life back then was hard, and everybody had to do his share to keep the family above water. But sometimes even that wasn't enough. His younger sister died of pneumonia because his family couldn't afford to take her to the doctor in the next village.

Both his brothers went to sea, so it was his job to take care of the family sheep. But he dreamed of exploring the world one day and discovering what lay hidden over the horizon, "there, where the sea was a blue that merged seamlessly with the sky."

He spoke with such wistfulness that Claire believed he probably had wanted to go to sea himself. But she didn't interrupt him so he could go on unhindered.

He spoke slowly and calmly at first, like somebody long preoccupied by the thoughts that were now coming out of his mouth. But the more he talked, the more emotional his speech became.

His voice had something hypnotic about it. This impression was enhanced by the smell of pine pitch from the trees on the logging truck that came through the car's vents. That sweet smell from her childhood made her imagination bloom more and more as she listened to George's story. The more he talked, the sharper the images in her mind became. They were vivid pictures of a time long past—a time of poverty and misery.

After the description of his life, he spoke of the fateful day when he drove his flock of sheep to pasture for the last time.

He told about the voice wafting from the bushes. About his otherwise so-faithful dogs turning tail and fleeing. And finally about the boundless fear he felt at the moment he was left alone with the sheep in the clearing.

Claire's heart beat faster with his every word. But in spite of her growing excitement, she didn't for a minute ignore the dark pull emanating from his story. It was a horrible fairy tale—a nightmare put into words, she realized. But unlike the campfire stories from her childhood, she suspected—*no,* she *knew*—that absolutely every word was true.

Either that, or he's the world's number one liar!

But she felt deep down that he was *not* a liar. After all, she'd seen with her own eyes how he'd been transformed. Seen a dozen gaping bullet holes in his chest, seen . . . *ENOUGH!*

She had seen enough to be sure he was telling the truth. She couldn't deny it any longer. The certainty was so overpowering that it almost took her breath away. She pushed her last doubt aside, once and for all, and concentrated on what was yet to come.

"I've forgotten her name," George went on, "but I'm sure the woman involved was the one who'd disappeared several months earlier."

A brief pause while he took a deep breath. Then he slowly released it. Claire could almost feel the tension he was under at that moment. It came in warm waves that washed over her. Her whole body was tense, and her fingernails dug harder into the steering wheel. But she was itching to know what happened back then.

"And then?" she exclaimed.

"Then she bit me," George said. "I fought her, tried to break away—but it was all hopeless. I couldn't do a thing. She was just too strong."

After stopping for a minute, he wiped his face with a hand and continued.

"I came to when it was dark, hours later. But I already sensed that I wasn't myself anymore. The lust for blood had burned itself into my guts and clouded my reason. And I wandered around in that fog for more than seventy years . . ."

CHAPTER 60

"YOU BELIEVE THAT bitch in the back?" Whitman asked. "Are you really serious, goddammit?"

They were on the move again, heading north. Before leaving the parking area, Bishop had ensured that nothing would happen on the road to Rockwell that he might regret later.

Instead of counting on Amanda retaining her present form, he'd given her another shot of tranquilizer just to be on the safe side. She'd crumpled and hit the floor with eyes wide open. They watched for several minutes to see if there was any movement, and since there wasn't, they got in the car and drove off.

"What else can we do, in your opinion?" Bishop grunted. "Maybe we should go back to New York, twiddle our thumbs, and wait for the woman or the vampire to pop up somewhere?"

"Not such a bad idea, if you ask me, chief. One of them's going to turn up sooner or later, and then we strike and bring them down. But now we're bumble-dicking around New England with a vampire in the back of an SUV. That breaks the Organization's rules, and you know it."

It appealed to Bishop more and more that Whitman despaired of the operation's success. He was amused by the finality of every one of his proclaimed decisions, as if the whole enterprise were a mathematical problem with only one solution.

But Bishop knew that you sometimes had to drill a lot of wells before you hit water. And those rules—he didn't have to lose any sleep over them, he'd decided, because *he* had drawn most of them up himself. And at a time when Whitman was still hanging from his mangy mother's tits. That colorful image he'd come up with put a broad smile on his lips.

"You don't have anything more to say about that?" Whitman asked.

"What is there to say, Charlie? Either we do this thing the way I think is right, or . . ."

"Or what, chief?" Whitman interrupted. "Are you threatening me? Do I really have to remind you that we're officers with the same rank, and I don't have to take orders from you?"

". . . or," Bishop continued as if Whitman's protest had fallen on deaf ears, "you can get out of the car right now and fuck off. Your call."

Whitman answered with a snort, then silence. He didn't want to throw oil on a flaming hot debate, so he simply kept his mouth shut and slumped back in his seat. That was how they drove the next several miles through the darkness of the interstate while the snow outside grew heavier.

A few minutes after they crossed the Connecticut-Massachusetts border, the radio on the dash buzzed. A little blue light signaled that the incoming call was from a satellite. And that could only mean one thing, Bishop recognized.

A message from the Vatican.

That very thought was enough to wipe the grin off his face. He unhesitatingly picked up the handset while turning off the loudspeaker so that Whitman couldn't listen in. Then he hit the ON button.

"*Buona sera, Cardinale Canetti. Come va?*" he answered. He hadn't been in Italy for years, but his accent was impeccable.

"Save your breath, Bishop," the voice on the radio said. "If I want to hear my mother tongue butchered, I'll go to the nearest restaurant and eavesdrop on American tourists ordering dinner."

"*Capisco,*" Bishop confirmed. "What can I do for you?"

"First of all, you can enlighten me as to how the operation progresses," the cardinal said. "I hope you've caught the vampire and the woman since our last communication. I trust you know how much depends on it. That vampire may help us eliminate this infernal plague once and for all. So how does it look, Bishop?"

So how does *it look?*

A moment's hesitation, because Bishop knew that the operation until now was the living proof of Murphy's Law: Everything that could go wrong had gone wrong.

But Bishop was fully aware that this wasn't the time to speak of the Devil. For one thing, it just wasn't done when talking to a cardinal on the phone. And for another, he didn't want to risk being pulled off the mission due to lack of success. So he chose his words carefully.

"We don't have them yet," he replied, "neither the woman nor the vampire."

"I fervently hope that is not all you have to offer me."

"It is not. We have located their hideout and are on our way there. It is all going according to plan. *Funziona tutto secondo il piano, Cardinale.*"

"I should hope so," came the reply. "This operation is far too crucial, and failure is not an option. After all, we've been looking for this damn hybrid for almost half a century."

Bishop hated the condescending tone the cardinal adopted every now and then. He'd known him for almost twenty years, so he recognized him for what he was—a narrow-minded bastard. An old fogey who couldn't even identify a vampire if it was giving him a blow job. Bishop kept these thoughts and feelings to himself, concealing them behind a façade of conscientiousness.

"I know how important this operation is, and I promise you that this business will be over in two days at the latest."

"Good," Cardinal Canetti said. "You will have two more days." A brief pause, and then:

"Is Agent Whitman in the car?"

"Yes," Bishop answered. "What do you want from him?"

The laugh coming over the handset reminded him of the cry of a hyena.

"*Alcun motivo di preoccuparsi,*" the cardinal assured him. "Let me speak to him, please."

Bishop handed the radio over in the direction of the passenger seat.

Whitman put the radio up to his ear. Though the cardinal said that Bishop needn't worry about it . . .

. . . *alcun motivo di preoccuparsi* . . .

. . . just the same, that was exactly what he did at this moment.

Worry, big-time!

What worried him most was that it was the cardinal talking the entire time and Whitman just listening. His partner didn't say a word but stared out into the night as he heard the cardinal's orders and instructions.

Huge worries!

Bishop knew it was a sure sign that what was said that was not intended for his ears. That conviction was a red-hot spike pushing deeper into his mind with every passing minute.

His hands clutched the wheel, and he gritted his teeth. A single thought reverberated through his brain like a never-ending echo.

Soon, Charlie, very, very soon . . .

Soon, Charlie, very, very soon . . .

CHAPTER 61

"AFTER THE FOG . . . then what?" Claire wanted to know. She looked at George and was surprised to see his face now. She was so engrossed by his story that she hadn't noticed the light dawning in the east. The horizon was a messy blur of shades of dirty gray, and one could only guess where the sun was.

"Then the things occurred that made me what I am today," George answered, "a goddamn hybrid life form. Half human, half monster."

He stopped his tale to ask, "How much longer?"

"A little over forty miles. I figure we'll be in Rockwell in an hour."

"Fine," George said, "that should be enough for the rest of my story."

Claire didn't respond, but thoughts tumbled around in her head. She had one hour to find out who George was. This hour was all there was for her to make up her mind whether to trust him or not. As exciting as his story was so far, it nevertheless had not yielded enough information about him. At least, not the kind of information she could entrust her life to.

So she had to learn more. Had to learn who this person sitting next to her really was. Because she knew that in an emergency so much—maybe everything—would depend on the decision she needed to make in the next sixty minutes.

As she considered this, George's story began again, and once more his words held her fascinated.

INTERLUDE I

After I was transformed into a vampire, I roamed through the woods for days without seeing a living soul. My desire for blood had taken over my ability to reason, like a thick, inescapable fog. All my thoughts revolved around finding blood as quickly as possible.

In my desperation I tried to satisfy my bloodlust with animals. But each time I had to confess that it didn't help. No fox, no stag, no forest animal could give me what my inmost yearnings desired.

I wandered through forests and canyons by night, driven by my madness and following my instincts. By day I'd crawl into caves to flee the sunlight. And if I couldn't find a cave, I dug into the ground or crept into a fallen tree trunk, where I could wait until sunset to go out on the prowl again.

Though my craving for blood robbed me of my reason, my instincts were on high alert. That is what initially prevented me from trying my luck at hunting in the daytime as well, and from having my body go up in flames.

After a week of searching and ambushing game, I had my first piece of luck, if you can call it that. Walking aimlessly through the forest, I spied my first victim.

It was a peasant girl, probably no more than fifteen. I came across her on a riverbank just after sundown. The western horizon was still aglow, and the first stars were already rising in the east.

She was absorbed in doing the laundry. Her hair fell over her face, preventing her from spotting me. I crept toward her, taking pains not to make the slightest noise that could give me away. The rustling of the river helped as well.

I approached her, step by step, until I was so close that escape was impossible. I grabbed her by the hair and pulled her head back. I can still remember how rough I was. Her neck tendons stood out, and her blood vessels throbbed under her skin. She emitted a high, thin cry, like a falcon's. Then she fell silent and looked at me with eyes filled with disbelief. Her eyes were blue—I remember that very well. Deep blue, like the sea just before the storm.

I stopped for a second and looked into those gorgeous eyes. A thought stirred deep within me. It was a final warning that what I was about to do was wrong. Wrong before God and man. But it was only a brief rebellion. Then my cravings prevailed.

I bent down and dug my teeth into her neck. She thrashed around and tried to free herself. She hit me, drummed her legs, and tried to scream. But she had no chance. Her voice was little more than a drowning gurgle, and her strength diminished with every heartbeat. Warm waves of blood spurted from her neck, and her body sank into my arms at last as she lost consciousness. I kept drinking until her heart stopped and not a drop of blood was left in her body.

After slaking my thirst, I vanished into the woods. I holed up in a cave and slept until the following spring. But it wasn't a proper sleep; it was a sort of paralysis that held me captive while my mind spun around like an infernal top.

When the temperature began to rise, madness seized me once more, driving me out of my hiding place. I went on the hunt once again.

That's how it went for years, Miss Hagen. Time and again I roamed through the night on the lookout for victims. My first meal had stilled my thirst for almost half a year, but the time between the need for one kill and the next grew shorter with every feeding. The stronger my instincts became, the greater my desire.

That's why I traveled greater and greater distances on the prowl for prey. I'd left Greece behind. But I didn't care. I knew no boundaries and no longer had a yearning for home. I'd become a shadow—a whisper in the wind, if you like.

The years stretched out before me. I wandered the world—like the messenger of death and damnation incarnate. Every new day my abilities grew; my instincts became sharper. I'd turned into one of the monsters from my grandmother's tales, and I knew deep down how true that was. But the worst thing about it was that I enjoyed it. I enjoyed hunting. I took great delight in my victims' fear, and I longed for their blood.

When the Austro-Hungarian monarchy went to war and punished the Balkans with suffering and misery, I grew obese from living off the proverbial fat of the land. Most men had gone off to war, leaving whole stretches of the country unprotected. Cities and villages were packed with women, children, and the elderly, who had no defense against me but their clasped hands raised to heaven and a few fleeting prayers.

Like a force of nature I went on a rampage during this time. I wiped entire mountain villages from the face of the earth. I was the biggest profiteer in that damn war, but the times moved on, and the waves of my madness abated.

I'd made it to Poland in the meantime, at that time a country of small villages and of deep, remote forests. I decided to stay there, just as a fox sometimes decides to remain in the vicinity of a chicken coop.

That country seemed to suit me perfectly. The people were all believers, of course, but not in any way that threatened. As pious Catholics they believed one and all in Jesus Christ their Savior. But unlike people in the Balkans, they weren't superstitious about creatures like me—and that was their greatest weakness, because their defenses against me were very limited without superstition to protect them.

When another great war engulfed the country, history repeated itself. Once again I lived through an age of unbridled activity as I raged about at will. I didn't dream, however, that my days were numbered. And as so often when a great upheaval occurs in one's life, it was by chance that my run of good luck came to an end.

The town I'd chosen as my headquarters was stormed by soldiers of the Wehrmacht just before evening twilight. Many of the citizens who'd managed to survive my madness fell victim to the soldiers. They were lined up against the wall and shot. Their blood colored the streets, and their screams reverberated through the oncoming darkness.

I crawled into the cellar of an inn and watched the spectacle through a street-level window. I still recall with shame how stimulating it was to see human blood splattering on the walls as bodies were riddled with bullets.

I thought I was safe and believed that I just had to wait it out. Since the soldiers were running riot outside, they surely would not bother about me. All the same, the sun had almost set behind the hills, and my strength was growing minute by minute. But my complacency was a huge mistake.

Shortly after the executions, the cellar door burst open and two soldiers raided my hiding place. I spun around to see them readying their guns. I still remember how ridiculous this gesture appeared to me, since I supposed that bullets couldn't hurt me. But it turned out they could!

One of the soldiers opened fire and put a dozen bullets into my chest. I tried to attack him, rip his throat out, and watch him drown in his own blood.

But nothing of the kind happened.

I couldn't move anymore and had absolutely no control over my body. I sank to the floor, and darkness enveloped me. I passed out, and never did discover how they were able to anesthetize me.

When I came to, I was somewhere else, in sterile surroundings like a hospital. I was tied to a bed and unable to move. I had just enough strength to lift my eyelids; there was no hope of escape.

Doctors in white smocks raced around, stuck needles into me, and administered all sorts of medications and serums. And all I could do was watch and wonder what the hell was actually happening. It took many months for me to find out.

Though my limbs were paralyzed, my senses were as sharp as ever.

I could hear the doctors and nurses talking, even through the walls. I followed their conversations, learning more about what had happened to me. And when they didn't say anything, I could read their eyes to see what was going on.

I guessed their plans and found out what they intended to do with me. Not only with me but with all the vampires they'd caught in the meantime.

It came to light that the Nazis had more than a romantic weakness for the supernatural, Miss Hagen. No, whole units of scientific personnel were detailed to target supernatural resources. Resources that were to help them turn their crude plans into action.

Hitler had given his personal orders to maximize research in this area, no matter what the cost. And over the course of time, it became clear that the results were indeed groundbreaking.

You're probably asking yourself, "But how did it come about?" That's precisely what kept me occupied during those endlessly long months when I was tied to a bed. Months when I had to put up with all sorts of medical tests, with my only reprieve coming sporadically with a supply of fresh blood.

The answer is as simple as it is terrifying.

When the Nazi death machine in Auschwitz was running full blast, several thousand people were murdered every day in the most bestial way. You've certainly heard how it usually proceeded, Miss Hagen. I don't think any details are needed. But let me add this: Once again it was chance that got things moving.

One day several dozen innocent people were herded into a gas chamber in Auschwitz. The doors were closed, and poison gas was piped into the room soon after.

This was the routine for soldiers on duty and the camp commandant at the time—one Rudolf Hoess. Everything was running along as always, and though it's hard to imagine, killing had become routine by that time, a bothersome chore that had to be done. The only difference from the countless previous executions was that this time something completely unusual happened. More than unusual, something downright incredible.

When the doors were opened, the soldiers didn't see what they expected. One man was standing there among the many corpses and faces distorted by the agony of death. He was grinning at the soldiers.

At first they believed that the amount of gas had been miscalculated and was insufficient to kill all the people in the gas chamber. A soldier drew his pistol, came up to the man, and shot him right in the face. As the shot echoed around the tile walls, the man grabbed the soldier's arm and ripped it off. Then he attacked him and slit his throat. The other soldiers had enough presence of mind to retreat at once.

They bolted the chamber door and blocked all the vents.

Word was they drew straws afterward to see who was going to wake up Commandant Hoess from his midday nap with the unpleasant news of this incident.

Hoess, a total psychopath but also an extremely fastidious bureaucrat, immediately realized the opportunity this event presented.

The rest, Miss Hagen, is history. One thing led to another, if you like. Hoess informed Himmler, who reported the amazing events to the Führer. Experts from all corners of the Reich were immediately commandeered to Auschwitz. They were to investigate the creature that was still held captive in the hermetically sealed gas chamber.

At some point—please don't ask me how they did it—they managed to sedate the vampire. Investigations began right away.

The scientists in charge had recognized that the vampire they'd caught was virtually invulnerable. Bullets couldn't hurt him any more than poison gas, hunger, or cold could. He and his kind were therefore the perfect soldiers Hitler needed to convert his sick ideas into deeds.

All the Nazi research focused on finding ways to control vampires and use them for their own purposes. They were trying to create an army of super-soldiers. An army to subjugate the whole world. At the same time they realized that more than one experimental subject was needed to fast-track their research.

The doctors attempted to create more vampires by themselves, of course, throwing the monster victims to feed on and hoping for transformations. Camp inmates were screened for this assignment in every way they could think of. But the vampire didn't play by Nazi rules. He killed one victim after another without performing the dark alchemy they so desired. And so a new source was needed, and specially trained Wehrmacht troops marched off to hunt vampires.

It was some of those troops that caught me by surprise and captured me in that cellar. Not only me, but other vampires were found as well. Though I never discovered the exact number, my guess is that research was carried out on several dozen vampires while I was a prisoner in Auschwitz. Very intensive research, Miss Hagen. As I said, my body was completely paralyzed all that time. I was one of many guinea pigs helplessly waiting to see what our tormenters would think up next. But although I felt so weak that I couldn't even open my eyes on many days, the sedatives the Nazis gave me didn't seem to have any effect on my senses. Senses were still as sharp as a predator's. And even if my body was lethargic and useless, my senses kept supplying me with all kinds of information. I could overhear the people in charge conversing—concrete walls three feet thick couldn't prevent me from following their plans and movements. So I knew all their secrets, Miss Hagen, and could smell the scent of their fear deposited in every corner, in the tiniest nook and cranny of the bunker where I was imprisoned.

Even when the end of the Third Reich loomed, the research kept going. Day and night, in shifts, without a break. The closer the Allies came, the more frantically the doctors and experts worked.

That's understandable, of course. Because even if those madmen didn't want to admit it, the war was lost long before 1944 was over. Vampire research was their last hope—the last desperate attempt to fight off the imminent end.

The day after Christmas, 1944, it happened. The doctors got lucky. They'd succeeded in developing a serum for *partially* turning vampires back to humans while retaining their supernatural powers. The serum was administered to me for test purposes. You've seen the results with your own eyes, Miss Hagen. It made me what I am today: a human being who still has a vampire's powers and faculties, but whose desire for blood has been completely extinguished.

But you might have already guessed their success came too late to help the Nazis. Thank God, because three weeks after I received the serum, the 322nd Soviet Infantry Division attacked the camp and liberated the remaining prisoners.

One of them was me.

That's my story, Miss Hagen. Or at least the part of it when I was still an out-and-out vampire.

CHAPTER 62

"SO?" BISHOP ASKED. "What did you and the cardinal talk about?"

He took great pains to make it sound like a casual question. He was trying to prevent Whitman from picking up on the uneasiness that had grown during the conversation and now had a firm grip on him.

"Frankly, chief," Whitman grinned, "that's private."

A short pause before Whitman continued with, "But I won't torture you—after all, we're partners. It was about figuring out my overtime. Something got screwed up."

Whitman's grin got wider with every word. Bishop didn't let on that he saw through his partner's little game. He just played along with it.

"Ahh, kiss my ass," he said, exaggerating his anger.

"You'd really like that, hey, chief?"

Bishop didn't respond. He clenched his teeth and grabbed the steering wheel with both hands. Nothing showed on the outside, but on the inside he was furious.

What the hell is that motherfucking cardinal thinking?
What the hell did they talk about?
What the . . .

Before his rage could completely overtake his thoughts, he took several deep breaths and calmed down. He knew it was pointless to lose control. He had to assert his command at any cost, not only because he felt it was the highest form of discipline but because this business had become far greater in scope than he had suspected at the outset. A lot depended on this mission, and for that reason he had to be cautious.

Very cautious.

He knew Whitman was a snake in the grass. And what did his father used to say?

You play around with snakes, and you'll get bitten.

INTERLUDE II

The killing didn't stop even after the Soviets liberated Auschwitz. Blood calls for blood, as the saying rightly goes, Miss Hagen, and many Nazi officers came to experience this painful truth on their own skin.

Many of them committed suicide right before the camp was captured. They hanged themselves on their own belts or took cyanide capsules. Others tore off their uniforms and slipped on prisoner's rags to escape the vengeance of Soviet soldiers. But all their efforts were futile, Miss Hagen. They were lined up against the barracks row by row and simply shot. At least those found the mercy of a quick death. Others who weren't so lucky had long felt that death was no longer a punishment but a merciful act of deliverance. Believe me, Miss Hagen, when I say the Russian soul doesn't necessarily live by melancholy alone. It can also live off suffering—its own as well as its enemy's. And in that respect, Miss Hagen, not one of the great writers exaggerated one little bit. Not Dostoevsky, not the many who came after him.

These terrifying events might strike anyone as odd at first— I only perceived them on the fringes of my consciousness. I had long been cut loose from mankind, and that's not the least reason I felt nothing but indifference toward their suffering. I didn't give a damn about the guards' pain and fear at that time; it was shortly after I'd gone through my final transformation. It was something that didn't affect my powers of reason at all; I was completely passive toward it all, like a beetle crushed under the heel of a shoe.

I was involved instead with processing the innumerable impressions that were pelting me. There I was, sitting on the floor with other prisoners and feeling the whole time like a goddamn wolf with its teeth pulled out. I was surrounded by myriads of people who talked at me in an overheated gibberish of many languages, apparently taking me for one of their own. One of their own—can you imagine? ME!

The sun was burning down on my skin and my limbs, warming them while memories of a long-forgotten time swirled around in my head. Memories of my life in Greece long ago. Of my family and of the person I'd actually been before all this craziness came upon me and turned me into a monster. And even though I'm not a believer, Miss Hagen, I think I know how Lazarus must have felt when he climbed out of his cave and had his shroud taken off, because although I was completely overwhelmed by all those impressions, I could still sense a tiny spark of hope being kept alive inside me. It was the hope that I'd finally left madness behind and would be a genuine human being again. Now we both know that my longing for this was maybe a little premature, but in the days after the liberation this thought was the driving force behind my behavior.

That's why it didn't take long for me to catch on that I had to get out of the camp as fast as possible. My thinking was that no matter how things proceeded, it wouldn't be long before the Soviets took an interest in the dark laboratories hidden many feet below the camp itself. And if it should come to that, I figured, then I could expect no mercy from them, because sooner or later they'd probably take a very keen interest in finding out what I was all about, me and the other vampires who had been held captive for months. And if things got that far, then they'd probably still take no pity on me.

Though I was fully aware of the danger, I still couldn't simply take off. My body was still worn out from the side effects of all the drugs—it was practically no good for anything. Escaping would have been mere child's play back when I was a monster. I'd simply have flown over the barbed-wire fence some night and killed anybody who got in my way. But for a human, an escape like that was plainly impossible—and you have to understand that I firmly believed at the time that I was a human again. Not only because I couldn't fly anymore, Miss Hagen, but because I was dead sure that it would take just one stray bullet and I'd be pushing up daisies.

Nevertheless, I didn't give up but did my best to improve my situation and get out unharmed. I roamed around the camp looking out for a suitable opportunity, and it didn't take long for me to discover one.

It presented itself in the form of an old woman.

Her name was Anita Pavlova. She was the sole survivor of a Polish merchant family from around Danzig. She was as old as anybody could be, and whatever old age might have still left to her, the torments of Auschwitz had ultimately taken it away. Her body was emaciated; she was almost totally blind, and as if that weren't enough, she seemed to have lost her mind. This was one reason it wasn't hard for me to make her believe I was Jacob, her grandson, the one she always went on about. She'd thought until that time that he'd been sent to the gas chamber right after he arrived because he was suspected of being a partisan and in the Resistance in Danzig.

I looked after Anita as best I could as she came out with ever more details about her former life. And even if her deranged mental state sometimes caused her to go off topic and get lost in details, I was usually able to ask specific questions to get her back on track. And so I gradually learned more and more about her family and, in the end, everything I needed to know about her grandson, whose identity was to become my life insurance policy.

The Soviets made a determined effort to comb through the camp inmates on the lookout for concealed soldiers of the Wehrmacht and SS henchmen. When it was finally Anita's turn, I'd already internalized so much about her life that it wasn't very difficult to make the Soviet officer in charge believe that I really was Jacob, her grandson. I'd slipped into a role, and since I'd long become an expert connoisseur of human nature, my charade was crowned with success.

They let us go, Miss Hagen. Shortly thereafter, Berlin was totally occupied by Soviet forces, and the Führer himself decided to emulate the cowardice of many of his officers and avoid capture by committing suicide.

Anita and I were living at the time in a little pension near Auschwitz that the Allies and the Red Cross had converted into one of several provisional centers and military hospitals for camp survivors. Only three weeks after the end of the war we received a telegram, Miss Hagen, containing three short sentences:

Dear A and J,
Thank God Almighty you are alive.
Tickets to NY reserved for you with all steamship
lines in Rotterdam Amsterdam London.
Look forward to arrival.
Regards C

Sometime later it emerged that "C" was Cyril Powell, Anita's younger brother. He used to be a textile magnate who somehow managed to feather his nest before the stock market crash in 1929 brought the whole country's economy to its knees and lost a lot of money overnight. Powell—he'd Americanized "Pavlov," his original name, naturally—was the name that in the end became my own.

What else shall I tell you, Miss Hagen? I did ultimately stay with Anita.

Why?

Not because I owed my release from Auschwitz to her. No, it had nothing to do with gratitude. I believe I was so overwhelmed by my brand-new humanity that there was nothing I could do but simply stand by her. Because that's precisely what the human spirit is mainly made up of, Miss Hagen: We're there for one another and give mutual support even in the hardest of times; we feel another person's pain now and then, letting him know that he's not abandoned to his fears and troubles all by himself. Aside from that, I must confess that it was all a damn cynical act of Providence as well.

It was an older woman who plunged me into disaster long ago, and after a very long time it was once again an old woman who helped me return to freedom. Perhaps that was the main reason I did not leave Anita's side, Miss Hagen.

She died on the passage from Rotterdam to New York. Her heart stopped beating somewhere in the middle of the Atlantic. She went peacefully to sleep as the sun sank below the horizon in a riot of reddish hues.

But that was *not* the drama that was played out on the high seas. I noticed shortly after Anita died that I'd been wrong to suppose that I'd become human again. Dreadfully wrong, to be exact. I was in an emotional state from taking leave of Anita and mourning her when I suddenly felt my old senses coming back to life.

First my hearing improved, and it wasn't long until I heard every single sound onboard, beginning with the mice eating through the insulation somewhere and going right up to the churning of the ship's propellers in the water. In short: From one second to the next I could hear everything and everybody.

A little while later I felt an old familiar easiness take possession of my body, the ease I'd only known before when I'd flown over great distances. The more time passed, the more my senses stirred and were once again superhumanly sharp. My old powers returned simultaneously, more and more. Suddenly I was able again to slip through any opening, no matter how small, and to blend into the shadows to defend myself against intrusive eyes.

And there was much more to it, Miss Hagen. My mastery over my capabilities was restored, and I'd be lying if I claimed it didn't make me damn proud to sense that boundless energy in my breast once more that I used to be in control of for such a long time—energy that exercised a dark attraction over me in spite of all the terror connected with it. But in spite of its appeal and the heady feeling that went with it, I suspected it would be only a matter of time when my thirst for blood would be reawakened.

In spite of my obscure apprehension, I lived for days in the certain knowledge that I wouldn't be able to fight it, if it went that far. So I sank even more into deep meditation, enjoying the supposed last moments left to me as a human being.

Meanwhile the ship had managed the crossing. Cyril took me into his home—like his own flesh and blood, as it's so nicely put. He was infinitely happy, though mourning the loss of his sister, because I, Jacob, at least, had survived the Nazi reign of terror. And since he had never met Jacob in person—he knew him just from a few yellowed photographs—it was a piece of cake for me to lead him to believe that I was his only living relative on the face of the earth.

I lived under Cyril's roof and ate at his table, Miss Hagen, until the day he died. All this time I was constantly waiting to see what might happen the moment my thirst for blood was aroused once again. I began to get to know New York during that time, a city that was, at least for me at that time, as enshrouded in legend as Atlantis was.

I lived every single day in dread that my newfound luck was only temporary and that it was only a matter of time before I reverted to the rapacious beast I'd once been. My fear was kindled as well by my discovery one day that I could be transformed again. It was as if I merely had to mentally throw a switch to change into a creature of the night. You've seen it for yourself, Miss Hagen, so you know exactly what I'm talking about.

But I did *not* feel any desire for human blood, even in that hideous shape, the shape of a primeval beast of prey from pre-biblical times. And the longer my awareness grew that I might stay this way from now on—always, forever—the more I nourished the hope that I could live a perfectly normal life. Be a human among humans—instead of an infernal plague stalking them night after night.

That was not the least reason why I started studying medicine. Since my life had been characterized for decades by living off people, hurting them, killing them, I wanted to give them something back in some way or another, wanted to help. A year before I became a doctor, Cyril died and left me the house in Tarrytown and the modest remainder of his once great fortune. I changed my name to George shortly after that, the Americanized form of the name my mother gave me. Way back then, for what feels like a million years ago.

What followed, Miss Hagen, was a quiet life devoted wholeheartedly to my mission as a doctor, a life that served the one and only purpose of helping and healing. I never had a wife and children, and only very few people I could call my friends. Then, too, Miss Hagen, unlike all other people, the tooth of time did not gnaw away at me. In fact, it looks as if time has knocked all its teeth out on me. I do not age, never get sick, or have to struggle with any complaints that sometimes unavoidably come with time. I don't know if I'm immortal, but I suppose that it will take rather a lot of effort to get me into the ground. The Nazis labored hard and long on that very task.

So there you finally have my whole life's story, Miss Hagen. I've left nothing out and glossed over nothing; I've described everything as it really was. I know it's not by itself sufficient to purge me of my old sins, but I hope you realize that I've nothing in common with the beast I once was. I've dedicated my entire life since then to people. I've helped them in any way I could and always treated anybody who couldn't pay for it. I've done everything to build a contrast to the many sins I committed when my lust for blood clouded my reason like a thick fog.

CHAPTER 63

THE VERY SECOND they passed the highway sign for Rockwell, George finished his story, after an hour of talking. When he stopped, it seemed to Claire that an uncomfortable silence spread through the car. An unbearable silence that compelled her to say something.

Anything at all.

But she didn't.

She had to think it over. The nearer they came to the center of town, the less time she had to make a decision. She still didn't know if she could trust George.

They passed Chestnut Peak, and Claire saw that the old Roberts house on the hill had burned down to the ground. A few black remains of the foundations stuck up out of the snow-drifts, like rotten teeth in an otherwise healthy mouth.

Claire was absorbed by the sight. The house was gone, the house and its history, grist for the town's gossip mill for years.

George's voice broke the silence in the car and pulled Claire back to the present.

"*Now* do you trust me, Miss Hagen?" he inquired. "Or do you want to get rid of me at the next opportunity?"

Claire stared at him with her eyes wide open. It seemed yet again that he might well have read her thoughts. As if he'd thumbed through them like a book. Anxiety overcame her, and one ice-cold shiver after another ran through her body.

He can read your mind. He can READ it!

"Don't be afraid," George said. "I can't really see what you're thinking."

There was a glint in his eye, and his gaze was frozen and hard. Claire's fear increased. But she didn't lose control.

"B-b-but . . . ?" she spluttered, her eyes riveted on George.

"Well," he said, "it's rather that your feelings spill over onto me from time to time. It's automatic, and I can't do anything to stop them. It's a kind of instinct, a sixth sense, if you will. I've come to regard it as one of the many sins I've inherited from my former life. I'm sorry if I've scared you."

While he was speaking, Claire's mind raced. She knew the time had come to decide. Downtown Rockwell was only a mile away, but that wasn't the determining factor. It was that George had seen through her plan. He'd looked deep into her mind and spotted her doubts.

He knew her intentions.

The charade was over.

CHAPTER 64

"CAN I ASK you something, chief?"

Bishop kept watching the road as if he hadn't heard Whitman. He was still stewing. The sure fact that the operation's parameters had been changed without his approval was eating at him, preying on his mind.

"I'll take your silence as a yes," Whitman followed up.

"Then go ahead and *ask*," Bishop growled.

More silence, so Bishop knew at once that he probably wouldn't like what Whitman was about to say.

"What do you plan to do? I mean after we get to this hick town? I don't think the woman's going to leave a trail of bread crumbs to her cabin. Assuming the cabin even exists. It's a big, fat lie, if you ask me. A red herring. We're wasting our time here."

Bishop knew Whitman's words might contain a grain of truth. But he wasn't dissuaded, let alone upset. He'd been hunting vampires since before Whitman could tie his own shoelaces.

Age wasn't his only advantage. It was his nearly unlimited experience. He was better informed about vampires than all the Vatican books and scholars. Throughout the years, he had acquired personal expertise that would beat that of anybody the Organization could ever find. The confidence that came with that knowledge assured him they were on the right path. They would find the cabin. It also had made him, over time, what he was today: the most trusted agent by far in the entire Organization.

Bishop had a passing thought that he ought to let Whitman in on his secret. He pondered this carefully and concluded that there was no risk in giving him a little peek. After all, he reasoned, Whitman's days were numbered. His partner wouldn't have an opportunity to do anything with that information or share it. It didn't matter if they found the cabin or not—Whitman wouldn't leave the woods alive.

"You've left one thing out of your calculations, my friend," he responded, "a damn crucial thing, to be exact."

"I'm not your friend," Whitman shot back, "but go on."

So he began to tell him, and every word that left his lips magnified the incredulousness written on his partner's face. Whitman went bug-eyed, and his jaw dropped.

Bishop was hugely elated at the sight and had great trouble concentrating on his driving.

CHAPTER 65

MINUTES ELAPSED while Claire wrestled to find the right words. By the time they arrived in downtown Rockwell, she still hadn't reached a decision.

"So what have you decided?" George inquired.

Claire didn't answer. She turned off Main Street, went past Olsen's hardware store, and parked in front of the general store. It was where she used to buy hunting supplies with her father when she was a kid.

Not until then did she turn to address George.

His eyes were glistening, and he still looked fresh and wide-awake despite the punishing trip. It looked to her as if the stress and strain had bypassed him without leaving a trace. His stubbly beard had grown a bit longer. She wondered for a split second what it would feel like to rub it.

Like sandpaper . . .

She shivered. But this time it wasn't fear that possessed her but a tingling sensation. A pleasant feeling like a weak electric current tugging at her nerve ends, making them vibrate.

It was a rash impulse, but Claire realized that was all it took. In that one brief, careless moment a critical insight had crept into her consciousness. She'd finally hit upon a way to see if she could trust George.

"What happened to Jack?" She came right out with it.

Her voice was calm and assertive. As she spoke, though, John's scared voice echoed in her mind like never-ending feedback:

Jack is dead . . . Jack is dead . . . Jack is dead . . .

She remembered the misgivings in John's face when he'd told her about Jack's death.

The doctors say it was a heart attack, but I've seen enough to know better . . .

Claire knew she had to get to the bottom of what had happened to Jack. But it was even more essential to find out whether George was involved with his death. If so, they'd be going their separate ways the next instant. She'd leave him behind right then and there and hide in the woods of Rockwell Heights all by herself.

"Who's Jack?" George asked. His eyebrows knitted together, and his look grew somber.

Claire watched his every movement. She could really see him, unlike last night. Now she wasn't forced to listen to him in virtual darkness in the hope that he was telling the truth. She could utilize all the skills and instincts she employed to earn her living. They could help convince her whether George was telling the truth or not.

"John's partner," she explained.

"You mean the other burglar? The guy with the man you met at the airport?"

"Yes. That's precisely the man I mean. What happened to him?"

George's face grew tense, just a bit. He wiped his face with his hand and sighed.

"What do you want to know about him?" he asked, his eyes fixed on Claire.

"Were you mixed up in his death?"

George looked at her for a second and pressed his lips together until they formed a thin line. Claire observed his every move with the utmost curiosity.

"Yes," he confessed, "yes, I was involved with his death."

Her heart skipped a beat.

Oh my God . . .

Fear crept into her thoughts again. But she did not lose control. She knew her life depended on what she was going to say or do next.

Before she could act, George continued talking.

CHAPTER 66

"YOU MEAN VAMPIRES can read people's minds?" Whitman asked incredulously.

He'd been quiet while listening to Bishop, and his expression grew darker with each minute. This did not stop Bishop from initiating his partner in the biggest secret of his professional career. A secret that he alone had discovered.

Bishop replied, "I'm one hundred percent certain of it. Those bastards have telepathic powers."

"There's not a word about it in the records."

"Forget the damn records for a minute," Bishop broke in. "For centuries they've been written by cardinals who presumed that they—and only they—had a handle on the truth. All those chronicles and reports are nothing but the Catholic Church's heroic self-adulation. Any truth about vampires in them is simply there by chance.

"But *I* have spent the best part of my life hunting vampires, and I can assure you I'm right about this."

Whitman made no response. He seemed to be thinking it over. He spoke up after several minutes.

"Let's suppose your theory is correct. How's that going to help us find the woman and the vampire?"

"That's easy," Bishop explained. "A vampire's telepathic powers are not universal. They are strengthened by direct blood ties."

"I don't get it."

"I mean that after these creatures are transformed, they often tend to attack their relatives first. That doesn't happen every time, of course, but strikingly often. Reports about this are in the Vatican chronicles—you've heard of them."

"Not that I know of, chief. Please enlighten me."

After a moment's pause, Bishop continued. "Let's assume a kid disappears somewhere in the world. As if an earthquake instantly swallowed him up. Several days after the search has been abandoned and those affected are slowly resigning themselves to their cruel fate, one of the kid's relatives suddenly has an inspiration. He thinks he knows where the kid might be. No, he not only believes it—he's *one hundred percent certain*. He sets out to look for the kid, and he, too, never comes back. Now do you see what I'm getting at?"

Whitman thought about it, and his face relaxed right away.

"I think I've got it," he exclaimed. "If your theory's right, then this bitch in the back will most likely lead us to the woman because it has a sort of telepathic link to her. *And* the woman is the one and only living relative this fucker has. Which seriously increases the likelihood we'll find her. That's what you meant, isn't it?"

"That's exactly how it is," Bishop admitted. "With a little luck this demon will take us by the most direct route to her sister and maybe to the hybrid."

CHAPTER 67

"I TAILED JACK. I wanted to play it safe after the break-in at my house. I *had* to find out what those two knew about me and see if they posed a threat."

"How did you ever find them?" Claire asked in a whisper. She was afraid of what George might come out with next.

He killed him! Oh my God, he killed him . . .

It was still snowing outside, without a break. More and more snowflakes fell on the windshield, gradually blocking Claire's view of the entrance to the general store.

"It was child's play," George answered. "I just took down the license number of the truck they escaped in. It was a rental—the company's logo was pasted all over the side.

"I went to the company the next day, counting on the staff's lack of concern about data protection. And I was in luck: After three hundred dollars had a new owner, I got the name and address of the man who'd rented the truck. Can you imagine? The guy actually was naïve enough to rent a car using his real name before committing a robbery. But his name wasn't Jack, it was Frank Murdoch."

"What next?" Claire urged him. She didn't want him to get hung up on details but to get straight to the heart of the matter— no matter how brutal and revolting it might be.

"From then on I monitored Frank around the clock. Followed him day and night to see if he was a threat to me. I even watched him hawking all my stuff. But I could see after three days that he wasn't any problem at all. He just went about his business, nothing else. So it was obvious he'd already put the events in my cellar out of his mind."

Claire concentrated hard but couldn't find any proof that he was lying. His facial expression, gestures, and tone of voice didn't provide any hints.

Everything indicated he was telling the truth.

Or he was a damn good liar . . .

"I've got to admit I was relieved that he wasn't going to reveal my secret. Maybe that was the reason I got a little foolish. Because instead of taking off and getting out of his life forever, I walked past him right out on the street. When he saw me, he opened his eyes wide and froze. His right hand went straight to his belt and grabbed his revolver. I was caught completely off guard and didn't know how to react. I wanted to talk to him and reassure him he had nothing to be afraid of, that everything was OK. But it never happened, unfortunately. He had—"

"—a heart attack?" Claire interrupted. "Am I right?"

"How did you know?"

"It's not important."

They said nothing for a time. The windshield was now completely covered in snow, blocking their view.

It seemed to Claire that they were completely cut off from the world. Not because of the snow on their car but as a result of the events of the past few days. Fate had brought them together in a weird way and demanded difficult decisions. Decisions their lives depended on.

She knew at that moment that the time had come to make one more decision. But now that she'd been able to get a clear picture of George and his motives, she knew he posed no threat. After all, he could have kept quiet about his connection with that man's death. And yet he'd been honest and told her about it.

She *would* take him with her.

It was George who finally broke the silence.

"I wanted to help him," he explained. "I called 911 and even tried to resuscitate him. It didn't help. He died in my arms. There couldn't have been a more senseless death."

"It's OK," Claire said, putting a hand on his shoulder. "There was nothing you could do."

Again her eyes fell on the three days' growth of beard on his cheeks, and again a shiver ran down her spine. It was a peculiar sensation—like a warm tremor emerging from inside her that muddled all her thoughts.

George looked up at her, and their eyes met.

"Well," he inquired, "what's your decision?"

Claire didn't say a word but slowly took her arm off his shoulder.

"Come on," she said, "surely you know already."

George made no reply. He just contemplated her as the grin on his face grew broader with every second.

Claire wondered how many of her emotions had "spilled" onto George. And the thought made her blush. Her cheeks glowed, and she suddenly felt hot all over.

"I'll take you with me," she finally uttered, without waiting for George's response. "And you can call me Claire."

"I know," he said.

CHAPTER 68

CLAIRE TURNED ON the ignition and the heat, and the windshield wipers sprang into life. Though the defogger was on warm, the flow of air cooled her hot cheeks. The wipers opened up a sightline to the store and brought her back to reality.

She took a deep breath. She got her purse and took a thick wad of hundred-dollar bills from a side pocket. After flipping through them, she gave George half the pile.

"What am I supposed to do with this?" he questioned.

"You're going in there," Claire pointed to the store, "to ensure that we'll have enough provisions for two weeks at least. Buy only nonperishables if you can, and get us backpacks, gloves, headgear, a good knife . . ."

She stopped to fish out a notepad and pen from her purse. She made a list of everything to buy so he wouldn't forget anything. Then she tore off the page and handed it to him.

"That should do for the time being," she added.

George scanned the list, and a sudden, baffled look appeared on his face.

"Don't you want to come too?"

"No," Claire stated, "I'd rather not. I don't want to take any risks. After all the things that happened in New York, I've probably been identified as a missing person or there's a search under way. Whatever—they know me here, and I don't want anybody to recognize me and phone Sheriff Decker. He could ask us a few questions we'd rather not answer. So you get to do all the shopping."

George made no reply. He folded the shopping list and stuffed it in his breast pocket. Some snowflakes drifted in when he opened the door a crack. Before leaving, he turned toward Claire and looked deep into her eyes.

"Don't worry," she said, "I'll still be here when you're done."

"I know," George said with a laugh before getting out and disappearing into the store.

He'd barely gone out of sight when she took her cell from her purse. She switched it on and called Arthur Flynn. He answered on the second ring.

"Claire, is that you?" he asked.

"Yes, it's me. Did you get my letter?"

"It came in today by express."

Claire heaved a sigh of relief. She closed her eyes and thought of the waitress. She'd kept her word.

Thank you, thank you, thank you, Marcy!

"Claire, you still there?"

"Yes, I am."

"Good," Art replied. "There was only one of those micro memory cards in the envelope. What's all that about?"

"It's the card from my digital audio recorder."

"So what do I do with it?"

"I'd like you to keep it in a safe place. If you don't hear from me after three weeks, you've got carte blanche."

"To do what?"

"To use the conversation on the card for a story in the *Review*. And, Art?"

"Yes?"

"It doesn't matter how crazy or screwy it sounds, everything is true. The man I'm talking to in that recording, by the way, is the dead man they found at the airport. I think the people who killed him are after me right now."

A moment's silence on the phone.

"What have you gotten yourself into, Claire?"

She thought that was a really good question.

A damn good question!

"Into something absolutely incredible," she replied and ended the call without a good-bye.

She knew he could be trusted. But what she didn't know was whether her tête-à-tête with John would be leverage enough to save George's life—and hers—in a pinch.

CHAPTER 69

THE CLOSER THEY CAME to Rockwell, the greater Bishop's quandary grew. It wasn't because of the upcoming operation; he could trust his instincts there. Everything would go well, he knew.

But he now had his doubts about knocking off Whitman. No problem with the technical side of it. There probably wasn't a method of killing anywhere that he hadn't used during his career. On a secret mission in South America, he'd once drowned a drug lord in a toilet bowl. It took ten minutes, but he didn't let go until that Colombian bastard wasn't moving anymore.

In a goddamn toilet bowl!

Whitman was a completely different matter. Not because of Whitman himself but because of the four men in the car behind. *Obviously*, he reasoned, he could rely on Petric. He was loyal and would probably keep his mouth shut even if he had to put a slug between his own mother's eyes.

His real concern was the other three men. Each one was a young soldier—ordinary rank and file, new to the Organization and constantly on the lookout for ways to get promoted.

They could *not* be trusted, that was for sure. So he had to find a way to lose them before they went into the woods. His mind was going at full speed as they neared Rockwell. And the more time went by, mile by mile, the clearer his thoughts became and the more his worries faded away.

He had a plan.

CHAPTER 70

IT TOOK LONGER to load up than they thought. George had to go back to the store several times and pack his purchases into the car. Claire wondered if they'd be able to lug all that stuff to the cabin.

By the time they left, twilight was setting in. It was just after four, and the snow was worse. Claire didn't think the march to the cabin would be as easy as she'd calculated.

But she didn't utter a word. She guessed that little part of her emotions had probably "spilled" over onto George too. After all, he hadn't said a peep since leaving the store. He just looked out into the growing darkness and emitted the odd sigh.

Claire left Rockwell via the main road, which snaked its way for some miles through the forest outside the town line. Their vehicle had no problem climbing, though the highway was barely plowed. The tachometer needle crept higher with each mile but was still far from the red zone.

After about ten miles Claire turned off the highway onto an unplowed dirt road. The lane was bordered by high snow-drifts on both sides. The treetops above were bending down under the weight of the snow, creating a kind of tunnel with not much snow on the road. The headlights worked through the increasing gloom as they crept along at walking speed. Claire kept her eye on the tach the whole time as it moved increasingly nearer to the red zone.

The motor had been like a whisper but now howled every time Claire stepped on the gas pedal.

Finally, after over two hours, the Subaru couldn't go any farther. The traction light was permanently on, indicating there was no traction. She knew what that meant: They had to get out and proceed on foot. The car went from a crawl to a full stop.

"Well, that's that," she said, turning on the interior light. "We've got to carry on by foot."

"Do you really want to start right now?" George asked.

"What else can we do?"

"We could at least spend the night in the car and start out in the morning."

"What's the point?"

"You've got to get some rest, Claire. You haven't had any sleep for more than thirty-six hours."

She knew he was right. Her eyelids felt as heavy as garage doors, and she'd noticed her concentration failing more and more. But still, she wanted to head out for the cabin at all costs.

"I can make it," she insisted, surprised at how pained her voice sounded.

"Quite likely you would make it," George agreed, "but it's also possible your circulatory system would collapse and you'd freeze out there in no time at all."

She mulled his words over for a minute and realized that his reservations made sense. The thermometer on the dash showed the temperature had fallen to twenty-four degrees and would certainly drop a few degrees more overnight.

Sober consideration, she reflected, would lead to the conclusion that an immediate start would be highly risky, mainly because they were just as safe from their pursuers on this remote forest road as in the cabin.

"Fair enough," she agreed. "Then we'll set off just before daylight. The tank's a third full, and if the motor's running, the heater will keep us from freezing."

"Good," George concurred and smiled.

They reclined the seats and slipped into the new sleeping bags. Claire turned out the light and huddled down in her sleeping bag so that only the top of her face peeked out.

At first she thought sleep would be impossible. Whenever she started to drift off, her thoughts returned to Amanda. That was the real reason she wanted to start walking right away, because the strenuous hike would stop her worrying about what Amanda was doing at that moment.

Here she was instead, snuggled up in her sleeping bag while the tension Amanda caused gnawed at her.

Where was Amanda? What's happened to her? Will I be able to rescue her?

Her right hand fingered the cross from John. She had a fleeting thought that saying a prayer might help. She vetoed the idea. She never had been a believer and probably never would be. She didn't know why she was wearing the cross anyway.

These and similar thoughts spun around in Claire's head while the wind whistled around the car, and the forest trees groaned under their burden.

But the steady noise of the motor mumbling away had a calming effect because of its familiarity. It ultimately lulled her to sleep.

Away from Amanda and away from her worries. Farther and farther until she went to sleep and forgot about everything.

But sleep didn't bring relief.

On the contrary.

CHAPTER 71

THE DREAM WAS IMMEDIATE and unrelentingly merciless.

First came the pain.

Unending, all-consuming pain. It devoured her body and smothered her thoughts. Every other feeling was submerged in the surging sea of pain.

It took some time to get adjusted to it. Only then could she deal with her other sensations. But that brought no improvement, because the more vivid the dream became, the more trapped she felt.

She was wedged in somewhere and unable to move, not even her arms. Blackness surrounded her. The darkness seemed to swallow her up.

She tried to work free, turned every which way, and tugged at her bonds. Nothing helped. Her body was ringed by iron bars that cut off any attempt to escape. She felt she'd been buried alive, and the very thought choked her up.

But another feeling was just as bad. A repugnant feeling Claire had never felt before. It was a painful ache from the murky depths of her subconscious that caused her whole body to cramp up.

It was an irrational, animal impulse. A primeval drive—a simple desire burning to be satisfied. And the more she yielded to it, the clearer the goal of her yearning became.

Blood!

She was dreaming of blood, longing for it—with every fiber of her being. The craving flowed through her limbs—she felt a tingling beneath her skin and a burning under her fingernails.

Blood!

There was no way she could fight it. Her thoughts were drowned in an undertow of desire.

Blood!

She sensed she was no longer a human being. She'd been transformed. She was now a beast of prey. With razor-sharp senses and sharper teeth.

And she was aware that every second brought her nearer to her victim.

The hunt was on.

CHAPTER 72

"NO, NO, *PLEASE*, NO . . ."

Claire thrashed around, tangled up in her sleeping bag. Her voice was pleading and her breathing labored. Her eyes flickered uncontrollably under her eyelids, and the corners of her mouth twitched. Then her whole face froze in pure terror.

"Wake up!" George shouted. "Hey, Claire, wake up. You're having a bad dream."

Claire opened her eyes and looked around. At first she didn't know where she was. Her eyes were glazed over and drugged with sleep. After her dream finally gave way to reality, she could recognize George.

He'd turned on the interior light and was leaning over her. The light flickered as if the battery would soon give up the ghost, and the heater fan had developed an asthmatic sound.

"Don't be afraid," he said in a gentle voice. "Everything's OK. Just a nightmare."

He unzipped the top of her sleeping bag to stroke her brow. His touch felt soft and warm. In the middle of all that snow and the insanity of the past few days, that little gesture soothed Claire more than she would have expected.

"No fever," George remarked nonchalantly, taking his hand away.

He was still leaning over her. Claire looked deep into his eyes. Her heart beat furiously, and she felt an adrenaline rush. And then a sudden impulse overcame her. An unforeseen inspiration, as strong as it was irresistible.

She peeled herself out of her sleeping bag, raised her arms, and wrapped them around George's neck. She could feel his neck muscles twitch for a second, as if it were a final protest from his reason, a last appeal to come to his senses.

But he relaxed instantly, and before he knew what was happening, Claire pulled him toward her. He offered no resistance; the ice was broken.

First she felt his breath on her face. Then his soft lips on hers. His stubbly beard scratched her cheeks, and the stinging sensation radiated through every part of her body.

"Are you sure, Claire?" George pressed his words through his lips. Claire didn't say anything. She just kept looking at him, looking very deeply into his eyes. Then she nodded and kissed him again.

She knew that what she was doing was insane. It was insane and maybe wrong, too. After all, they were on the run, and they hardly knew each other. She knew practically nothing about him and wasn't at all sure he was even human. And yet, in spite of all her doubts and fears, if felt so good.

Too good for words!

All her qualms melted away when George took her tightly in his arms and pressed her to him. Soon his hands were everywhere, exploring her body, caressing it, and holding it tight.

Finally the interior light died and the heater fan along with it. The motor gurgled on for a bit before it gave up the ghost as well.

Claire and George were oblivious to it all.

CHAPTER 73

THEY DROVE INTO ROCKWELL just before dawn and stopped at a gas station. Bishop saw it was time to put his plan into action. He had to get rid of the other men if he was to ensure that Whitman wouldn't leave the woods alive.

They parked the two SUVs in single file.

"What next, boss?" Petric asked.

"Listen up, men," Bishop barked in a military voice. "We'll take a short break and stock up on supplies. Then Whitman and I will drive into the woods. The rest of the crew will take up position in the town and await further instructions."

Whitman turned to him with eyes blazing. Lamplight gave his eyes an orange sheen, like a rabid dog's.

"How the hell will that help?" he snarled. "The men are coming with us, goddammit. We *need* them."

Bishop grinned at him dismissively.

"Negative," he responded.

"*Negative*? What the hell does 'negative' have to do with it?"

"You understood me perfectly well, Charlie. The men stay here. They'll be the rear guard in case things don't go according to plan."

"You're forgetting one crucial point," Whitman countered.

"Which is?" Bishop inquired.

"We're officers with the same rank, and I don't have to take orders from you. Not a single one, you get me? That's why I say the men are coming with us."

Bishop wasn't fazed by his argument. He'd had several opportunities to study Whitman's character during the whole operation. So he knew his partner had a quick temper. But he knew just as well the one thing he did *not* have at all: the power of self-assertion.

For him, Whitman was just one of Cardinal Canetti's lapdogs. Lapdogs who loved to bark but didn't have the balls to bite when they had to.

For that reason he wasn't worried that his plan wouldn't come off.

Not worried in the least.

"No, Charlie," Bishop corrected him, "you're the one who's forgetting one crucial point. You forget the woman knows the terrain here better than we do. She knows a thousand paths and secret roads, while we've got to rely on information from a damn animal. In case she shakes us off again, we'll at least have a rear guard to cut her off."

Whitman eyes looked as if they were about to drill right through him.

"Besides, you've forgotten another very important thing. Something I've already explained to you."

"And that is?" Whitman said through clenched teeth.

"I don't fucking give a shit about your opinion, my friend. Either you do what I ask, or you can fuck off. *Got that?*"

Whitman snorted like an enraged bull. His steamy breath clouded his entire face, blocking his view of Bishop. Then he turned on his heel, got into the car, and slammed the door.

Bishop knew of course that under normal circumstances he should not let himself go after Whitman so ruthlessly. But the certain knowledge that Whitman would have no chance to lodge a complaint against him reinforced his roughness. That, and the fact that he would be a living legend in the Organization after this mission. A legend who wouldn't catch any shit for such mere trifles. Because when all was said and done, *he* would be the agent who managed to capture the damn hybrid.

All by himself!

Petric looked at Bishop, a smile on his face.

"Looks like our shrinking violet's having her period, hey, boss?"

Bishop didn't respond. He turned to the other men instead to outline what they had to do next.

CHAPTER 74

BY THE TIME the gray dawn appeared in the east, they were almost halfway to the cabin.

They were making good time despite the heavy gear and the slight incline. Partly because the snow had let up during the night, visibility was fine, allowing Claire to get her bearings effortlessly. And because the low temperature had completely frozen the top layer of snow, they could walk easily through the terrain without snowshoes.

But Claire knew that the favorable conditions weren't the only reasons for their quick advance. Constant physical strain guaranteed that she had no time to dwell on her thoughts. And that was precisely her aim.

So she repeatedly quickened her step and pushed herself to her physical limits. The more her muscles hurt, the less she could concentrate on the chaos raging inside her.

But she suspected that she wouldn't be able to evade her thoughts in the long run. No matter how hard she pushed back, they always resettled on the events of the previous night.

That made no difference to her physical torture. The fact that George had hardly spoken a word didn't make it any easier. He just trotted along behind her and said nothing. At times, he seemed to be aware of her doubts and worries, and she guessed that explained his silence.

Claire was not naïve.

She knew the past night was meaningless. After all, in the twenty-first century you could sleep with anybody without having a relationship. She'd had the random hook-up experience often before—probably like most people in New York City. Flings with people who were little more than anonymous figures, the search for the occasional human contact in everyday life. *No*, she concluded, *last night meant nothing at all*.

Though the analysis sounded reasonable, she found it unsatisfactory. Deep down she knew it was a lie, a crafty chess move in a game of self-deception. Nothing but an evasion to keep her from making very complicated things even more complicated.

Contrary to her rationalizations, she couldn't help admitting to herself that some things had changed. Fundamentally— whether she wanted to believe it or not. Because after last night—the night they'd shared—George was no longer the stranger he'd been a few hours earlier.

She couldn't exactly gauge the extent of her feelings for him. The only thing she could state with any certainty was that it was lovely to lie in his arms.

And that was just the tip of the iceberg . . .

"How much farther?" George's question snapped her out of her thoughts.

She stopped and waited for him to catch up. When he reached her, she turned and looked into his eyes. And she smiled at the same time. At least, she thought she was smiling, since her face had lost all feeling because of the cold. When George returned her smile, she knew it had worked.

"What's the matter?" he asked.

She didn't answer. She raised an arm instead and pointed to a hill about a hundred yards in front of them. It was a little hill above some low-lying ground and ringed by conifers.

He looked where she was pointing. He squinted and frowned as he scanned the landscape ahead. Then his face relaxed into another smile. Claire had been so lost in thought that she hadn't noticed they were almost at their destination.

At the foot of the hill, in a small clearing, stood her father's cabin.

They'd made it.

CHAPTER 75

WHITMAN WAS ON EDGE.

Bishop could tell by the way his eyes kept darting to the rearview mirror. But even those observations didn't provide any relief. He squirmed around on his seat, threw fleeting glances into the backseat, and checked his pistol constantly to see if the safety was off.

"Why does the thing have to sit behind *me*, chief?" he asked, giving Bishop a look of pure horror.

"She's got to be put somewhere, right?" he answered. "After all, she knows the way to the goddamn cabin."

"Is she properly tranquilized?" Whitman ventured.

"Sure she is. She's up to the eyeballs in tranquilizers."

That wasn't the truth, of course. He'd given Amanda a tranquilizer shot before letting her out of her cage. He'd paid scrupulous attention to the dosage. He didn't intend to knock her out completely for the next few hours.

His goal was to keep her in a state of lower responsiveness.

A state where she wouldn't cause any trouble but would still be able to guide them.

But he didn't expect Amanda to play by the rules, so he'd tied a heavy steel chain around her neck and fastened it with a heavy padlock. Petric helped him wrap the other end of the chain around her several times and lock it in place. As if that weren't enough, he'd ordered Petric to sit beside her and not take his eyes off her for an instant.

After that they got going. Northward. In the direction the cabin was said to be.

"What happens if she transforms?" Whitman asked. "Did you think of that?"

"If she actually does that, then she's shit out of luck," Bishop replied, "because she'll burst into flames in a split second. After all, it's daytime."

Bishop felt some uneasiness on this point. The sky was gray and gloomy, and not a ray of sunshine broke through the clouds. Furthermore, the car's rear window was tinted, presenting an additional potential risk. He didn't really believe it was bright enough in back to turn Amanda into a human torch.

If she did, *she'd only give off little puffs of smoke . . .*

But he kept these misgivings to himself. He knew they were close to their goal, so he found this safety risk defensible in light of their imminent success.

The town lay several miles behind when he turned to Amanda for the first time. He wanted to be sure they were going the right way.

"Amanda, can you hear me?"

"Yes," she growled.

"Are we going the right way?"

"Why the hell should I help you?"

Bishop thought fast about a reward for Amanda's coopera-tion. He knew he had to choose his words carefully. He assumed that a vampire's telepathic powers were restricted to family members, but he didn't discount the possibility that they might actually be universal.

And if so, then one wrong word could spell doom. He sur-prised himself with his rather quick answer to her question. It was as if it had been on the tip of his tongue the whole trip.

"Listen," he said, "if we find your sister, then she's all yours. I've no use for her. I'm only interested in the guy she's with. You can do anything you want with her. How's that work for you?"

Amanda stared at him in the rearview mirror. Her one, immobile eye was fixed on him, and Bishop couldn't pick up any movement.

"I've got another idea," she said in a dull, bubbling voice. An animal sound, with nothing human about it.

"Let's hear it," Bishop responded.

"Go to hell."

At that moment the sound of tearing cloth came from the backseat, together with the loud rattling of the chain. Every-thing happened with lightning speed. Before Bishop could react he felt something warm pouring down his neck, and the rusty smell of fresh blood filled his nose. A snarl roared through the car, followed by violent thrashing that rocked the SUV.

"Shit, she got loose!" Whitman screamed.

Bishop turned around. His partner was right.

Amanda had torn open her straightjacket, and her arms reached out through the coils of the chain. Her face was com-pletely smeared with blood.

Petric sat crumpled beside her. His throat was ripped open. Blood spurted from the wound like water from a fountain and sprayed all over the inside of the car. His face was frozen in an expression of naked horror.

Bishop moved fast in spite of the shock. He took a hand off the wheel and went for the tranquilizer gun in the middle console. But just as he was curling his finger around the trigger, he was seized by a funny feeling:

What the hell?

For a second it felt like he was weightless and about to float upward.

A second later the world started to tilt before his eyes. The moment was suspended in midair, and time came to an abrupt halt. But it didn't take long for reality to catch up with him.

The impact was so great that Bishop banged against the steering wheel with full force. The gun slipped from his hand, and he lost his bearings.

The car rolled over several times, crashing through the underbrush and rocketing against tree trunks. It finally came to rest lying upside down.

There was a moment of absolute silence. For the first time in years, Bishop wondered if he were dead.

But the gears in his brain immediately kicked in. He opened his eyes and looked around. Although the world was upside down, he could see that Amanda was not in the car. The next thing that caught his eye was Whitman wriggling out of his broken seat belt and trying to get out. Bishop didn't hesitate for a moment and did likewise.

"What the hell happened?" Whitman yelled as he helped Bishop to his feet.

"The rear end swung out of control," Bishop muttered absentmindedly. "We must have hit some black ice." Not until then did he see what had really happened: They'd shot over a hilltop and skidded downhill into a steep embankment. A swath through some snapped-off tree trunks marked the SUV's path before it stopped.

"That's it," Whitman groaned. "The bitch is gone, and we won't find this damn cabin without help. I'll try to contact the guys back in town to come and get us."

Bishop forced a smile in spite of the pain and shock.

"What?" Whitman asked.

"Nothing's over, Charlie," Bishop answered, reaching into his jacket pocket. He took his hand out, and Whitman stared in disbelief at the object he was holding. His face darkened as he stood there open-mouthed.

Bishop's smile grew broader.

"It's only over when I say it is."

CHAPTER 76

THE CABIN WASN'T particularly big. It had two small rooms, including a bedroom. It also had a low cellar storeroom lined with shelves.

It had no electricity or running water, and the people who stayed there had to relieve themselves outside.

Despite these inconveniences, there were advantages. The most important was the stone fireplace that kept the cabin dry and warm in the worst part of winter. As long as there was enough firewood, you could hold out in the cabin even in the fiercest blizzard.

They were in luck. The whole south side of the cabin was piled high with firewood covered by a plastic tarp. Claire couldn't remember when her father last came out here to hunt. But she saw he'd followed his iron rule anyway: to leave enough firewood for next time.

She bet he didn't have an inkling back then that his morning cough was more serious than a slight cold. On that last trip, he wouldn't have known that the cancer had spread to all of his inner organs. He wouldn't have known that he'd never go hunting again.

Cigarettes had laid him in his grave with the sureness of a bullet, but without its speed. His death was a blessing in Claire's eyes, putting an end at last to his ordeal of suffering. She felt a sharp pang of grief at the thought of him. But that didn't keep her from getting on with her work.

She laid a fire in the fireplace and checked its draw. After that she emptied the backpacks and stored their contents in the cellar. The monotony of the tasks quickly made her forget her worries.

That was a good thing, she admitted. For when all was said and done, they had made it. They got to the cabin, and on the whole everything had been easier then she'd assumed. Now they just had to wait it out until things blew over.

Claire paused and reflected. How long would it probably take until things blew over?

Two weeks? Four?

Would her life ever be normal again? And what would happen to Mandy in the meantime?

Before she could probe these questions further, George stuck his head through the trapdoor to the cellar.

"Everything OK down there?" he asked.

"Yes," Claire replied. "I'm almost done. If we ration out the supplies properly, then we can hang on until spring."

George knitted his brows and sent her an exaggeratedly critical glance, and Claire knew right away that he wasn't serious. She couldn't help herself—she had to smile.

"I'm happy if it lasts the next four weeks" was George's rejoinder.

"Well, I've got a little something that should help."

"What do you mean?"

Instead of answering, Claire squatted down and pulled out a wooden box from under the bottom shelf. It was rather long and rather dusty. But she knew by its weight that her father had followed another of his rules before going hunting for the last time.

One of the most important rules ever . . .

Claire took off the lid and showed George what was in the box. Then she looked back up at him.

"Now we can hunt," Claire smiled.

George didn't reply. He just grinned. He stared steadily at the object in the box.

It was a Ruger Mini hunting rifle with a mounted sight, along with several boxes of cartridges and a complete cleaning kit. The smell of gun oil permeated the cellar, telling Claire that her father had oiled and cleaned the gun well to keep it from rusting. He'd done a fine job and left nothing to chance.

Thank God . . .

Claire was delighted, but when she looked back at George, she could see how casually he was inspecting the rifle. It was almost as if he were looking at a primitive tool from the gray dawn of prehistoric time, maybe a stone knife with so many flaws it was almost useless. And the longer Claire thought about it, the more she was convinced it was actually true. After all, she reasoned, wouldn't he probably get along damn well without the Ruger? Judging by what George had told her about himself, he'd probably be a better hunter than she'd ever be, even without a gun.

Certainly he would . . .

His strengths were far greater than hers. And strictly speaking, Claire realized, her father's rifle wouldn't change anything all that much.

But she was still overjoyed to have that gun in spite of this momentary doubt that made her a little uneasy. No matter what might happen, she reckoned, at least she wouldn't be standing there completely empty-handed facing the whims of fate. And this thought was by itself enough to drive away the dark clouds and put her in a happier frame of mind.

Everything was going according to plan, she concluded.

But she had no hint that things would soon get completely out of hand.

Very soon, in fact.

CHAPTER 77

"WHAT'S THAT?" Whitman asked, his eyes glued to the object Bishop was holding.

Bishop knew there was probably no better time to take out Whitman, who was still all over the map after the accident and earlier events. But he rejected the idea, primarily because he wasn't dumb enough to try his luck a second time.

If there were unforeseen problems at the cabin, it would be better to have an extra man along who was very handy with a gun. So he decided to let Whitman live at least until the job was done.

A shadow of a doubt flashed through Bishop's mind, which ruined the thrill of anticipation. He wondered why he was so keen on killing his partner anyway. He admitted he couldn't stand him any more than he could trust him.

It was only a brief prompting of reason that flitted through his mind. Then a corner of his consciousness that was inaccessible to such concerns took over. A corner that did not stop and think about his actions and therefore needed no justification.

That instinctive part of his personality was responsible not only for his meteoric rise within the Organization but for the fact that he was still alive. Whenever it came to the crunch, that part of him took control of the situation and saw to it that everything went according to plan.

And, Bishop thought, it was no different this time. Everything was going according to plan: Whitman and he were alone in this godforsaken forest with no witnesses for miles around.

"Didn't you understand the question?" Whitman asked.

"Of course I did, Charlie," Bishop rejoined. "But I think you know very well what this is."

He raised his hand and showed Whitman the object in it.

"A GPS tracker?"

"Amazing, isn't it?" Bishop said. "Although I may be old enough to be put out to pasture, I do know how this type of thing works. Seems you aren't the only techno-freak on this team, Charlie."

It was a small triumph, but Bishop savored it to the last drop. After all, he knew how much Whitman hated not knowing about everything all the time.

"Where did you put the transmitter?"

"We planted it in the straitjacket collar while the demon was unconscious. It's a micro transmitter, the size of a button battery."

"Well?" Whitman smirked. "Do you have a signal, Mr. Genius?"

Bishop hit a button on the instrument, and it suddenly came to life with a peeping sound. The display lit up for a few seconds until the satellite connection was established.

"Oh, yes," Bishop replied, "clear and distinct. She's heading north-northwest. The cabin must be that way. C'mon, soldier, shoulder arms, and forward march."

"Ah, bite me!" Whitman retorted.

Nevertheless he did what Bishop ordered. He went to the rear of the SUV, stuffed the necessary equipment into a back-pack, and loaded up with ammunition. Bishop did the same.

It wasn't five minutes after that when they started out.

Quick march, direction north-northwest.

CHAPTER 78

"CAN I HELP YOU?" George asked.

He came up to Claire and laid a hand on her shoulder.

She was at the table in the cabin's living room, cleaning the gun. She'd dismantled all the parts. Springs, screws, and other components were lined up in front of her on the table. George's touch knocked her off stride, causing her to pause momentarily.

"Do you know how to clean a rifle?" she inquired, looking up at him.

"No," George replied. "Unlike you, I'm not a gun nut."

"Well then, let me think of what else you can do for me," Claire said.

She was aware of the ambiguity resonating in her words. And that was a good thing, she felt. Because every second that George's hand was on her shoulder increased her desire to do something rash again . . . something irrational. A certain something for which there were nicer places than the folded-back seat of an imported SUV.

Before her desire could take over, she remembered it would soon be dusk, and some matters had to be dealt with before then.

Since the cabin had no running water, one of them had to go to the creek and fetch some. And Claire knew it wasn't going to be an easy or pleasant job, given the temperatures, to extract a few jugs of water. The creek would be completely covered with a thick layer of ice, and the water had to be lugged up a slight rise for almost a hundred yards back to the cabin.

In light of the onerousness of the task, Claire decided she'd rather George did it.

"You can go fetch some water while I finish with the rifle," she suggested.

"Consider it done," George replied.

She gave him directions to the creek. Then she handed him two plastic jugs and walked him to the door. They stood there and looked into each other's eyes. And then, quite unexpectedly, he bent down and gave her a fleeting kiss on the lips.

She was so taken aback that she couldn't muster a response.

"That's been overdue all day," he said.

Claire was still taken by surprise—by the kiss and the warm quiver that raced through her body when their lips touched.

Before she could get a word out, George turned and vanished into the gathering gloom. Claire shut the door behind him and stayed there for a moment as if rooted to the spot before returning to the table.

She picked up from where she'd left off. The only difference was that now her face was glowing.

And as so often when Claire was by herself, her thoughts took on a life of their own, running wild like a team of ornery stallions. Sure, she thought, the stress of the past few days had been real hard test on her nerves and pushed her to the limit.

No wonder she was so upset at that moment. *That* was probably the reason, she decided, for that bit of idiocy the previous night. But she knew it wasn't so simple, because even if she set aside all the terror she'd experienced, she couldn't deny the sure fact that George held an uncanny kind of attraction for her. She had no idea where that attraction might lead. And even if that feeling, the loss of emotional control, was rather exciting, there was one thing that dampened her good mood, something that all her happy feelings couldn't flush out of her mind.

It didn't matter a damn how she twisted and turned the facts: George was a murderer.

Maybe not according to the traditional definition—but he had killed people nonetheless. Countless innocent people had fallen victim to his voraciousness over the years, and this was a tough nut for Claire to crack. But the deeper she dug, the more she thought her subconscious was looking for reasons to justify George's earlier character and to acquit him of any guilt that he'd once taken upon himself. Whatever he'd done, Claire reasoned, he'd done in a former life when he'd followed his nature, just like beasts of prey.

Suddenly, as if her mind were finally trying to put an end to her confused thinking, she recalled her father's advice that he'd given her to take along in life:

It's never done anybody any good in life to keep looking back, honey. If you keep looking backward, you fall forward. Keep looking ahead, and let the past be . . .

These few words were just enough for Claire to calm down for a bit.

At least for the moment . . .

Of course she knew that subject wasn't off the table yet. But she believed that she had better things to do at this specific moment than racking her brains to figure out what George's life looked like more than half a century ago. Instead, she had to spruce up the damn gun and see to it that it was in perfect shape for its next shot.

Because it might well be that her life would depend on it some day.

She had no trouble cleaning the gun, though it had been years since the last time. She knew every component, how to strip it, and what needed special attention. She was so absorbed in her task that she forgot everything around her. While her hands were busy with the brush and gun oil, her thoughts kept circling back to George.

She was therefore even more startled when a sudden crash sounded through the room: a hollow bang as if someone had thrown a brick against the outside cabin wall. At first Claire thought it was a gust of wind catching a shutter. But when she looked out the window, there was no wind. Snowflakes fluttered down to the ground almost vertically.

Before she could wonder what that meant, the sound was repeated. A violent knocking. But this time Claire could locate the source.

It came from the cabin door.

"Who's th—?"

But she never finished her sentence. The door burst open with such force that it bent the hinges in the frame. Claire saw a dark figure in the doorway, staring at her.

In spite of the blazing heat of the fireplace, her heart instantly froze into a block of ice.

She stared at the door, unable to move, as the figure slowly came toward her. It approached, step by step.

Its feet shuffled over the floor, each step accompanied by a ghostly rattle.

Clank, clank, clank . . .

CHAPTER 79

BISHOP SET A STEADY PACE, although he hadn't trekked over terrain like this for years. But that didn't matter, he thought. After all, he'd grown up in Montana, in a shack in the foothills of the Rockies.

He'd spent his childhood and teenage years hiking through forests and climbing mountains. In an environment like this one, he had internalized the fundamentals that would make him an excellent soldier later in life.

He'd learned to hunt, shoot, and make his own decisions. Sometimes his life depended on them. Whatever he learned in the Marines later was just the finishing touch that steered his available potential in the right direction.

So his profession was his vocation. He had no doubts about that. Everything he did came from the inscrutable depths of his consciousness. He didn't have to think things over for long; decisions just came to him. His instinct allowed him to survive completely hopeless situations unscathed.

Panama, Colombia, Afghanistan, Somalia, Bosnia, and Iraq—stages in life he'd gone through with little more than a few scratches. His instinct had protected him, always keeping him alive while his former comrades had bled to death in some grave or other.

At exactly that moment his instinct piped up to say it had been a mistake not to kill Whitman right after the accident. Not to put a bullet in his head right away. It was only a brief impulse that flashed through his mind.

But before he could give it more thought, another impression dominated and drove all his qualms away. Not only regarding Whitman but the whole operation.

About three hundred yards in front of them he could make out the outline of a cabin. It lay at the base of a small rise in the middle of a clearing that sloped off to one side. But that wasn't enough for him to throw all his misgivings overboard. Even at this distance he could see a column of smoke rising from the cabin's chimney. And Bishop knew what that signified.

They had made it. The cabin was occupied. The woman and the hybrid were holed up inside, unaware and unsuspecting.

They'd reached their goal.

A feeling of triumph surged through him, letting him forget his doubts completely.

He switched off the GPS tracker and stuffed it in his jacket pocket.

Then he reached for his automatic and released the safety.

CHAPTER 80

CLANK, CLANK, CLANK . . .

Claire was paralyzed.

She was still sitting at the table, unable to tear herself away from the sight in front of her. The dark figure came closer and closer. It crossed the room, step by step, sending snowflakes spinning through the air.

Fear and terror took her breath away. But she realized she must act. Though she didn't recognize the intruder, she sensed the real and present danger emanating from it like an invisible ray.

She instinctively looked for a way to defend herself. She first thought of the rifle. She saw immediately that she couldn't assemble it in time.

But she wasn't completely helpless. She held the gun butt in her hands. It was as long as an arm, made of polished hardwood, and easy to hold. Even an act of pure desperation, Claire knew, could inflict considerable damage if she attacked cleverly. If she used it like a baseball bat, she might be able to keep the intruder at a distance. Her hands instinctively tensed up around the gun butt. Hope gave her strength.

Then she went on the offensive.

She sprang to her feet, jumped to one side, and wound up for the swing. Her legs were spread, her arms raised, ready to strike at any moment. But before she could move, the intruder attacked. And in a way that destroyed her defenses.

"Did you miss me?" the figure growled. Its voice was deep enough to set the air in the room vibrating. Then it took another step. The light from the fireplace illuminated its face, an indescribable picture of devastation.

It was charred in several places. Skin hung down in tatters, and an occasional skull bone stuck out from beneath singed clumps of hair. One eye was completely blinded, while the other glowed red and drilled its gaze right through Claire, like a red-hot lance.

But in spite of all those wounds, Claire knew at once who the intruder was.

Amanda! Oh my God, it's Amanda!

Claire could feel her strength dissipating. An ice-cold shiver ran through her, right into her bones, so that she couldn't move anymore. At the same time, she sensed her mind clouding over and all her thoughts coming to a standstill. Dark spots whirled around in her field of vision, and she had trouble staying on her feet. Her head grew dizzy, and everything around her started to spin. She could feel herself blacking out quickly.

Nonetheless, she did *not* quit.

She clung to consciousness like a drowning person clings to a piece of driftwood. The first onslaught of terror crumbled, and she took a deep breath. The dizziness subsided; the dark spots before her eyes faded. She had herself under control again.

For the moment.

Amanda still came toward her, relentlessly. The chain around her body jangled with her every move. Her arms were stretched out in front of her, ready to grab Claire. When she was just a few steps away, Claire knew it was time to act.

"Please forgive me, Mandy!" she begged.

Then she let the gun butt rip, giving it her best shot. She packed all her strength into her swing with her eyes closed. In spite of its swiftness, her swing seemed to take forever.

The large end of the butt thundered against Amanda's temple. The force of the blow vibrated through the wood, traveled up Claire's arms, and reverberated to her shoulders. She could feel her sister's head reeling from the blow. She heard Amanda's stunned body slump to the floor.

Claire opened her eyes. She was ready for anything.

Amanda was laid out at her feet. She seemed a little dazed but conscious. Her first movements were hesitant and awkward. But she recovered quickly. In spite of the huge wound on her temple, she resumed her assault.

Amanda leaped forward before Claire could move. She grabbed Claire's ankles in her claws and pulled. Claire's feet were ripped so violently from underneath her that she was powerless to stop it. She wheeled her arms in the air, trying to catch herself.

The rifle butt slipped out of her hands, flew across the room, and banged against the wall. She sailed through the air right after it, hitting her head on the floor tiles, then lying stunned beside the fireplace. But once again desperation compelled her not to give in.

In spite of her dizziness she propped herself up on her elbows and looked at Amanda, who'd released her grip on her ankles and started to crawl toward her.

Claire looked around. She had to find a weapon to defend herself, because she suspected that trying to stop Amanda with her bare hands wouldn't work.

Her eyes scanned the room and landed on a poker on the wall next to the fireplace. It was solid steel and had a sharp end that could split a thick piece of wood down the middle. Claire knew this was her one chance if she wanted to survive.

She turned and reached for the poker. Her fingers slipped on the warm steel but couldn't hang on. It was beyond reach. She tried to stretch farther, but Amanda's weight pressed her to the floor, making it impossible for her to move. Claire was not about to surrender. She stretched out one last time. Her fingers slid up the poker and made it move.

Yes, yes, yes . . .

But instead of falling toward her, the poker skidded along the wooden wall, jangled onto the floor, and finally fell out of reach.

Claire gave up.

She turned and stared at the disfigured features of the creature that had once been her sister. They were face to face, eyeing each other.

Claire's nose picked up Amanda's rotten breath, causing her stomach to rebel.

"We'll soon be united, Claire," Amanda snarled, "*forever!*"

Then she took another leap forward. Her claws grasped Claire by the wrists. She pushed her to the floor and bent over her. The strength she had was overpowering.

Claire turned away. She could see out of the corner of her eye that Amanda's shark-like mouth was coming closer and closer. Her teeth sparkled, like curved daggers.

Oh my God . . . no!

The creature's horrible face came nearer and nearer. Claire saw there was no escape. That was the last thought that whirred through the convolutions of her brain. The very last thing was fear. Naked, all-consuming fear.

But that wasn't right. There was one more feeling. One impression that Claire had paid no heed to until now. A warm sensation that seemed to originate in her heart. The nearer the creature approached, the more this cozy warmth turned into searing heat. Finally it turned into a blaze that burned the skin on Claire's breast.

The pain was unbearable as it flowed through her whole body. But Claire couldn't fight it. She was trapped in a giant thumbscrew, unable to move. Then she clenched her teeth and closed her eyes.

She abandoned herself to her fate.

That same moment she felt the creature's lips on her neck. Curved teeth scratched her skin, as a cold tongue searched for a suitable place to bite.

But suddenly it stopped. The grip on Claire's wrists relaxed, and the creature pulled back a bit. A second later it emitted a scream so loud that Claire felt her left eardrum burst. At one stroke she'd become completely deaf on her left side. The pain was unspeakable, like a red-hot thorn boring right into her brain.

And still she took hope.

She could feel the creature's body go limp. It retreated, slowly at first, then more and more rapidly.

Claire was completely taken by surprise. She didn't know what had happened. She sat up and stared nonplussed at the creature as it kept scrambling backward. It eventually leaned against the wall separating the living area from the bedroom.

Then it raised its right claw and pointed to Claire's breast. "What the hell is that?" the creature growled.

Not until that moment did Claire lower her eyes and look down at her breast. And the sight she saw once again took her breath away.

The little gold chain around her neck was aglow. It was the necklace from John, and right now it was literally smoldering. It emitted a reddish glow and an indescribable heat that seared Claire's flesh. Fiery red welts appeared on her chest, and she could smell burned skin.

But she felt pain only on the margins of her consciousness. Her mind focused on the memory of John. On him and all the things he had mentioned at the airport.

. . . the cross is the most effective protection against vampires, so anybody wearing it doesn't have to be afraid . . .

She instantly realized that John had spoken the truth. But that by itself was not as important as the second insight that shot through her mind at the same time:

He had not only told the truth but had saved her life. Without that crucifix she would probably be dead.

Or worse—she herself might be . . . *a vampire!*

The thought renewed Claire's strength. Deep down she intuited that the creature could no longer harm her. It was still huddled against the wall, and its ferocious stare didn't leave Claire's chain for one second.

Anybody wearing this cross has no need to fear vampires . . .

But her personal safety wasn't the most important thing for Claire at that moment. She wondered whether John had been right about *everything* he confided to her at the airport.

No question that the business with the gold crucifix had worked, she granted. But what about the two vials that were supposed to put an end to a vampire's transformation process? Would that work? Could she rescue Mandy? Could she stop that process?

Claire didn't know.

The one thing she knew for sure was that it was worth a try. She stood up, grabbed the poker, and walked toward the beast. As every step brought her closer, the crucifix around her neck got hotter.

Claire didn't know what she was to do, but her goal remained—to rescue Amanda.

She at least had to try.

She had to do everything in her power.

CHAPTER 81

AN ANIMAL CRY echoed through the woods, and Bishop flinched. He and Whitman exchanged glances, and then kept on going. The sun had almost set. Darkness was taking over, and the forest shadows melted into one another, forming an impenetrable black tangle.

They passed the halfway mark and would reach the cabin in less than ten minutes. They could of course have moved more quickly. But Bishop knew they had to be careful.

Very careful!

You never could tell what might be lurking in the dark—ready to pounce on you at any moment.

CHAPTER 82

THE CREATURE HAD **different ideas.**

What it was planning, Claire didn't know. But it didn't want any help—that much was obvious. Claire had barely made it halfway to the creature when it jumped to its feet and ran toward the door. Claire realized that it was trying to flee. She took off after the beast in an instant and grabbed the chain around its chest.

She pulled very hard to keep the creature from escaping. But it didn't take long for her to gather that she was no match for its uncontrollable strength. She felt like someone trying to capture a raging bull by grabbing its tail.

It was hopeless, Claire thought.

The demon was simply too strong. Claire could feel her fingers slipping off the chain. A second later the creature had worked itself free. It ran toward the door, hurtling across the room with lightning speed. The creature was so quick that its feet scarcely touched the ground. Claire could only watch the thing that used to be her sister and pray for a miracle.

Then she saw that she didn't need one. The one thing she did need was standing in the doorway and blocking the exit. It was a black figure barely discernible in the gathering darkness. Claire recognized right away who it was.

George.

He was in the doorway, looking back and forth from Claire and the creature.

"Everything OK?" he asked. His voice had a growling undertone that reminded Claire of the evening they first met.

"Yes," Claire said, "yes, it's OK. But *please*, George, don't hurt her. It's Amanda, my sister."

George nodded in reply to her instructions. Then he fell upon the creature that had once been Amanda.

His attack was quick as a flash, leaving Amanda no time to react. George grabbed the chain and swung the beast around.

His move was so quick that Claire's eyes could only register it a bit at a time. One minute George was standing in the doorway, and a second later he was whirling Amanda in the air. Claire just stood there, observing the spectacle, unable to budge.

George's attack turned wilder and wilder. He spun more and more rapidly around his axis. At the highest point of his swing he let go of the chain. The creature flew across the room, banged her head against the cabin wall, and sank to the floor. A dent in the woodwork bore witness to the force of her hitting the wall.

"Quick," George commanded. "The trapdoor to the cellar!"

His words had barely died away when he flung himself on the creature again. He didn't want to give it a chance to recover. It still lay on the floor, looking somewhat dazed.

In spite of all the commotion, Claire caught on right away to George's plan. She instinctively fell to her knees and pulled open the trapdoor.

George got to work again fast. He whipped the creature around in circles as quickly as he could. Its feet swept through the air as its paws tried to scratch George's face. Its black claws hissed through the air.

But she couldn't get at him. He was too quick. He spun her around the room and got ready to jump. Before Claire knew what was going on, he flew headfirst down the trapdoor, dragging the creature behind him.

Tied together, they sped past Claire with the raging force of a freight train going full speed. A second later they crashed onto the cellar floor. The impact shook the whole cabin. All the windowpanes rattled in their frames.

Then came a moment of perfect quiet. Then the racket under Claire's feet started up again.

She looked through the trapdoor into the cellar but could make out only a confusion of shadows in the darkness. Shadows constantly recombining in various ways. Snarling sounds reached her ears, making her cringe. She didn't know whether they were Amanda's or George's.

But it didn't matter right now, Claire realized. She couldn't back down. She had to know what was going on down there.

She jumped up, ran to the table, and snatched one of the two flashlights George had bought in Rockwell. Back at the trapdoor, she turned it on.

The darkness in the cellar gave way instantly to the glaring gleam of the flashlight, revealing to Claire a sight she hadn't anticipated.

CHAPTER 83

AMANDA LAY ON HER STOMACH on the cellar floor, her arms and legs bent toward her back with the chain wound around them several times. A large knot ensured she couldn't move. She yanked at her bonds, of course, attempting to get free, but Claire saw right away that it was hopeless. The knot around her limbs hog-tied her tightly—she didn't stand a chance.

George had done it.

He leaned over her and held her by the neck with both hands. His strength pushed the creature's face into the dusty dirt floor. She snarled, screamed, and swore—but George showed her no mercy.

"I think I've got her under control," he announced, looking up at Claire, smiling. But she couldn't help but notice that his eyes had a reddish glow. She knew he was on the point of transformation.

"What now?" Claire asked. She'd scarcely uttered the words when she feared she already knew the answer George might give.

What if he decided that the only right thing to do was to kill Amanda then and there? Twist her neck like a chicken's and hope that would prevent suffering?

No, no, no . . . please no!

Though that course of action seemed absolutely realistic, Claire hoped it wouldn't come to that.

George was still looking up at her. His smile had gone, and his eyes looked normal again.

"She's not completely transformed," he said. "I can still feel a heartbeat. It's weak, but I think there's still a ray of hope."

"What do you mean?" Claire asked. Her heart speeded up, and her hands tensed around the flashlight.

"It's not too late," George asserted.

"What for?"

"To save her. I think I can do it!"

I think I can do it!

The tension drained out of Claire's limbs and all her strength along with it. A sigh escaped her. It was a hissing sound that seamlessly turned into a laugh. It wasn't a pretty laugh but a foreign sound that scared her. It was an agitated, high-pitched sound almost ending in a sob.

Claire was afraid that the horrors of the last few days had pushed her to the brink of madness. Maybe, she reasoned, she was on the point of losing her mind and simply burning out, like a dead lightbulb. The very thought made her heart seize, and an icy shiver ran through her limbs.

"Claire?" George asked. "Everything all right?"

His voice jerked her back to reality. Her laughter promptly dried up. She looked down into the cellar where Amanda was tied up on the floor.

"I think I have to try it," George said "What do you think? I mean, what have we got to lose, right?"

"Try what?"

But George didn't answer. Instead, he rolled the right sleeve of his parka up to the elbow. The skin on his arm looked pale and lifeless in the glare of the flashlight.

"George," Claire insisted, "*what* are you going to try?"

Her voice trembled. As did her whole body.

"What are you thinking of, dammit?"

George turned around one more time.

"I'm going to try to save her."

A thousand questions flooded Claire's mind. But before she could deal with even one, George had gone to work. And from that moment on she couldn't do anything but watch and hope that everything turned out well.

With his sleeve rolled up, he leaned over Amanda and flipped her onto her side. The flashlight lit up her face to reveal a mask of pure hatred. At the same time it showed the true extent of her wounds: Her whole body was a mess of flesh and blood.

That did not deter George. He kept at his work. He leaned closer to Amanda and did something that Claire wouldn't have thought possible. The tension was so great that she didn't have the courage to breathe.

CHAPTER 84

IT HAD GROWN TOTALLY DARK. They'd worked their way to the cabin step by step, constantly on the lookout for an ambush.

They'd crept to within about fifty yards of the cabin when there was suddenly a loud racket inside. They instinctively cringed and huddled down behind a chest-deep snowdrift.

They exchanged a quick glance.

It was enough for Bishop to realize how tense Whitman was. His face was like stone and his eyes glassy. He clutched his rifle, aiming it at the cabin, ever ready to open fire.

Bishop was keyed up, too, but he didn't show it. He tried to imagine what was going on in the cabin at that moment.

A number of scenarios rolled around in his brain, and he couldn't tell which was the most likely.

The only thing he knew for certain was that Amanda had found her sister.

And from what he knew of Amanda, he didn't think it had been an affectionate reunion.

CHAPTER 85

CLAIRE WAS STILL STARING into the cellar. Despite the questions whirling through her brain, she kept quiet. She was rooted to the spot. Meanwhile George went on with his work.

He leaned down closer to Amanda, loosening his grip on the back of her neck. She turned over, lifted her head from the dusty floor, and eyed him with her one, blazing eye. Her lips curled back to bare a terrifying set of teeth.

For a moment time seemed to be at a standstill. Then George did something that Claire never thought possible.

What the . . . ?

After bending over Amanda, he shot out his arm with the sleeve rolled up. He held it out to Amanda, so close that it was easy for her to snap at it.

And she didn't wait for an invitation.

Before Claire could comprehend what was happening, Amanda tore her teeth into George's arm in one lightning-fast motion. She bit down with all her might while emitting an animal hiss. Her eyes blazed more than ever, and her whole body quivered.

She sucked on George's arm, shook her head back and forth, and kept on growling. Slurping noises rang through the dusty cellar air. The grisly scene lasted several seconds, ending as surprisingly and abruptly as it began.

Amanda suddenly stopped. Her eye opened wider, and her body went limp. She dropped George's arm and fell back onto the floor. She heaved a deep sigh, and total calm returned to the cellar.

Claire snapped out of her frozen state. She still didn't know what she had just witnessed. But that didn't matter. Deep down she trusted George and believed in what he was doing.

Nevertheless, she was afraid.

She kept her eyes focused on Amanda, who lay in the harsh glare of the flashlight without moving a muscle.

Meanwhile George had gotten to his feet. He inspected his arm and rolled down the sleeve of his parka. Then he turned to the ladder and began to climb out of the cellar. Claire knelt beside the trapdoor looking down at her sister.

"Did it work?" she asked George.

He gave her a tired look. It seemed as if the procedure had cost him an unbelievable amount of strength. For the first time since she'd known to him, he looked exhausted and crushed.

But Claire couldn't make any allowances for that. She had to know what was going on with Amanda.

"George!" she demanded. "Did it work? Will she get better?"

"See for yourself," he responded.

Claire turned back to Amanda—and was bowled over again by an incredible sight that made her gasp. She was powerless to do anything else—she just had to keep staring.

She could feel her energy dropping with every passing second. The sight before her eyes was fascinating and terrifying at the same time.

The flashlight fell from her hands. It fell into the cellar, tumbled and rolled over, and wound up lying in a way that put Amanda in the center of its beam.

Amanda's wounds were healing.

Bits of skin rolled back into place, piece by piece, and fused with the rest of her body tissue. The burns on her face paled, burst, and dropped from her forehead and cheeks, falling away like fine sand and quickly dispersing into the air. Skin appeared where her burns had been, a bit red but unblemished. There were no scratches, and not a single scar was left.

She was in one piece and unscathed.

Every wound disappeared, healed up, and grew over, as if a ghostly hand were stretching skin over every place where there'd been an open wound a moment ago.

Mandy's blind eye woke up to a new life. It blinked incessantly, reminding Claire of a butterfly just emerging from its cocoon. And she secretly knew that the comparison wasn't so very wrong. Because at that moment she was witness to an unbelievable transformation—a supernatural metamorphosis.

Finally, Amanda grew a new nose. The tissue pulsated as it grew and grew—first bones, then cartilage, and finally flesh and skin.

When the spectacle was over, Amanda looked as if her madness during the last few days had never existed. But that wasn't quite right, and Claire knew it. For in spite of the speed of her healing, there were nevertheless some uncorrected flaws. Amanda's hair was mostly burned off, and her scalp was visible. With a few long, scattered strands and all her bald spots, she looked like a plucked chicken.

But Claire couldn't care less right then.

An indescribable feeling of happiness flowed through her, washing away every other emotion in no time at all.

It worked! Oh my God, it actually worked!

Tears welled up and she did nothing to hold them back. A steady stream rolled down her cheeks. She turned to George, who was still standing beside her, and lifted a smiling face up to him.

"It worked." She got the words out. That was the one single thought running through her head.

George returned her smile.

"Yes, Claire," he added, "it did w—"

Before he could finish his sentence, half his head blew up.

CHAPTER 86

THE BANG WAS DEAFENING. Claire shuddered and instinctively flattened herself against the wall nearest the fireplace.

George's lifeless body sailed through the air as if in slow motion and thudded onto the tile floor.

Though Claire was in shock, she recognized at once the full extent of his wound. The left side of his head was a crater in which clumps of hair, bones from his skull, and parts of his brain had become mashed together into an opaque pulp.

The horrific sight brought a stabbing pain that blocked all thought.

Meanwhile two dark figures came into the cabin, walked across the room, and stopped in the light from the fireplace.

Oh my God, what's happened?

"Good shot, chief," the younger of the two men said, breaking the eerie silence in the cabin, "but was it really necessary? We could have taken him alive. Then we'd have found out more about him."

"Of course we *could* have," the older man said, "but no need to get bogged down when a tissue sample from this bastard is enough for working on an antidote."

"Whatever you say, chief," the younger man added. "Then let's take some samples and scram. I can hardly wait to get out of this goddamn forest."

"Right away, Charlie. I'll just take care of this woman in a minute."

He took a step forward, raised his gun, and pointed it at Claire's head.

"Caused us a lot of trouble, sweetheart," the man said. "I'm almost sorry it has to end like this."

His penetrating blue eyes stared at Claire as a smile lit up his face. Claire saw the index finger of his right hand slide onto the trigger.

She knew that escape was futile. She was alone, unarmed, and in no position to defend herself. She knew she was going to die. Not at some time or other, but right now, at this very moment.

They would kill her, and Amanda after that. Just the way they'd killed George. And John.

For a split second she wondered if she would see the flame from the muzzle before the bullet hit her. It was one of those banal thoughts that for some inexplicable reason frightened her more than the certain death she was facing.

Claire resigned herself to her fate, with no thought of making a break for it or of self-defense. Her opponents outnumbered her, and the situation was completely hopeless.

She closed her eyes.

She gritted her teeth and waited . . .

CHAPTER 87

EVERYTHING WAS GOING AS PLANNED, and Bishop knew it.

Now it was time to get the kiddies off the street once and for all, he thought to himself. And that meant finishing this woman off and Whitman right afterward.

He'd taken the safety off his gun and put it on full automatic fire. His plan was to waste the woman with one shot and turn around in one smooth motion and let Whitman have it. Surprise would be on his side, he calculated. Besides, the gun's expanded magazine held fifty rounds.

More than enough for the job!

Whitman would slump to the floor before he even knew what hit him.

That little shit can hardly wait to get out of the forest, he thought. Whitman didn't have the slightest idea that it would be his final resting place. He'd rot in these woods.

Assuming of course that the wolves didn't get to him first.

A grin spread over Bishop's face, and the thrill of anticipation was intoxicating. He placed a finger on the trigger, then squeezed it a little until he was halfway along his two-stage trigger.

He began a silent countdown at the same time.

When he got to zero, he thought, this farce would be over and done with.

Over and done with.

Five.

Four.

Three.

Two—

CHAPTER 88

THE SHOT WAS ENORMOUSLY LOUD.

Claire could sense her strength leaving her body in a flash. She slumped down the wall and landed beside George. The idea of her certain death enveloped her mind with chains of fire that nipped every other thought in the bud.

She kept her eyes shut and waited for her mind to go dark. She waited for death with composure.

Her head finally fell to the floor. The rough wood pricked her cheek, and her good ear could hear crackling in the fire-place. She felt the warmth from it a few seconds later.

The one thing she did *not* feel was pain.

She concentrated as hard as she could—but came up with nothing. Except for the wood in her cheek, she was all right.

There was *nothing* wrong with her.

Hope flared up inside her.

She opened her eyes and immediately witnessed something incomprehensible.

The older man was stretched out on the floor, one hand on his throat. Blood spurted through his fingers and squirted into the semidarkness of the room. His eyes were wide open and staring at the other man.

He tried to say something, but his voice dropped as his throat emitted a rattle. Blood trickled out of his mouth and down his chin.

The other man stood there eyeing him. He had a high-caliber revolver in his hand; smoke was still coming from the muzzle. The gun was cocked, and a strong stench of gunpowder filled the room.

Suddenly Claire realized what had taken place.

The younger man had just shot the older one. He'd hit him from behind, straight through the throat.

Though she didn't know the whys and wherefores, her hope grew. Maybe the other man was an ally, she thought.

Maybe . . .

She lay there without moving a muscle, anxiously following the bizarre drama in front of her.

The man with the revolver took a step toward the wounded man. He'd slung his rifle over his shoulder in the meantime. It was long and towered over his head like a lance.

"End of the line, chief," he spoke at last, a grin playing at the corners of his mouth. He looked delighted. His face glowed with triumph.

The wounded man propped himself up and tried to speak one more time, but his voice made a gurgling sound again, and only a few fragments of words could be understood.

". . . son of a bitch . . . dir-ty *snake in the grass* . . . I'm gon-na *ki-ll* ya."

The effort to talk caused more and more blood to spill out of his mouth. Claire could see he was rapidly getting weaker.

The other man seemed totally uninterested. He squatted down next to the wounded man and pressed the muzzle of his revolver against his temple.

"Oh, yes, there's one more thing," he said. "A little message from Cardinal Canetti I'm supposed to give you."

The wounded man had stopped trying to talk. Pure hate blazed in his eyes.

He breathed laboriously, and blood poured through his fingers with every gasp.

Claire saw that his free hand was feeling around on the floor for the gun that had fallen out of his hand. His movements were quick and frantic. But she could also see that the gun was out of reach.

He didn't stand a chance.

When the young man noticed what he was doing, his smile died, and his eyes turned cold.

Then everything went very fast.

"You're fired, chief," he said, and pulled the trigger.

The wounded man's head flew apart. Claire saw the flame from the muzzle exiting the back of his head, followed by a mess of bone, blood, and brains that splattered over the wall with a wet smack.

The man's body went completely slack. His upper body was flung back by the force of the shot and dropped to the floor.

His eyes were still open and staring at the ceiling. Claire saw that they'd already turned completely dull.

Even the fire mirrored in them looked cold and unreal.

CHAPTER 89

CLAIRE PULLED HERSELF TOGETHER and tried to get on her feet. But she was barely in a squatting position when the man started talking.

"Keep still," he cautioned in a friendly and calm voice. But the revolver in his hand spoke a completely different language. Claire stopped immediately and stared at him.

The man stared back.

The other man's body lay at his feet, and George's body was right in front of Claire. She found the sight so grotesque that her mind was almost unable to process it.

She felt for a second that she was drowning in the unreality of the situation. She knew she had to fight that feeling.

Because her life depended on it.

Her life and Amanda's.

"Stay where you are," the man ordered, raising his revolver. The muzzle was huge—much larger than the other guns. Yet Claire sensed for some inexplicable reason that there was still hope.

It was a funny feeling, almost as if she had a word on the tip of her tongue that she wanted to say. But what tickled her consciousness wasn't a word; it was something she'd overlooked until now. Something that had completely disappeared in the confusion of the last few minutes. A crucial sign that had escaped her.

She had to figure out what the point of all this was. And the best thing to do in this situation was to play for time.

"What do you intend to do?" Claire asked.

The question seemed to amuse her tormentor, because her words had barely died away when a smirk reappeared on his face. He was mocking her—no doubt about it.

"What do you think?" he taunted.

Claire didn't give an inch. Instead, she looked around for ways to give herself time to process whatever she was on the verge of understanding. She spotted the poker, but it was too far away. Her eyes then fell on the dead man's gun, which was also beyond reach.

But she didn't let up.

She was sure she had overlooked *something. That* she was sure of.

"No answer? That's OK too," the man with the revolver said. "I'm going to kill you, my dear. Just the way I shot this old piece of shit here. I wish I could tell you it won't hurt, but I think that would be a lie."

His smirk grew bigger. But Claire was undeterred by that. Her searching eyes scanned the room. All at once she recalled that she still had a little . . .

. . . *tiny* . . .

. . . ace up her sleeve, and now was the time to play it. After she'd learned how dangerous her persecutors were, she didn't think she could stop them. Not in the way she'd tried, she thought, but with a little bit of luck she could still buy a bit more time—time she urgently needed to reach something crucial. A thing she still supposed might just be a figment of her imagination.

"You can't kill me," she asserted. Her voice sounded self-assured and firm.

Her tormentor raised his eyebrows, and his face registered momentary surprise.

"And why not?"

Claire's eyes were flashing.

"Because you'll blow your cover. You and the whole damn Organization," she argued. "There's a secret tape recording of my conversation with that guy at the airport, John. It's loaded with incriminating facts about you nutcases and . . ."

The man burst out laughing. And he wasn't faking it. It was a loud, echoing sound. He really seemed to find Claire's threat funny.

". . . and then what?" he joked. "Are you going to bust the evil Organization? Is *that* what you're threatening me with? Is *that* your little scheme?"

Claire didn't respond. If she'd figured him out correctly, then he'd prefer to answer his rhetorical questions himself. And that would give her more time to look for that minute piece of the puzzle that she'd overlooked so far.

Once again her eyes darted over the room. They settled on the attacker's corpse and saw a pistol in his shoulder holster. Claire mulled over that possibility for a moment and concluded it was futile. Even if she were to jump up and grab the gun, there wouldn't be enough time to release the safety and fire.

Her gaze wandered over to George. She felt a spasm in her heart. Tears came to her eyes at the sight of him. He was lying on the floor, eyes wide open and a huge hole on the left side of his head.

Inspecting his body more closely, she saw that he didn't have anything on him that could help her at this moment.

No gun, and nothing else.

Absolutely nothing.

Still, Claire's eyes were glued to him.

Meanwhile her guess about the man with the gun pointing at her was confirmed: He was apparently a person who savored each triumph to the last drop. Either *that*, Claire reasoned, or else he was a thoroughgoing sadist. A sadist who liked to see his victims stew in their own juices. She judged that both options were correct.

Very definitely!

"Is this some kind of joke?" he asked. "You think you can blackmail *us*? You can't blackmail us, let me tell you. We're the most powerful by a long shot . . ."

The man chattered on, but Claire wasn't listening. For a brief moment it felt as if she'd found the solution to the puzzle. But she wasn't quite able to recognize it.

George lay on his back—motionless, lifeless, dead.

He wouldn't be able to help her.

Nonetheless her feelings at that moment were overwhelming, and she forced herself to examine his corpse more thoroughly.

Very thoroughly.

Her eyes came to rest on his face. At that moment her feeling that she'd overlooked something was so strong that it was truly preying on her mind. A powerful shudder ran through her, begging to be stopped.

She still didn't see it.

The seconds went by . . .

C'mon, goddammit, concentrate . . .

And then, all of a sudden Claire saw what she'd overlooked.

The sight of it took her breath away.

But she didn't tip her hand.

Because that would have been her death sentence.

CHAPTER 90

CLAIRE REALIZED AT ONCE why she hadn't seen it right away. The change was minimal, so small it could hardly be seen at first glance.

George was lying there without moving. Everything looked the same. But when Claire took a closer look she could see that nothing was the way it was before.

Not the slightest thing!

George's eyes were still lifeless and rigid, but something was different. Claire at first thought it was the reflection of the fire in the fireplace and had dismissed it. But now she was absolutely certain that wasn't the case.

Because George's eyes were shining. It was a feeble, reddish shimmer. A subtle sparkle, barely perceptible.

That wasn't all. His mouth was open a crack, and Claire could see that his teeth were also different. They weren't the nice teeth in his smile of a few hours earlier but an animal's teeth eager to bite into a victim. His canines in particular protruded below his lips—they were long and curved.

Claire could see that clearly.

But not only his face had been transfigured. When Claire looked at his hand she saw black, curved talons at the end of his fingers scratching the floor over and over, leaving deep grooves behind. The sharp talons effortlessly sliced into the wood like a hot knife through butter, hardly making a sound. Claire knew at once what that meant.

George was *not* dead.

He's alive.

Claire reflected on this, as hard as she'd ever pondered anything in her life. Her life depended on what she'd do next. Not only her own life but her sister's, too.

She weighed the possibilities and thought some of them through, only to toss them aside. Her thoughts were whirling around ever more rapidly, combining then scattering.

But she didn't give up.

He's alive! Oh my God, he's alive!

And then, out of the blue, she thought she'd found a way. A way to save herself and Amanda.

Yet she wasn't at all sure it would work.

CHAPTER 91

"DID YOU UNDERSTAND WHAT I SAID?" the man with the gun wanted to know.

Claire stared at him while her thoughts spun around in her brain.

"Does it make any difference?" she asked.

"No," the man conceded, "probably not."

He raised his gun and aimed it at Claire.

Claire shook her head.

"No," she pleaded, "just one last wish."

"And what's that?"

Claire's hand pointed to George's dead body.

"I'd like to say good-bye to him before . . ."

The man squinted as if trying to interpret her words. Claire's heart was in her mouth. She knew that everything now hung in the balance. The merest doubt, and he'd shoot her immediately.

Seconds ticked by. Then the man's face relaxed. He pointed his gun at George's body and told her:

"Go ahead, do it. I'll give you one minute."

One minute.

Claire jumped right up and leaned over George. She kissed his cheek, but it wasn't out of a fit of tenderness. She wanted to confirm that his eyes were *actually* glistening and it wasn't only her imagination.

Please, please, please . . .

She was in luck—a brief moment, and she could tell it wasn't her imagination. George's eyes really did glisten. But that wasn't all. His pupils flickered and moved. They were two black circles that alternately closed and dilated—like a predator's pupils. Claire knew at once what that meant: George was alive and reacting to visual stimuli. His eyes kept refocusing. The bullet must have wounded him horribly, Claire thought, but didn't kill him. At that moment he was probably fully conscious but unable to move.

This line of reasoning struck Claire as logical but didn't make her any more confident that her plan would work. It could just as easily turn out that absolutely nothing would happen.

But what did she stand to lose? If she ventured nothing, she thought, then she and Amanda were dead for sure.

So she pushed her doubts aside, hard as that was—especially because she felt time slipping through her fingers like fine sand. In the next minute that madman with the gun could choose to kill her.

One minute.

Claire didn't believe he'd keep his word. She abandoned herself to her instincts.

She bent down over George and covered his cheek with kisses. She moved her right hand toward his face, slowly, so as not to arouse suspicion.

Her fingers touched George's chin, his lips, and then his

pointed, razor-sharp teeth. But she wouldn't stop. Her hand kept sliding farther up, so far that she was finally able to shove the side of her hand into George's mouth. It took a lot of energy and self-control because every time she moved she felt his teeth boring deeper into her flesh. It was like pushing her hand into a heap of shards.

Though she felt a warm stream of her blood pouring into George's mouth, she didn't feel any pain. She was under too much stress to feel any pain.

When she'd finally accomplished what she'd intended, she did the only thing she could.

She waited.

And hoped.

CHAPTER 92

SECONDS WENT BY, and nothing happened.

George didn't move and didn't show any signs of life.

Her plan had failed, Claire conceded, heaving a sigh. It was all for naught.

She was going to die.

She gave George one last kiss, moved by affection this time. Her lips had scarcely touched his cheek when she felt a tingling throughout her whole body, like an electric current coursing through her limbs. Claire stopped and tried to locate where this unique feeling was coming from.

She closed her eyes and surrendered to her fate. She sensed that a minute had gone by. Soon the man would cock his revolver and kill her.

She lay there for several seconds, lying on George and fully aware that her death was imminent.

She couldn't think straight because of the pain. Second by second it flared up and sped through her body like an all-consuming conflagration.

She opened her eyes and fell backward in a reflex motion. She wanted to get free. Wanted out of here, away from the source of her terrible hurt. But she couldn't. Her hand was in the grip of George's jaws, and he was biting on it with all his might.

Claire could feel his teeth rubbing against her metacarpals. The crunching passed from her arm along her nerves to her brain. She simultaneously felt his ravenous force as he sucked blood from her hand.

It was a steady stream that made her feel faint after a few seconds. She pulled and tugged but couldn't work herself loose. At that moment the chain around her neck began to glow.

Claire looked up at the man with the revolver. His eyes were wide open, as if he couldn't believe what was happening.

"What the hell's going on?" he shouted.

Then he raised his gun and opened fire.

Claire flipped herself around to evade his first bullet, which whistled over her and into the wall. A second one zoomed just above her head and shattered the window behind her. Though her hand was still stuck, she tried her best to move. She hurled herself onto her other side. The pain in her hand was beyond words, but she fought on nevertheless. Desperation lent her strength.

But it didn't help.

The next shot hit her with full force and spun her around. At first it was like a warm, stabbing feeling below her collarbone; the round drilled her in the shoulder. Her mind immediately sank into a seething, hot lava flow of pure pain.

She collapsed and lay on the floor without moving. That same moment George's jaw released her hand.

In spite of her pain and fear, there was nothing else Claire could do about it—she *had* to see what was happening. She lifted her head as far as she could and stared at the scene before her.

George was no longer lying on the floor. He was sitting up and looking ferocious, staring in the direction the shots came from. His eyes were ablaze, and his face was distorted. Claire could see his head wounds slowly closing. They grew together bit by bit until they were nowhere to be seen.

The man returned his stare for a second. Then he leaned forward, pressed the gun against George's temple, and pulled the trigger.

But nothing happened. Just a soft click sounded in the room. Claire knew what that meant.

The revolver was empty.

The gun was completely useless.

The man immediately pulled back. He reached over his shoulder for his rifle, a quick and perfectly routine move. But he wasn't as fast on the draw as George's hand was—it lashed out and grabbed the man's ankle to make him stumble and lose his balance. The gun fell out of his hand, and his arms thrashed through the air. He fell backward and crashed to the floor with his full weight.

George was on him in a flash. One leap, and he pushed the assailant to the floor. The man screamed and raged, his flailing legs thrashing around like a chicken with its head cut off.

But it was no use. He didn't stand a chance. One yank, and George had ripped off his head. The screams stopped abruptly. The man's heart beat a few times, covering George's face with blood.

Claire was still unable to move because of her fear and pain. She witnessed everything. How George transformed into the beast he'd told her about on the trip from Rockwell. How he raged and delighted in his victim's screams, grinning nonstop, like the Devil himself.

But that passed. The man's blood had barely run out when George turned to Claire. Not until that second had she realized how abysmally ugly he was. There was no longer anything human in his face. His eyes were two blazing holes, and his mouth was a horrible abyss, a sight that almost drove her insane. His entire visage was soaked in blood—rolling down his cheeks and dripping off his chin.

He was a walking nightmare, and Claire sensed his thirst was not yet stilled.

Not by a long shot . . .

He left the man behind and came directly at her.

Step by step he came nearer.

His eyes glinted, and his bloody cheeks constantly twitched like a dog's.

Claire knew she'd made a big mistake. She'd saved George's life but realized he was no longer the man he was before he'd bitten her.

He'd become a monster once again.

And now he was coming after her.

CHAPTER 93

"STAY AWAY FROM ME!" Claire screamed.

Her voice quivered, and tears ran down her cheeks. She could barely move. Her right hand was completely torn to pieces and of no use. Besides, the pain from the gunshot wound had spread from her chest to her whole body, paralyzing her.

"I said stay away!"

But George wasn't listening.

"So *make* me," he snarled. The words came in an unbroken stream. It was a thunderous sound, like the motor of an old sports car churning in neutral.

Claire quickly figured out that words alone were insufficient to make George keep his distance. She reached into her décolletage and pulled out the little chain. It was her last chance, she thought.

She swung the pendant between her fingers and held it up to George. The crucifix sparkled in the glow from the fireplace and promptly brought him to a halt.

His expression darkened as he let out a terrifying scream. He was rooted to the spot, his eyes fixed unwaveringly on the cross.

"Get away from me!" Claire repeated.

Her voice was barely above a whisper. She felt the light gradually fading. She knew she'd lost a lot of blood and felt some still coming from the wound in her shoulder.

Her clothes soaked up more of her blood with every heartbeat. She knew she'd soon pass out. That's why she hoped all the more that George would leave before it came to that.

"Go away," she whispered, "*please* go away, George."

The chain slipped from her fingers, but she grabbed it again. She could see George backing off. He retreated slowly in the direction of the door. His face became darker and darker as he got farther away from the fireplace, so far that only two blood-red eyes penetrated the dark and stared at her.

"We'll meet again," he growled, "and then I'll rip your heart out of your breast alive, Claire. Revenge for turning me back into what I am now."

Then the eyes vanished into the dark. The shadows drew together.

In a split second, he was gone.

Claire's strength left her not a minute later. She slid into unconsciousness, certain that she was dying. She would bleed to death before dawn.

But at least I did it! I saved Amanda!

The thought consoled her. This moment was her safe haven in a raging sea of fear.

Shortly afterward, she didn't feel a thing.

CHAPTER 94

CLAIRE DIDN'T BELIEVE she'd ever recover from the events she'd lived through at the beginning of November.

She knew the memory of them would fade with time and that she might even be able to lead a normal life again sometime. But she anticipated it would be a fundamentally different life from the one she'd led up until then.

From now on, fear would be her constant companion. She had stared into the abyss, and the abyss had changed her. Nietzsche's pearl of wisdom was reaffirmed by her grotesque example: The darkness of the abyss had crept in and laid claim to a part of her soul forever. All she could do was come to terms with it and accept the things that had happened.

But Claire knew that wasn't quite right. She could still do something different. Something she'd done all her life to earn a living.

She could write, place her fears into a story, at least to try to create space for some relief. She could banish them to her writing pad and hammer this craziness into some sort of shape.

And that is precisely what she ultimately did.

EPILOGUE

THE FOLLOWING PAGES are Claire Hagen's personal records. They were found in the cabin by Charles Decker, the sheriff of Rockwell County.

At the present time they are an important lead in the search for Claire and her sister, Amanda. There is a police manhunt under way for the two of them. And there is still no trace of either one.

Must get my mind off it. The pain is driving me crazy. Can't think straight. Amanda still hasn't woken up. Must force myself to eat—I feel my energy level dropping. Wound is inflamed. Fever is burning me alive. And then the dreams. Those terrible *dreams . . .*

Fever has subsided. Shoulder pain has eased. I still can barely move my arm. I've felt the spot several times and don't think the bullet hit my shoulder blade. I won't be sure until I've had an x-ray. At least I'm certain I don't still have the bullet in me. It went right through. I found it in the wall of the cabin and picked it out with a knife. It was a full metal jacket, misshapen, but I could see it was intact. In any case the fever hasn't returned for two days now. I've got my appetite back in the meantime. But I'm still awfully worried about Amanda. I still can't wake her up. I'm afraid she's fallen into a coma. Scared she's going to die.

Amanda is awake. I'm beside myself with joy. She just sits staring at me. Her eyes keep closing. She doesn't talk and doesn't eat. Still, I'm hopeful. At least a little.

NOVEMBER 26

Amanda's been getting better. Initially she slept almost all day and would get up only to go to the bathroom. She would look at me without saying a single word. There's a dread in her eyes that reminds me of a wild animal. But she's been getting better since yesterday. She's eating again, even if she is little picky. She says a few words now and then. As time goes by I can understand her better. Even her hair is slowly growing in. I have real hope for her.

───────

NOVEMBER 27

Amanda told me how it happened. She described it for me word by word. Recited it like a kid who memorized a poem. She was on her way home from a club when it happened. A man attacked her. He wore rags and looked like a homeless person. At first she thought he was trying to rape her. But he bit her instead. After that he haunted her and drank her blood several times. How long this nightmare lasted exactly, she couldn't say anymore. I think the memories of these events have left ugly scars on Amanda's soul. I pray that she can recover from them. Please, dear God.

───────

NOVEMBER 28

Addendum to November 16:
I dragged the two bodies outside (delirious with fever and at the end of my strength—but I couldn't bear the sight

of them!). I left them in the snow about fifty yards from the cabin and hoped that nature would do its job. And it certainly did. That same night a pack of wolves was all over them. I heard them snarling and scrambling to get the best pieces. It must have been a good-sized pack because the next morning only bones were left from the older man, and there was absolutely no trace of the younger one. Even their heads had disappeared. I know they'll never find them. Wolves leave nothing behind. But I must look out and never go outside without my rifle now that they've stuffed their bellies with human flesh. I've always got one of the men's automatics on me. It's light and comfortable in the hand. And that's a good thing, because I still can hardly move my arm.

DECEMBER 1

I'm giving Amanda the wild rose oil I got from John. I don't know what the results will be, but I'd rather be safe than sorry. I mix a few drops in with her food without her noticing. At least, I think she doesn't see me do it. (Does it make a difference anyway?) I've figured out what happened the day I visited her in the hospital, when she was transformed after I wiped her forehead with my hand. John had probably some oil on his hands—no—I'm sure that's what must have happened! Because the scent I smelled at the airport is the same as the wild rose oil. He passed it on to me when we shook hands. That tiny drop on her skin was enough to drive Amanda insane, and to burn my fingers. The whole story is so confused and hard to understand that I sometimes wonder how much of it really happened. I suspect deep down that I'll never be able to work out the whole truth.

———

Today was my first day hunting. I shot a stag on the hill behind the cabin about two miles off. I dressed it on the spot, exactly the way Daddy taught me. As I knelt beside the bloody carcass, I suddenly felt an indescribably strong desire to sink my teeth into the raw meat. The sight, the smell, the steaming warmth of its guts . . . it all practically drove me out of my mind. I wanted to lie down and roll around in the stag's blood, and I swear to God I almost did. Since then I've been putting some wild rose oil in my food as well. Better safe than sorry. After all, George did bite me! Only once, of course, but I think even that was enough to bring about a little change. I'm terribly afraid. And those dreams on top of it. Those horrible nightmares . . .

———

I've turned over the bedroom to Amanda. I sleep in the cabin's "living room" on an improvised cot beside the fireplace. I have my rifle handy, beside me all night. Sometimes when the wind creeps around the cabin, I seem to hear whispering in the room. It sounds like a hiss, like someone calling me. I lie awake for hours staring at the door. Usually sleep overtakes me when it's already getting light out. But it brings no relief: I see those diabolical, hideous faces dancing around a huge fire deep in the woods. They bare their teeth, and their eyes bore right into me. Their bodies are little more than shadows flickering before my eyes, like mirages at the end of a long street in summer. One of them is George, that I know for sure. His face is bathed in blood, and he keeps growling the same words:

"Come to me, Claire. Come to me."

My wounds are improving daily. The bullet wound hasn't broken open again, and I can move my arm a little. Not much, but still, it's something. Getting better has inspired much more confidence in me. It gives me strength. And yet my dreams are getting worse night by night.

I sacrificed George and grieve terribly over it. I'm so sure of it that it's been gnawing away at me these days more than my pain and fever put together. He paid the price for my life and Amanda's. And I'm afraid it was a high price. A very high price.

But what else could I do? He'd already been mortally wounded. (It must be because he had healed Amanda just before he was shot. I think his actions had made him temporarily vulnerable.) Who would benefit if Amanda and I had died too? Please forgive me, George. Please, please, please forgive me. I didn't know what I was doing . . .

My writing pad is almost filled up. There are only two pages left. I must record only the most important issues now. This is my last note. The crucial thing: I have terrible fears. My nightmares are getting worse, and when I'm awake I can't tell dreams from reality. Shadows dart through the underbrush around the cabin, and I don't know if I'm imagining them or if something's really out there. Something just waiting in ambush. What's more, I'm afraid of the transformation that's happening to me. I still feel OK, and I'm not afraid of the cross around my neck or bright sunshine. But there's reason to worry: I ate a piece of raw meat yesterday. My craving was so strong that I couldn't fight it off. I threw up right afterward, several times, and since then I've felt as sick as a dog.

I've only half a page left—get to the point, goddammit!

I have a horrible sense of dread. Because of what was and what might be coming.

I'm most afraid of the child growing in my womb.

It is George's child.

No, it is our child.

Flesh and blood of us both.

And it is growing, I can feel it.

It is growing incredibly fast.

ACKNOWLEDGMENTS

Dear Readers,

Writing is usually a very lonely job. So I call anyone fortunate who is helped onto his feet a bit now and then. I was lucky enough to have this happen to me. All the more reason to record my thanks here to all those who were involved in any way in the creation of this book.

I owe many thanks to Maria Gomez of AmazonCrossing, who made an author's wish come true by accepting my manuscript. (Thanks, Maria!) Further thanks are due to David Pomerico, my editor at 47North, who always lent a sympathetic ear to my concerns and supported me tirelessly in word and deed. (Thanks, David!) A great debt of gratitude to Gerald Chapple, my wonderful translator, whose hard work far exceeded my wildest expectations. I can't thank you enough, Jerry, for your commitment and help that went far beyond the call of duty. I would also like to express my sincere thanks to Clarence Haynes for his editing work, and to Stewart A. Williams for his marvelous cover design. A thank-you as well to Sarah Tomashek and Verena Heerdt of AmazonCrossing for our very nice productive conversation in Leipzig—your invitation really meant a lot to me. A huge thank-you as well to all others who were in any way involved with this book and whom I cannot list by name. Thanks to every one of you—you've done truly magnificent work.

I would also like to thank my parents, my sister, and my fiancée, to whom this book is dedicated. Every single hour I spent writing and editing this book was carved out of our usual free time together, which is why I stand greatly in their debt. A final expression of gratitude goes to Christian Angerer, Matteo Rodriguez, Heidi and George Dersch, and to Sylvia and Hinnerk Feja. Every one of them was in some way involved in the creation of this book. Thank you.

Finally, I would like to express my very sincere thanks, also on behalf of all my many friends who are writers, to Jeff Bezos, whose vision of self-publishing has smoothed the path for so many authors throughout the world and has opened up a unique way of publishing books and finding readers. As in my case. Thank you, Mr. Bezos.

Munich, November 2013

ABOUT THE AUTHOR

Daniel Dersch is the pen name the author uses to ensure that readers don't knock on his door in the middle of the night to ask him about vampires. Born in Munich, he's the author of three number one best-selling German-language Kindle horror titles. In his other life, Daniel is working on a PhD and collects mechanical watches.

ABOUT THE TRANSLATOR

Gerald Chapple is an award-winning translator of German literature. He received his doctorate from Harvard and went on to teach German and comparative literature at McMaster University in Hamilton, Ontario. He has been translating contemporary German-language authors for over thirty-five years. His recent works in prose include two thrillers for AmazonCrossing, *The Zurich Conspiracy* by Bernadette Calonego and The Russian Donation by Christoph Spielberg; two works by the Austrian writer Barbara Frischmuth, *The Convent School* and *Chasing after The Wind*, both completed with his co-translator James B. Lawson; Michael Mitterauer's probing history of Europe from 600 to 1600, *Why Europe? Medieval Origins of Its Special Path*; and Anita Albus's wonderfully idiosyncratic book, *On Rare Birds*. His poetry translations have focused on Günter Kunert for almost twenty years. He lives in Dundas, Ontario, with his wife, Nina, an architectural historian, and a black Labrador. He can often be found studying birds, butterflies, and dragonflies, or listening to classical music. He can be reached at geraldchapple@post.harvard.edu.